this is how you remember it

Also by Catherine Prasifka

None of This Is Serious

this is how you remember it

catherine prasifka

CANONGATE

First published in Great Britain in 2024
by Canongate Books Ltd, 14 High Street, Edinburgh EH1 1TE

canongate.co.uk

1

British Library Cataloguing-in-Publication Data
A catalogue record for this book is available on
request from the British Library

ISBN 978 1 80530 099 1
Export ISBN 978 1 80530 102 8

Typeset in Bembo MT Pro by Palimpsest Book Production Ltd,
Falkirk, Stirlingshire

Printed and bound by CPI Group (UK) Ltd, Croydon CR0 4YY

MIX
Paper | Supporting
responsible forestry
FSC® C171272

This one was for me. And you.

You do remember this, don't you?

Why don't you?

One

The path down to the beach is precarious. You can see it from the window of the car, framed on either side by weathered stone walls. You unbuckle your seatbelt and fish your right shoe out from under the seat. It slipped off as soon as you got into the car and you've only just realised. You pull the buckle tight against your ankle, until the glittery purple plastic digs into your skin. The shoe is too big for you but your mum is sure you'll grow into it. You wiggle your toes in all the free space at the end.

The video camera is stowed between you and Evan in the middle seat of the car. It's wedged between a folded towel and a water bottle. You pick it up carefully and stroke the black plastic of the case as you would a frightened animal.

'Be careful with that,' your dad says to you.

'I will,' you say, slipping the strap over your head.

You open the door and get out of the car. Both your feet hit the road at the same time and the momentum carries you forward. You catch yourself with your arms outstretched on either side. The video camera careens out in front of you, then returns to hit you in the thigh. Your father doesn't see.

You take the camera out and swing the empty case across your body. It's huge in your tiny hands, too big for you to comfortably hold, the metal design sleek and smooth. You run your fingers over the raised buttons, pressing them as though you're playing an accordion. You imagine it's alive in your hands, the wires and springs functioning as an artificial nervous system.

You flick out the little screen and press record. The camera beeps and a light on its body goes red. You leave your parents behind and start walking. The gravel crunches under your feet before giving way to earth.

The lane curves to the left and every step you take reveals more, the world unfolding before the camera lens. You breathe deeply, smelling the air. You move the camera from side to side, trying to capture the entire experience. Your purple shoes appear and then vanish in a flash of movement.

'This is the way down to the beach,' you say.

The camera is looking at the blue sky, examining the wispy strings of white cloud just below the sun. It's a hot day, the hottest all summer. Your mum smeared sun cream on your face before you left the house, and you can still taste it.

You don't notice the exposed rock breaching the grass as you approach it. The tip of your shoe hits the edge and you stumble. The wind rips through your yellow and green cardigan, the one your grandmother knitted for you.

'I've tripped on this rock before, last year,' you tell the camera. 'I should have remembered.' You zoom in on the smooth expanse of grey rock until it fills the entire screen. There's a patch of something white and a little puddle of rainwater. A yellow butterfly lands next to it. 'That was silly of me.' The camera lingers, then moves on.

The stone walls on either side of the path hold back tangles of blackberry bushes. The world is thick with colour: rich purples, bright yellows. You stop to search for any ripe berries. You push the lens of the camera into the bush, and your cardigan catches on a thorn. A piece of yellow thread is pulled loose as you yank yourself free. In the next field over, a pony watches you silently, its tail flicking.

As the lane dips and then rises again, there are stalks of montbretia as tall as you are. You run your fingertips over the soft orange petals, the long green leaves, showing them to the camera. You want it to understand what this place is to you. You find a spider web glistening with small droplets of dew, too fine to show up on the screen. The spider is a small brown smudge. Already you can hear the sound of the sea, the quiet whispering of the waves.

All at once, you arrive at the beach. The Atlantic Ocean stretches out wide in front of you, bigger than you could imagine. The deep blue waves are capped with white horses. The camera doesn't immediately adjust to the light of the sun on the water, and for a moment everything is white, and there is no difference between the sea and the sky. You blink, and the world comes back into focus.

You know this beach, this small strip of sand stretching between the fields and the rock formations that protect it from the open ocean. You know how to walk down the rocks to the sand, how to test each one before putting your entire weight on it. You expertly balance the camera, never once afraid you're going to drop it. It's easier to hold it sideways, with the lens facing down. On the little screen, the world falls away and stones fly by.

You recognise the people here; most of them are members of your extended family. You tell the camera who they all are and how they're related to you. You forget some of the names, or perhaps you never knew them, so you make up new ones. You take special care pointing out the people you don't know and the ones from other families who you barely remember from last year. You know, of course, that this is a public beach, a popular holiday spot, but it doesn't feel that way. It feels like it belongs to you alone, at least for one month a year.

The camera pans towards a significant spot. It's sheltered from the wind on two sides by a large rock. Small pink and white flowers grow along the top of it. You can't see the tidal pools behind it, but you know they're there.

'This is where Lorcan's family sit,' you tell the camera. You zoom, amplifying the vacancy of the space. It feels huge to you, unquantifiable in its nothingness. 'They're not here yet.'

You'd been hoping Lorcan would have arrived already, it's part of the reason you rushed down from the car. You have little interest in talking to anyone else. You hold the camera even more tightly. You associate this beach so heavily with him, with your two families here every August, that his absence drains something essential from it.

'Lorcan's not my real cousin, but he basically is. Our parents are best friends. And no one else is my age.'

You scan over the beach to emphasise your point, too quickly to get a clear image. Most of your cousins are teenagers, or else newborn babies. The camera stops on your grandmother, who is sitting in her chair reading a book, a red chequered blanket draped over her lap, a cigarette in her hand. She waves when she sees you, and you wave back. You love your grandmother, but she frightens you, the way that ageing does. Distance develops slowly, yet suddenly it's there. It has stopped being easy and natural to hug her.

As you take in the scene, you notice some people have bought new chairs, or blankets. Some of them are sitting in new spots. You don't like the taste these changes leave in your mouth. This is a place that never changes, that will always be here, and you don't like seeing newness brought into it, as though one red towel emblazoned with a cartoon car could alienate you from the whole place.

A storm has washed in great clumps of brown seaweed, which now litter the beach. You don't like seaweed, not since Lorcan told you that things like to hide in it. He'd made a face as he was telling you that frightened you so badly you'd had nightmares about it.

You approach one clump slowly, warily. The camera watches the progress of your feet. The shells are white spots in the sparkling sand.

'I don't think anything is hiding under here, do you?' You're afraid of the seaweed, but the camera makes you braver. You hold it out in front of you and watch the screen carefully. Tentatively you nudge the seaweed with your foot. It's firmer than you'd anticipated, dried as it is from the sun. Something about the texture feels off to you, the brittle crackle as the strands of seaweed break apart. A fragment makes its way between one of the gaps in your sandal and lodges itself between your toes. You snap the camera closed and stop recording.

You sit down and take off your shoes, stopping between the left and the right to swirl your fingers in the sand. You wonder if this sand remembers you, if it's the same sand as last year, and if it missed you too. You close your eyes and listen to the sound of the waves.

When you open your eyes, your parents have arrived with Evan. They're heavily laden down with buckets, spades and picnic items. One of the buckets is yellow, and it's yours. You'd begged your parents to take it with you when you left last year, and it spent the winter rolling around underneath your bed.

You watch them, your father holding Evan's hand, your mother carrying the cooler. The towel on your father's shoulder catches the wind and takes flight, landing in the sand. You run and grab it. Your foot tangles in one of the folds and you stagger, before regaining your balance and yanking the towel out from under you.

'If you need anything,' you say, running up to them, 'just let me know.' You've heard other people say these words. They come easily to you. You drop the towel in front of your mother. It falls in a pile in the sand. 'Anything at all,' you say. 'I can look after Evan if you want to go for a swim.'

'That's great,' she says, stepping over the fallen towel, her tone not conveying an acceptance of the offer. Your parents begin setting up your area on the beach. You pick up a folding chair. It's heavier than you thought and stiff with age. The blue fabric is sun-bleached and torn on the top right side. One foot of the chair knocks over your mother's flask as you wrestle with it. The flask is sealed tightly and doesn't spill.

'Can I do anything else?'

You pull at her legs to make sure she's heard you. Now that you're seven, you want to show them you're responsible. You're very excited to be seven. It felt like you were six for ever. You like the shape the number seven makes on the page as you write it. Your mother nods and picks up the fallen flask. She turns away from you and embraces your grandmother. The two of them are laughing, as they have done on this beach together many times. You find watching them fascinating. Your father is methodically unpacking things from bags, not saying anything. No one is paying attention to you.

You scan the beach looking for something to do. You pick up a fishing net. It's heavy in your hands, the weight of it concentrated a metre from your body, and instinctively you swing it around in a wide circle. The blue netting blurs in the wind, the rod nimble in your adept hands.

'Don't hit Evan with that,' your mother says, suddenly alert.

'I'm just helping,' you say. She looks at you, and you drop the net at your feet. Defeated, you sit down and begin to build sandcastles, but they fall apart as soon as you lift the bucket. You think your bucket was changed by its stay under your bed, that it no longer works. Or maybe it's the sand that is the problem, the whole beach itself wrong somehow. You flatten the crumbling civilisation at your feet.

You're bored, something you're not used to feeling in this place, which upsets you. This could be a sign of growing up, that you're going to lose your imagination like your mother always tells you she did. 'I wanted to be an artist once,' she sometimes says, the beginning to a story you're not old enough to understand.

You walk to the top of the beach, camera in hand. You don't have the words to tell the camera how you're feeling, you won't know them for another while yet. Instead you take sweeping panoramic shots of the beach, zooming in to the places where rock meets sea. The white water froths and foams, like a creature's mouth.

Just then, as your mood is threatening to break like a storm, Lorcan and his family arrive at the beach. You haven't seen him since last year. The last thing you remember is his car pulling away, his waving hand visible through the back window. You'd felt like your world was ending, the lump in your throat too big to swallow around. Now you're uncertain and confused.

He's holding a body-board, which is nearly bigger than he is. When he sees you, he puts it down on the ground and waves. You watch him and his family as they unfold and unpack their items. You've become shy, unsure of what to do next. The camera is limp at your side. You put it away.

You look over at your family. Evan is fussing, refusing to settle, and one strap of his dungarees is twisted. There are long tracks in the sand from where your parents dragged folding chairs. You pause and examine the straight lines in an otherwise chaotic landscape.

Your dad sees you falter over the top of his newspaper. He rustles it and looks at you. 'Oh great, the Ryans are here,' he says. 'Let's go say hello.' It's the only encouragement you need. You jump over the twin lines in the sand as you run, your arms pumping at your sides, your fists balled. You father follows behind, slower.

The first thing you notice is that Lorcan is taller. He's taller than you, which is something you resent. You'd always been the tall one.

'You're tall,' you say to him.

'Well, I'm older than you,' he says. He sticks his hands in the pockets of his swim trunks. They're new too, patterned with green and blue fish.

'Only two years, that's nothing,' you say. For some reason this upsets you, although you don't know why. 'It's not even a full two years.'

Now that you're closer, you start to notice other small changes in Lorcan. His face is different, you think, and his hair too. You're overcome by these changes which make obvious the differences between the two of you. It makes you feel small and young, like Evan.

'That's everything,' he says. 'Mum says I can get a phone next year, when I turn ten.'

'That's not fair,' you say. The brag annoys you. You've always wanted a phone. Your dad never lets you play on the one he got for work, even though he doesn't know how to play any of the games on it. You hold all the high scores on Snake.

You want a brag of equal importance. And you have one.

'Look at this,' you say. You swing the case around and hold it up in front of you, reassured by the weight of it. You allow your eyes to go wide, your eyebrows retreating high into your hair. You're putting on a show for him, you want him to be impressed. You already know how he's going to react, you can see it in your mind's eye. It takes your fingers a moment to catch the zip and pull it open. The camera drops into your hand. 'Mum says I can film the whole holiday, as a time capsule.'

You don't really know what a time capsule is, but the concept excites you. You turn the camera on and focus it on Lorcan. His blonde head fills the frame. Behind him, the shifting forms of the adults move. He sticks his tongue out at you and you laugh. You zoom all the way into one of his eyes and then all the way out.

'Tell them who you are,' you say.

'Tell who?'

'You know,' you gesture vaguely, 'the people who will watch this.'

'I'm Lorcan,' he begins, 'and I'm really cool.' He pauses, his thumbs pointing at his chest. 'I don't know what else to say . . .'

You turn the camera off and hold it by your side. You gently knock it against your leg, thinking. Lorcan holds his hands up in an exaggerated shrug gesture. You're disappointed with how bad he is at this, you'd been hoping he'd be a good subject for you.

'Can I hold it?' he asks.

You stand, considering. You take him in from head to toe. His hair is shorter than last year, more serious somehow. Lorcan is the only person not in your family you'd trust with something so precious. You know he'll be careful and your mum wouldn't mind him holding it.

'Okay, but only for a little while,' you say. Your grasp on time is loose, but your grasp on power is strong. You like the sound of the words, the way he looks at you when you say them. You hand the camera over, watching the weight of it transfer from your hands to his.

You make a game of it, unlike any game you've ever played on this beach. The lens of the camera makes everything more real. It's the vehicle to another world entirely, one better and more lifelike than this one. You wonder how this camera, this small metal creature, could possibly understand the world. And yet when you watch the footage back, there the world is.

You start by describing the rocks, naming each one. The names developed slowly over the years, based on particular grooves or plateaus, or the rock-pool formations and the creatures that inhabit them. You show it how to walk between rocks, where you need to make a big jump, which rocks are wobbly. There are a few things you've been a little bit afraid of before, like going from one rock to the next, but you do it perfectly now.

On the screen, you are tiny, and yet you nearly fill the whole thing. Behind you, the beach is a yellow expanse dotted with greens and browns. You see it all reflected in the circular black lens. Lorcan isn't as steady with the camera as you are, so you bounce in and out of frame. At one point your head is cut off, but you don't notice.

Your confidence grows. You start to speak like they do on the news, with each syllable clearly annunciated. Any trace of your accent gets lost somewhere in the Atlantic. You begin to get a sense of how to fill out the space, the boundaries of the screen etched on the sand. You imagine the beach disappearing behind you, shrinking to fit into a box over your right shoulder.

You arrive at the biggest rock on the beach. It stands guard at the edge of the beach, sheltering it from the worst of the waves, allowing the small bay to form. It's possible to swim around to the other side of it, but your parents won't let you. You have to stay in the bay where they can see you. The brown incline appears smooth and steep, but you know the grooves your feet can slip into. You find traction easily, your toes strong. When you reach the halfway point, the beach two metres beneath you,

you stop and stand, your hands on your hips. You know this is impressive.

Lorcan follows you as you take the camera over the other side, to the secret place you like to come to. The beach is lost behind you, the adults a world away. On this side of the rock the surface is broken up into different ledges, eroded into a landscape which moulds your imagination. It changes from grey, to brown, to yellow and speckled with barnacles. You point out the parts you shouldn't walk on without shoes. Further along and to the left, you reach the place you're looking for.

'This is where we like to play,' you say as you sit down, the stone warm beneath you. From here, you can see the cascading headlands of the coastline, the Aran Islands and the great expanse of water beyond.

'I don't play any more, though,' Lorcan interjects from behind the camera. You make a face at him, both because of what he said and the fact that he said anything at all. He puts the camera down and stops recording. Without the eye of the camera on you, your movements are too grandiose. You put your arms down at your sides, where they remain still. Lorcan looks away, out to sea and across the horizon. You sigh, and his gaze snaps back to you.

'Okay, fine, let's do another take. *Action*!'

He says the word like a proper director. He holds the camera up again, and you're at attention. Your arms spring back out from your sides. On the screen, you are perfectly composed. You relish the opportunity to get it perfect this time.

Lorcan directs you deftly, telling you to move your hands to emphasise what you're saying, showing you how to pronounce the big words the adults use. He's older so

12

he knows a lot more than you do, although you don't tell him this. You start to craft different stories: in one a sea monster is just out of sight along the horizon, in another you pretend to nearly fall off the rock and into the sea below. You're a great team. Then the camera says it's running out of memory.

'We can keep going,' Lorcan says, 'and just not record?'

The fact that he even suggests this is preposterous to you. You lie down on the rock, your legs starfished out in front of you. The thrill had been in the recording, in knowing that what you did was being preserved. In watching it back and seeing how you look to the outside world.

'What's the point?'

Lorcan stops recording and hands the camera back to you. You watch the videos together. You are totally absorbed by the screen, you can hardly believe it's something you're able to hold in your hands. The tide is well in by this point, so you and Lorcan sit side by side, your feet dangling over the ocean. Every so often, a wave crashes against the rock and hits your feet. Together, you scream and laugh at each recording and you can barely breathe.

'Do you think we could send this to the TV people?' you ask. 'Do you think we could get it in video shops?' The idea is too exciting to contain. The moment you say it out loud it becomes real. You imagine the cover of the case, the advertisements that would play before it starts. People fast-forwarding and rewinding to the good bits.

'I don't know, probably?' Lorcan says.

'Let's ask Mum, it's her camera.'

You carefully put the camera away in its case and make your way back to the other side of the rock. As you crest the top of it, you realise you've misjudged the tide. You're surrounded by a river of ocean. You know the camera can't get wet.

Slowly, you descend the rock. It's trickier than going up, and at any moment your body weight could carry you face first into the water. You clutch the camera close to your side, eyeing the waves below you. A foot before the waterline, you stop, your toes wedged into a groove.

'Let me take it,' Lorcan says. 'I'm taller now.'

You contemplate this and see his point. You hand the case over to him, making sure he secures it around his neck like your dad showed you.

'I'll be careful,' he says.

'Let me test the water first,' you say solemnly. You dip your toe in; it's freezing. Across the beach, some people are swimming. You steel yourself, waiting for a moment where you feel particularly brave, and then jump in.

'Oh.' The water is only just past your knees. 'Phew.'

You hold out your hands, and Lorcan passes the camera back to you. For one devastating moment, when the camera is in the space between his hands and yours, you think you're going to fumble it and drop it into the sea. You yelp, but then the camera makes contact with your hand and you hold tight. Lorcan places the strap over your head and you keep going.

'I wasn't going to let you drop it,' he says, but you ignore him.

When you make it across the beach, it's hard to get the adults' attention, and then harder still to communicate why what you're talking about is important.

'You were gone for ages, what were you up to?' your mum asks, although it doesn't seem like she's actually interested in your answer. She has that concerned expression on her face, the one that annoys you. 'You know I don't like you wandering off to where I can't see you.'

'Look what we were doing.'

You hold the camera out to her, but she doesn't take it from you.

'I hope you didn't get any water or sand into that, you know it's delicate.'

You sigh impatiently and snap the camera closed. You look over at Lorcan, but he's no help. You and he have different ideas about what you spent the last hour doing, so it's all coming out jumbled. Lorcan is telling them that you'd been making funny tapes, but you hadn't been joking for any of it. It all felt so real.

Lorcan's dad ruffles your hair with his large hands and says he'll watch the videos with you, but it's too late.

'Hey,' he says, 'cheer up. You'll be seeing a lot more of us, I think.'

'What?'

Your mum says, 'Lorcan and his family are moving to Dublin.'

'That's where we live,' you say.

You're too young to understand the shift this presents in your relationship, how simple things like time and space can affect something so essential to you. It all feels very abstract, now. The videos feel concrete.

When your older cousins come over and ask Lorcan if he wants to go swimming, Lorcan loses interest in the camera entirely. You feel his attention shifting like a physical thing. By now the tide is far enough in that people can jump off the rocks into the deep tidal pool on one side of the bay. You clutch the camera in your hands and watch him leave. He disappears beneath the water in a great splash.

You want to join them too, even if you're afraid of jumping. Before you can ask, your parents say no. They can see the look in your eye that you're not aware of. The blow is crushing, even if part of you is relieved.

'You're too young,' your dad tells you.

'Lorcan's not that much older than me.'

'But he's a boy,' your mother says.

You sit down on the sand in a huff and open the camera again. You show your parents some of the videos you'd filmed, the one of you sitting on your special rock ledge. Your mum looks at you finally and says, 'You shouldn't sit like that.'

'Why? I'm sitting like that now.'

'It just looks different on camera,' she says.

Your legs look perfectly fine. You mimic the position exactly, with your legs starfished out, but you still don't understand what the problem might be. Your legs are covered in sand up to the knee from where you'd got them wet crossing the water. You rub it off, revealing your bare skin. Suddenly you're thinking about them in a way you never have before.

You sit in the sand, a sea of newspapers around you, and pretend to film the boys jumping into the sea. You hold the camera in front of you and zoom in and out. You even sing a soundtrack. One by one, you watch as they hurtle off the rock and out of frame. It's difficult to capture both the jump and the splash as they hit the water, you have to move your hand so quickly the image blurs. After a few tries, you begin to get it right.

It all strikes you as very unfair. You begin to feel hollow, lesser somehow, as though the sheer feeling of lack is boring into you, causing you a pain in your stomach. You tell your dad you're not feeling well, but he tells you to stop complaining. The camera runs out of battery. You stare into your own eyes for a second, reflected in the blacked-out screen, and then you put it away. The world loses texture.

You remember how it felt to be behind the lens of that camera, how enthralled you were by your own face. Seeing yourself from the outside, as though you're a stranger to yourself, was exciting. Being able to go back and reshoot, to make each take better, to delete the ones where you said the words wrong. Your mum recognises something in the camera too, although you're not sure what exactly it is that she sees. All you know is that what you film with the camera becomes something other than real life.

You wonder if you'll have to wait until you're ten to get a phone, if your parents will ever relent. Maybe they'd let you get your own video camera. You sit there in the sand and think about all of the things you could preserve, how you could best present them to the outside world. If there is a way you could better present yourself as well. You're thinking about it still when you leave the beach, and when you return home after your holiday. The thought never leaves you.

Two

The house phone rings and your dad yells, 'Can someone get that?'

The blue marker falls from Evan's hand and he clumsily pulls himself up, leaning his whole body weight on the kitchen table, but you call out 'I will!' and jump out of your chair before he's fully risen. You like being the one who answers the phone. Something about it distorts time and space, disconnecting your voice from your body and making you feel much bigger than you are. It fills you with a sense of purpose and authority.

The phone rings out again. Evan flinches.

You get to it just in time. You always wonder if someone is on the other end of the line, even if no one's called. Sometimes you pick up the receiver and put it to your ear and just listen. You're never sure if anything is listening back. This thought enters your mind as the phone makes contact with your face, and you're nervous.

'Hello?'

'Hi, it's Pat, can you tell your dad I'm just on my way over now?'

'Sure,' you say, 'no problem.' You twirl the phone's

coiled yellow cable around your index finger. It cuts off your circulation and your finger begins to change colour. You release it in one go and it springs loose. You glance over at Evan, who is watching you intently from across the kitchen.

'I shouldn't be more than a few, I'm going to get in the car now in a minute.'

The phone is too big for your head, so his voice sounds far away. You picture him as very small, perhaps small enough to fit inside the receiver. Much smaller than you are.

'Okay,' you say simply, because his discussion of time has confused you. 'See you soon.'

You hang the phone back up, and the wire coils around itself like a snake. One of the twists sticks out at a funny angle. You pull at it to try and get it to go back to normal, but you only make it worse.

Your dad walks into the kitchen. You hide the phone cord with your body, tongue-tied. If he picks up the phone he'll see what you've done. Your vision flashes white. Pat could know, he could have sensed it. There's nothing you're more afraid of than getting into trouble, although you're not quite sure what trouble is. You just know how your dad reacts to it.

'Who was it?'

Your dad is wearing the striped t-shirt that you like, the one with the pocket on one side. Your mum gave it to him for Christmas. Your memories are very important to you at this age; each one is fresh. There is still room in your life for big ones to form without forcing you to let go of others. There is room for insignificance. Your dad takes one step towards you, and then Evan drops something, distracting him.

'Pat?'

'Oh great, what did he say?'

'That he'll be here soon. In a minute.'

'Great.'

You're not entirely sure who Pat is, but you're aware that you're supposed to know, and that makes you too embarrassed to ask. You have an impulse to pick the phone back up, in case he's still in it, but you know that's not how phones work; it just feels that way.

You wait until your dad has his back to the phone before you return to the table and open your maths copy again. Physical distance creates emotional distance, and you forget about the phone wire. When Evan isn't paying attention you pick up the blue marker and use it to shade in a box. Just as you're finished he says 'Hey!' and pulls the marker out of your hand. It leaves an elaborate flourish on the page, like a tick.

You close your eyes and rub your temples, replicating a motion you've seen on TV. It's supposed to be calming, you've gathered. Evan is sometimes like a whirlwind, uncontrollable, and you hate how he disrupts your space. You wish you could silence him as easily as a phone call. You imagine plonking the receiver on his head.

You open your eyes when Evan asks, 'Who was in the phone?'

The fact that he misunderstands how the phone works annoys you, even though you secretly think the same. You know better than to say it out loud. He has his hand splayed out on his drawing, holding it down as he colours in the sky. He keeps rotating the page to get a better angle, resulting in numerous crosshatchings that border on unpleasant. You've tried to show him how to colour neatly, but he doesn't care for it. The more he colours the squeakier and drier the marker gets.

'No one was *in* the phone, someone was *on* the phone.'

'Oh. Who?'

'No one you know.'

'I might.'

'You don't. You don't know anyone.'

He starts to look upset. You know from experience that once Evan gets upset there's no cheering him up, and it'll be all your fault. You'll have to be the one to console him. He always comes to you, teddy bear in hand, tear-streaked face. Your mum tells you it's nice he loves his big sister so much. In your head, you hear something like a dial tone ring out. You leave him at the table and go to see what your dad is doing.

In the hall you find a miniature cityscape of cardboard boxes. Some of them are blue and some are white. Most have geometric designs on them. In one, a man smiles out at you. The skin of his face is a perfect white expanse, his shirt a deep navy. He's holding something in his hand, but it's covered and you don't know what it is.

You stand next to the tallest box and rest your chin on it. You have to stand on your tiptoes to do it. You grip the edge with your fingers for balance. The box is glossy, and one corner catches the fabric of your t-shirt. Some of the rhinestones have fallen off, but you won't let your mum get rid of it yet. You wear it most days, so you haven't noticed you've started to outgrow it. You haven't yet fully understood the concept of change and how it applies to things other than the seasons.

Your dad comes down the stairs. He's holding a paper

booklet, folded over and open on one page, and he's excited.

'Hey, Dad, look!' you say, chomping up and down with your mouth, your chin not leaving the cardboard. You feel the bones of your jaw working like an alligator. As you move, your chest rubs off the edge of the box and the t-shirt design makes a rippling noise.

'That's nice,' he says, patting you on the head.

Your dad walks by you and the boxes. Pivoting on your feet, head still on box, you turn to look. The corner is now digging uncomfortably into your face. Through the frosted glass of the door you see a shadowy figure. It reminds you of something you'd seen in a cartoon once; something you know to be ominous, though you're not afraid. The bell rings and you stop making the noise, curious.

'Hi, Pat,' your dad says, opening the door, 'come in.'

It's Lorcan's dad. Of course the name had sounded familiar to you. You didn't recognise it because Lorcan never uses it, and he sounded different on the phone. That small voice is nothing like the large man who stands before you. He's wearing a long brown coat that's missing one button at the top, revealing a yellow polo shirt beneath. You're surprised to see him. It feels like months since Lorcan's been here, but in reality it's only been a few weeks. You've been seeing him more frequently since his family moved to the area, but the times between seeing Lorcan always feel long to you at this point.

'What are you doing here?' you ask him, without malice. You remove your chin from the box because your position is muffling your speech and step away. You play with the plastic band around one of the boxes, slipping your fingers underneath it. It's tight, and you draw your hand away when it starts to pinch.

'I'm here to help set up the computer.'

That makes sense to you. Your mum had once told you that he worked with computers. When you'd asked Lorcan about it a few months later he'd said he made chips that went in people's brains. You're pretty sure he was joking, but then he'd told you about movies he'd seen with robots and zombies in them, and then you were less sure. Horrible images swim before your eyes. You want Lorcan to tell you he was joking.

'Is Lorcan with you?'

None of your internal panic must show on your face, because Pat responds calmly: 'No, he's playing football. Him and the old ball and chain will be around later for dinner though.'

The words he says are funny and you don't understand them. Your brain starts drawing up possible meanings. None of them make much sense to you. You're picturing Lorcan dragging a giant football behind him on a chain, which he may or may not have won at football training. You're familiar with the chains they clamp on prisoners. A lot of how you understand the world is through TV. You think of the coiled phone wire and how there's a kink in it now.

'Like a football?' you ask, head cocked to the side.

Pat's face changes. His eyes flick over to your dad, whose gaze is fixed on the boxes before him. Your dad shrugs, the responsibility of answering the question bouncing between the two of them like a tennis ball. You watch the spaces they are watching, your question unanswered.

'Dad, what does it mean?'

Your dad is crouched over one of the boxes, prying it open, so he's nearly eye level with you. Pat is examining a box, and not paying attention.

'He means Mary, Lorcan's mum. You know Mary.'

You frown, clutching the edge of the open box, inches from your dad's face.

'Why didn't he say that?'

You look at Pat accusingly now, unsure why he'd want to confuse you. It would have been much simpler if he'd used her name. You hate when adults deliberately hide things from you. They think you can't tell, but you can. The football swells in size and then pops in the golden light of the hall. You don't like feeling foolish, and now you do. You don't know if it's your fault, or Pat's, and now you think that asking the question had been a bad idea in the first place.

'It's just an expression.'

'Do you use that expression with Mum?'

From upstairs your mum yells, 'He'd better not.' You hadn't realised she'd been able to hear everything you've been saying. You whip your head around, embarrassed, like you've forgotten your lines in a school play. You don't like feeling like there's an audience you weren't aware of; you haven't learnt to like it yet.

The two men laugh then, and you don't know why so you laugh along with them. It feels good to laugh, much better than the unease you'd just been feeling. You exaggerate each noise you make for the benefit of your mum upstairs, playing up for the audience. Laughing releases tension from your belly and lets you feel more in control.

Pat turns to your dad quietly and says, 'Maybe you should, what?'

Something you don't have a name for yet passes between the men, some secret meaning far enough below the surface that you can't comprehend it. You just keep laughing, sitting on the staircase, watching from between the banisters as the men pull bubble-wrapped rectangles of grey plastic from the boxes. They leave them discarded at the front door in a heap.

'This thing will change your life,' Pat says. 'It's about time you finally got one.'

'That's what they're saying,' your dad says back.

Pat turns to look at you. Your face is pressed up against the gap in the banisters. It nearly fits through, except for your ears. 'You're so lucky, you have no idea. You're going to have computer skills people like me couldn't dream of.'

You sit on the staircase and your dad hands you a piece of bubble wrap. You run it through your fingers, not pressing hard enough to pop. Once you start, you know you won't be able to stop; everything will pop. You hold it against your face like a pillow, testing how much pressure it can handle.

Evan comes in from the kitchen. His hands are covered in swatches of marker. He's managed to get some on his white top too. You move over to the side of the staircase so he can sit beside you. He waddles over, getting under the men's feet before finding his way to you. You put your hands on either side of his torso as he sits down, so he doesn't fall over.

'Stop,' he says, fussing and pulling your hands off him. 'Stop!'

'I'm just helping,' you say.

The two men take the computer parts into the sitting room. There's a thump when they place each one on the ground. With the hall empty you are free to investigate the boxes. You pick up a smaller one and pull the top open, then lift it over your head to see if you can fit inside. It goes on easily and then falls around you. You sit for a minute in the claustrophobic darkness, your knees tucked against your chest. Then there's the sound of small fists on cardboard.

'Let me have a go,' Evan says. A pause, then, 'Please?'

You roll your eyes in an exaggerated manner, even though there's no one to see it, and push your way out of the box. Evan is knocked over by the movement. His little form hits the floor and the box falls on top of him. He lets out one sob, so you say, 'How about we make a castle? And play a game?'

His hand appears in the gap between the box and the floor. You lift it off him.

Evan's face is still cast in shadow. 'You promise we can play?'

'Of course.'

You take the box into the kitchen and find the scissors and tape. You carefully craft windows and doors. Evan tries to help you, but he's not very good at using scissors yet. You invent a game where you're the queen of the castle and he's your servant. You sit on a box throne and he expertly gets you biscuits and glasses of water. You don't mind playing this game with him.

'Be nice to Evan, he's only small,' your mum says to you. She's stirring something in a big orange pot, her brown hair tied up.

'I am, we're playing!'

It takes longer than you thought for the men to set up the computer. You send Evan into the room several times to see if it's ready yet. You're excited by the prospect. Pat seems to think it's special, or you're special; or even, it could make you special.

You've seen the computer they have at your school, but you've never used it. It sits in the corner of the classroom, and sometimes when people have finished their work early they're allowed to play games on it. Once, it had been your turn to use it, but when you sat down in front of it the computer wouldn't turn on. The teacher had to call the handyman, and no one has been allowed to use it since. You don't understand how a big plastic piece of furniture could be so fragile.

Evan's lost interest in your game. He's sitting inside one of the boxes, and you've made him a hat. Dinner's starting to smell nice, so you're sitting at the kitchen island and watching your mum cook. She hums as she stirs and lets you taste things off little spoons. Your dad comes into the kitchen. Your parents exchange looks: for as long as you've been alive, they've been able to communicate silently, or exchange hushed tones that you can't comprehend. You're not sure what's passing between them now, but you know something is.

'Come look at this!' your dad announces.

Whatever excitement you'd lost in the waiting comes flooding back. You scoot across the floor in your socks and follow him into the sitting room.

There's a small alcove in the corner of the room, evidence of a removed doorway, that last month your dad had decided would house the computer desk. It's a fine wooden unit, all golden-brown and full of shelves. Earlier today, it had been an empty skeleton. Now, the computer is a hulking mass of dark grey plastic and wires colonising it. Pat stands beside it, plugging in things and moving boxes around on the desk.

'These are speakers,' he says to you, holding up one of the small boxes. You reach out your hand to touch it. The grey fabric on the front is soft and gives way under your fingers.

'What do they speak?'

'No,' he laughs, '*speakers*. Sound and music and things come out of them.'

'Oh,' you say, not knowing what else to do. You put the speaker back down on the desk, disappointed it won't actually talk to you. Pat laughs at the expression on your face, but you don't know that's what he's laughing at. You wonder if you should laugh too.

Your dad bends down in front of the box on the floor. You balance yourself by holding on to his leg, watching.

'This is how you turn it on. It's the power button,' he says.

You're familiar with the concept of a power button, it's what you use to turn on the TV. You reach for it now; you want to know what it would feel like to push it, so you do. The button lights up green and fans begin to whir from somewhere inside the machine. It sounds like breathing. The monitor lights up and announces itself with a chime.

Your dad sits in the new chair your parents bought especially for the computer. It has wheels and spins around, unlike anything else you have in the house. He lifts you up onto his lap so you can see the screen properly.

The screen begins to show colours, different blues and greens and bits of writing. Lines snake their way across it. It reminds you of the video camera, the way it turns on with a burst of colour. You look closely at the screen and wonder if it could be looking back at you. You straighten your back, just in case.

Your dad tells you words for things that are so alien they might as well be gibberish, but they linger in your brain somehow. It's like watching Evan learn how to read. Slowly these words become part of your vocabulary. Things that couldn't possibly have names suddenly do, and you know them.

The keyboard is vast. The keys click pleasantly under your fingers. You have to read every button before you press it, and you have to press each one with more effort than you've ever had to press anything before. There are lots that don't make any sense to you, random letters jumbled up. You try to read the keys straight off, making words from them. You run your fingers in great swooshes over them, pressing whole rows at once. You wonder if this means anything to the computer, if it knows something you don't. You hope you're not accidentally upsetting it.

The mouse is too big in your hand. You pick it up and play with it, running it along the foam mat it sits on. You watch it with suspicion until your dad tells you to look at the screen. You can't quite connect the movement of your hand to the movement of the cursor.

You push yourself off your dad's lap and watch him use the computer. Your mum helps you bring a chair in from the kitchen. You sit on it, watching the movements of your father as Pat tells him various computing secrets. He is utterly still, except for his arm which moves occasionally, pushing the mouse or clicking a button. Sometimes the fans of the computer scream so loudly you think it might be broken, but the men don't react.

You have too many questions to ask him, which means you don't ask him any. You watch your hand as it moves a phantom mouse. Later, you will realise this is the first and only time your father had to show you how anything worked; everything else you will learn from the computer. But it's impossible to understand that at this point, when it feels like an alien creature and not an extension of self.

'See if it's connected now,' Pat says.

'Alright, let's see.' Your dad clicks an unassuming icon and then turns to you. 'What's your favourite animal?'

'A cat?' You say it uncertainly, as though it's a question.

He types something into the bar in the middle of the screen, and suddenly there are hundreds of kittens. Millions of kittens. You scroll together, and he lets you type into the box. You start searching for horses, then ponies, then unicorns. No matter what you type into that box, no matter how you spell it, images blink into existence. It's listening to you.

Your mum calls something, and your dad and Pat leave the room. You pull the chair close to the desk, eyes glued to the screen. With some of the unicorns, there are images of women; fairies, witches, fair maidens. Some of these women have long swathes of sheer draping fabric clinging to their bodies, but you don't notice them. You haven't learnt to notice these things yet. You think they look beautiful, and you want clothes like theirs.

The doorbell rings, but you don't move. You've forgotten that Lorcan is coming over. He doesn't exist to you right now, no one does. It is just you and the screen. No one is here to witness you discover all of these things, to be perhaps the first person in the world to see such amazing images.

Three

You dump your bag in the hall, kick off your shoes and run to the computer. You sit at it, your knee-high socks rolled down to your ankles, your grey school jumper draped over the back of the chair. The padded arms are starting to fray, and you dig your nails into the groove where the stitches are. Blue thread comes loose in your fingers.

Your grandmother follows you into the sitting room and sets your bag down next to the coffee table. She's older now, but not as old as you think she is. To you, she is ancient. She fixes her glasses and crosses her arms when she turns to look at you, gathering vast swathes of her shawl as she does it. You know what she's going to say, you hear the words before she utters them. 'Do your homework before you start playing on that thing.'

Your grandmother doesn't understand the computer; for a while you'd been able to tell her it was educational, but there have been articles in the paper and topics on talk shows. It's the only thing you've ever fought about, the spark that's about to burn the already rickety bridge of your relationship. You don't know that now, though, not with the flattened perspective of youth. You've heard her arguing with your dad about it, when she's babysitting and you're supposed to be asleep. Your father has never had easy conversations with your grandmother, even at the best of times. Later, you'll wonder if you got this part of your personality from him, if there is an embedded coldness being passed down your family line, inescapable.

You unfold yourself and walk over to the coffee table, just as the computer flashes on. You're disheartened when you hear the chime and groan as you take your books out of your bag. You sit down at the brown leather sofa and start working. Out of the corner of your eye, you see the computer prompt a login. The glow of the screen calls to you across the room.

Your grandmother brings Evan in to sit next to you. He doesn't have homework, so he sits on the floor, his legs under the coffee table, eating toast and watching you. Crumbs fall on the corner of your page. You blow them away but some of them get caught in the binding of your book.

This is your routine with Evan when you come home from school. You do your homework, and he waits for you to pay attention to him. The pen cramps in your hand as you write out the answers to your Irish homework. Your writing is a nearly illegible scrawl; you'd asked your teacher if you'd be allowed to type up your answers but she said no. The ink from your cartridge pen smears across the side of your hand.

When you're finally done, you go in to your grandmother and ask her if you can use the computer. When she says yes, you don't thank her, you just leave her sitting at the table smoking a cigarette and reading the paper. She watches you through the double doors between the kitchen and the sitting room. As soon as you re-enter the room Evan rushes to the chair and climbs up, taking up the entire thing. You ask him to move, pushing him gently and then more forcefully when he doesn't budge. He doesn't understand sharing, not really, so you have to be firm with him. His eyes are fixed on the screen, and he doesn't react. When you squeeze in beside him he decides he would be more comfortable sitting on your lap. He leans across you and grabs the mouse, pushing himself off your chest with his other hand. You peer through his arms and type the password into the computer. Your fingers pull up the homepage of the virtual pet website without conscious effort, acting out of pure muscle memory.

Evan doesn't like it when you play this game. It's too complicated for him, too girly, he complains. But he likes quietly watching you from the couch, though he pretends he doesn't. He'll sit on the sofa and talk to you, saying things like, 'Well, you can tell me what you're doing, but only if you want to.'

Today, you've decided to let him make his own pet. You log into your account and navigate to the pet generator. It prompts him with various colour options, all of which come with a numbered code he doesn't understand. He refuses to listen when you try to explain it. He clicks 'Create', and his cat comes out a mucky grey colour. He's crestfallen, devastated. He climbs off your lap and goes into the kitchen to your grandmother. You print out a picture of Jerry the cat for him anyway.

Now it is just you and the screen. There is a new language in this space, one that has taken you a long time to learn. Sometimes it feels like there is a whole world on the other side of the screen, and you are only just pressing up against it. But you are pressing up against it nonetheless, about to fall in.

You spend the afternoon talking to people you don't know; who don't know you. There is a role-playing forum, where you pretend to be certain pets or characters from movies and TV shows. All of the characters are extensions of yourself, self-inserts into the story that is unfolding. You picture yourself doing everything you describe.

Then you spend a while curating your own profile. Moving images and text boxes around. You like how you can be anyone you want, to anyone on the site. You can change your personality with a few clicks. You haven't told any of your friends at school about this website. You like that this world is yours alone; you like being anonymous.

A message arrives in your inbox, and you know it's from Nelly. She's normally online at this time. She gets out of school later than you do. Her username is JellyNelly123, but she told you her actual name is just Nelly; that her real friends call her Nelly. She's the only one on this site who knows your real name.

You can talk to her about anything. She doesn't know any of your friends, she's not even from the same country as you. She tells you she's twelve, and you pretend you're twelve too. Lying is easy, and you've had people on this site stop talking to you once they find out you're only nine, but you're not sure why.

You like being friends with Nelly. You trade virtual pets and items back and forth. She sends you a gift on your birthday. It's nice to have someone to talk to who understands this website. Your mailbox is full of conversations with her, and you start to miss her if you can't log on for a day. She trusts you to feed her pets when she's away on holiday. You know her login and she knows yours.

Her message is a response to an ongoing thread you have. You're not sure what the original message was about, and the subject line has been lost long ago.

Re: Re: Re: Re: Re: Re: Re: Re: Re: Re: Re:
17:47 *JellyNelly123*
   Don't act like u don't see it too1!!
   20:15 *i_luv_pink*
   haha noooooooo
   20:15 *JellyNelly123*
      omgg when are you to going to get married already
      20:14 *i_luv_pink*
      Sorry I have to log off, ttyl!!!!!! Lorcan's really good at maths tho
      20:12 *JellyNelly123*
         Uuuuhhh it's OK. I hate maths!!!!11!!
         20:10 *i_luv_pink*
         That's okay, I've been busy 2. How's school?
         20:05 *JellyNelly123*
            Sorry I was gone 4 AGEESS.
            Let's talk (u pick the topic)

37

Your dad comes in as you're trying to formulate a reply to her. You didn't notice your grandmother leaving; the smell of smoke still hangs in the house. You're confused when you look away from the screen, and lights dance across your vision. You didn't notice it getting dark either. For the past few hours you've barely had a body.

You quickly click into one of your other tabs. You instinctively hide parts of this website from your parents; you know they wouldn't like it. When your dad looks at it, all he sees are the cartoon creatures. To him it's like all the time you used to spend looking at Google Images. He doesn't understand. It makes it easy to evade the questions you know he'd like to ask, if only he could.

'Want to see my pets?' you offer, before he asks you anything else. Over the last few weeks you've acquired as many pets as the site allows you to have. You've arranged them in colour order, but you're thinking of changing that.

'It's time to get off that thing, the Ryans are coming over.'

You go red, because you're thinking of Nelly's message to you. The glow of the computer screen hides it, and he doesn't notice. Your heartbeat thumps in your ears.

The tether you have to the site snaps when Lorcan rings the doorbell. You run to the door, pulling up your socks as you go. You see his form through the glass, flanked on either side by his parents. For the first time in a long time, you're not thinking about your pets; you don't see them behind your eyelids when you blink. You're full of the kind of excitement you only feel when Lorcan is around.

A rush of cool air enters the house, and Lorcan and

his parents step inside. They're bundled up in raincoats. Lorcan's mum shakes a black and white umbrella three times before stepping into the house. Your dad hangs her coat up, embraces her, and holds out his hand to shake. It's a joke he's been trying out lately; acting like Lorcan is an adult. Pat claps you on the back, and you stumble forward half a step.

The adults go through to the kitchen, and you're left with Lorcan. You stick your tongue out at him as soon as his parents are out of sight. He sticks his out as well, and you both laugh. You like it best when it's just the two of you. You can't remember your life before Lorcan moved to Dublin any more; it feels like it's always been this way. He asks you about school and tells you he just got a new bicycle. You're desperate to learn, but your parents say they're too busy.

'I can teach you,' he says, 'sometime after school maybe.'

Sometimes, when your grandmother is busy, Lorcan's mum collects you and Evan and you wait outside the gates of Lorcan's school for him. Sometimes you eat dinner at his house too. Lorcan's dad works late most nights, or that's what his mother tells you. At this point, you don't have a reason to doubt her.

You grab Lorcan by the arm and pull him into the sitting room. The two of you approach the computer together. You don't have to discuss it; it's routine. You're wary this time. Nelly's message is weighing heavily on your mind. You read it off this screen, and it seems perfectly possible to you that some after-effect of it could still exist there, its essence somehow plainly visible. You're afraid that Lorcan will be able to take one look at the computer and know the secrets you've been whispering to it. You're not aware that they're secrets, you just know that you don't want anyone else to know them.

Your mouth is dry, and you're conscious of every movement Lorcan makes. Every time he types something into the search bar, you're worried it will suggest your virtual pet website. No matter how many times you have played on the computer with Lorcan, you've never shown him the site.

When your mum comes in with Evan, he kneels in the chair and insists on playing too. Lorcan is infinitely more entertaining to Evan than you are, and he doesn't mind you knowing it. The two of you are constantly in competition for Lorcan's attention, and even though you know it's not serious, the fact that Lorcan entertains it makes you insecure. Evan is treated gently in a way that you are not. You want something to be just yours for once. You want it with a panic that is inexpressible.

'Move over,' Evan says, rolling the chair into your side and causing you to lose the game you've been playing. His movements echo yours, the countless times you've had to force him to move, but it feels different. Your hip bone smarts. It sparks something inside you, which threatens to ignite all the kindling you've been holding on to. The emotion you've been storing up comes out, sharp.

'Lorcan's my friend, not yours,' you say. 'Go away.'

'That's not true,' Evan replies. There are tears in his eyes, and you throw your hands up in exasperation. Lorcan doesn't come to your defence. He doesn't react at all. He continues to play the game on the screen, showing Evan how to win a tough level. The tension remains. You're not sure if Lorcan can sense it. Your hip throbs, and you're lost to the emotions writhing inside you.

'Do you know any pet games?' Evan asks Lorcan, when the game is over.

'Pet games?'

'Yeah.' Evan sounds smug, much too smug for a seven-year-old. He nudges you in the shoulder. You're tense, your muscles a hard wall that does not give under his touch. Neither of the boys have noticed your change in stance, how coiled you are.

You narrow your eyes. You're not sure if what Evan did was deliberate. You hadn't thought him capable of reading social cues, let alone weaponising them. But maybe he had been paying attention. Maybe he knows how boys act when things are pink and purple, and this is his attempt to usurp your friendship with Lorcan.

You decide he's not going to win and you're going to prove it once and for all. You show Lorcan your site. You pretend it's cool, emphasising the money you've managed to make and the general regard the community holds you in. All the while, your pulse jumps in your throat and you're afraid. You have a message in your inbox. The notification frightens you.

'Oh, I used to play a game like this,' he says. 'The pets looked different, though. This one seems more complicated.'

His compliment makes you confident, self-assured, the way that only Lorcan's recognition does. Evan is forgotten, a ghost of a presence at your side fighting for attention you refuse to give him. You're not sure what makes you tell Lorcan about Nelly, maybe simply the fact that she's on your mind and you need to let it out in some way. When you do, he rolls his eyes and says she's probably not real. You hadn't even considered that. Beneath your thin layer of confidence is a canyon of self-doubt. You can sense the cracks forming, the fall inescapable. You're annoyed at both boys now. You set your jaw and hold back tears.

'Or she could be lying about who she is and she's actually a forty-year-old man. In school they told us that's really common.'

'Shut up,' you say.

'Don't use rude language, I'll tell my dad.'

The threat annoys you, you hate how Lorcan babies you and treats you like a child sometimes, even though he's not that much older than you. You hate how everyone makes you watch Evan, and you hate that everyone thinks this website is silly. You just want to be understood. All at once, you're furious with Lorcan. You know words way worse than that.

'Fuck you,' you say. Your first swear word comes into existence, and you feel it. You'd heard it in a movie once, and your parents had laughed. You've never said it aloud before, never dared to. This is the first time you've done something you know you're not supposed to. And it isn't the last time.

Evan gasps and puts his hands over his ears, wide-eyed. He looks as though he's about to run to your parents. You see it all very clearly; the smooth wood of the computer table, the blank expression on Evan's face, the warm grey plastic of the mouse. Every sensation is so pure.

'Don't you dare,' you say to Evan.

You're not sure what's come over you. You never talk to Evan like this. He doesn't know how to react to it. No one says anything. You stand up and leave them at the computer. You walk slowly to your bedroom, close the door and breathe in little shallow gasps. You don't let yourself cry. If you cry, they win.

Instead, you hold yourself tightly and stare at your face in the mirror. You clutch your edges, as though you're at risk of falling to pieces, or vanishing entirely. You let the intensity of the emotion run through you, the white-hot rush and cold chill of it, but you let none of it show on your face. You swallow it all, and it settles somewhere in your stomach.

Lorcan doesn't speak to you again that day. Dinner is a silent affair, with the adults looking between themselves, asking each other what happened. You hitch a smile onto your face and pretend you're okay, and after a while it feels like you might be.

OMG LORCAN

20:42 *i_luv_pink*

> I just had the WORST fite with Lorcan tonite. I even swore for the first time!! He didn't say goodbye. He told me u might not be real? Or ur lying to me?? How ridiculous is that??????????????

You wait days for Nelly's reply, but it never comes.

You're patient and good at coming up with explanations, but her account remains inactive, and you never speak to her again. She's changed her password. You watch the virtual pets in her account slowly die. It's heart-breaking. You can't believe she's forgotten about you, about this game. Maybe it meant something entirely different to her.

The site now becomes lonely for you. You don't reach out and message people about their fun usernames or cute pets. You wait and wait and hope your friend will come back online.

Sometimes you read the message over again and wonder if you could have phrased it better. When you're feeling extra lonely, you send a follow-up 'Hello?', but the silence only extends. Maybe what Lorcan had said was true, and Nelly had been lying to you. You dismiss it, but then realise that, of course, you'd been lying to her the whole time. She never knew the true you. You'd crafted a much better persona.

You stop playing. It doesn't happen all at once, but slowly. The joy of the game is gone. You've conquered it, sucked all the marrow from its bones. One day you just log on to feed your pets. Another day there is a special event so you play for that. Some days you forget to play at all.

One day when Lorcan and his parents are over, Lorcan teases you about how much you enjoyed your silly virtual pet site. After he leaves you log on and see all of your pets have died.

You never log on again.

Four

You're sitting at the computer with your legs under you, one hand on the mouse, the other absently pulling at the flesh of your arm. The afternoon is just fading into evening, and your face is pale in the glow of the screen. Luna, the family's new kitten, is sitting on the desk watching the cursor dart across the screen. Her pupils are huge in her green eyes as she tracks the movement. You and Evan had begged your parents for months to get a pet, but you're ignoring her now. Your parents are upstairs somewhere, but they feel miles away.

You type in a single letter and the web address autofills. Lately, your class has been obsessed with an artificial-intelligence chatbot. You print out funny conversations to show off in school.

Hi!
Hi, how's it going?
I'm good! How are you?
Good. You?
Good. You?
Good. You?

It's funny to watch the computer get stuck in a loop like this, repeating the same answer over and over again. You copy and paste your response into the chatbox, watching the conversation move down the page, the clicking of the keys rhythmic. It's not a conversation, just a reflection; what you don't understand is that you're the one providing inadequate content; you're the one trapping yourself here.

When the string of text fills the screen you stop and scroll back up to the top. You tap your fingers on the desk. Luna startles at the noise, then paws at your hand. You push her away absent-mindedly, not looking in her direction. She jumps from the desk and leaves the room in one quick movement. You don't notice her going, your eyes are fixed on the screen, and you're barely aware of your surroundings.

You clear the chat and start again, trying different prompts. Like:

Tell me a joke.
Okay. Why did the chicken cross the road?
To get to the other side.
Nope. To get to the other side.

Or:

What's it like inside the computer?
You tell me.

Some of these responses are troubling. There is an uncanniness in them, and in the moments when it actually feels like you're talking to another human. You're unsure of the things that make up consciousness and the philosophy of being. It doesn't seem impossible that this chatbot really thinks and feels, the same way that you do.

You hit print on the chat you have now and catch the piece of paper as it falls out of the printer. You lean back in the chair, stretching. On Google Images, you search for funny conversations. It's easier than coming up with your own, and the girls at school don't notice the difference. It is simple to give your creativity over to the machine; fun even. You click on one to see if it'll enlarge and accidentally select a link.

The website it leads to is a mixture of grey and blue hues, which seem very grown-up. Instinctively you know how to use this website. It reminds you of the virtual pet website you used to love. With this context, you navigate to the first comment on the thread, scrolling past images and text posts.

Users are talking about the conversations they've had with the bot. One user says that the bot is getting better at replicating human speech, citing an example of some slang that it used perfectly. You don't know what the word means, so you search it and end up on a community-sourced dictionary. It's similar to websites you've used to look up words before; it's blue and orange and official-looking. There are more words here you don't understand. You recognise them as English, mostly, but they are imbued with new significance. Each hyperlinked blue word only raises more questions. You form the words on your tongue but don't say them aloud, tasting them to see if their meanings become clearer.

You leave the website open in another tab and return to the forum, confusion brewing. This is a habit you've picked up quickly: turning to the internet for answers. The computer has become an extension of yourself. You no longer form conscious intents, you simply act.

In reply to the previous comment, another user says that the bot will never fully feel like a human, because it's blocked from using certain words. They post a list, so you copy and paste them into the dictionary too. A few of them are swear words, and you laugh as you read the descriptions of what they mean. You try to remember them so you can whisper them to Maggie in the playground tomorrow, behind the trunk of the large chestnut tree so no one else can hear. You don't dare to print them out, just in case your parents or your teachers find it, or the printer has some way of tracking the things you send through it. You are aware of the concept of surveillance only loosely and have no conception of how you're actually being watched. You may never fully understand it.

You return to Google. When you type into the search bar, nothing autofills. You lean forward in your seat. When you click search, you are met with hyperlinks and strings of letters. You click one, curious.

At first, you're not quite sure what you're looking at; the image is so strange that you confuse shadows with hard lines and lose sense of the shape of everything. The image is peach; brown; pink. You think you see a face, maybe, and some skin. It's like an optical illusion. It reminds you of raw chicken, something you've seen at the butchers.

You turn your head to the side and then back again. You realise it's a woman, kneeling down with the camera above her. She emerges out of the meat of the image. For a moment you picture yourself holding the camera, as you have many times before. You imagine the scene as it exists outside of this image, if you were in it.

Her hair is pushed back from her face, and it's greasy. She is wet and red and not wearing any clothes. You stare at her, not having a frame of reference for what you're seeing. You run your fingers over the flesh of your arm again, which seems so different to the thing you're looking at on the screen. Something heats up inside you. You've never seen anything like it; you're fascinated. At this age you're encountering so many new ideas and experiences that you have no idea what you should and shouldn't be exposed to. It's all so shiny and curious.

You glance around the room, suddenly aware that you're in your sitting room and not wherever this woman is. You can hear your heartbeat in your ears. You're alone, but it doesn't feel like it. It feels like you're on stage, with a million eyes watching you. You don't know what you're looking at, but you're certain that your parents wouldn't like it. You know this is another secret you have to keep. You hear a neighbour close their back door somewhere nearby and a dog bark.

You close your eyes and then return to the screen.

You click the image, and it enlarges, revealing more detail. You turn your head to the side, trying to understand it. The cursor moves, and the page zooms in and scrolls to different parts of the picture. It fills the entire screen now, seemingly larger than life. The image is pixelated, not meant to be blown up or inspected. It adds to your confusion around the definition of the shapes, about which parts end where.

Transfixed, you follow the image to a website. The background is black, which makes the video thumbnails and pop-up ads stark in comparison. Hundreds of images are vying for your attention, flashing and changing colour. You don't understand the video captions, or the tabs along the top. You're familiar with websites, but not websites like this.

You're not sure where to click first. Something makes a noise when you click it and you jump out of your skin. You turn the dial on the speakers all the way down, holding one to your ear so you can make it out faintly. You think it sounds like screaming.

There's a thick taste in your mouth, like a burnt tongue. People are contorted, doing things you weren't sure were possible. Seeing them makes you uneasy in your own body, as though you had never really thought that you were flesh and blood before. You're painfully aware of your physical form and how it doesn't look like any of these; how you want it to look like these. You want it so badly that it burns a hole in your stomach.

In one video, a disembodied hand slaps the face of a naked woman. You put your own hand on your face, mimicking its placement. Her face is red, but she doesn't cry. You rewind the video, the sound of the slap echoing in your ears. A man off-screen asks her if she likes it, and she says yes, and the hand comes down again. You return to the homepage.

You begin to feel something akin to panic, something that causes you to get short of breath and lose all perspective. There's a creak in the house and you jolt upright. You remember your family upstairs. Several distinct and contrary feelings shoot through you and meld together: curiosity, shame, hunger, disgust. They become impossible to disentangle. Your body goes icy cold and you close the window you have open. Now you're looking at a blank desktop, unsure of what to do.

You hear a door open and then footsteps on the stairs, each one reverberating throughout your whole body. Your dad calls out hello to you and you respond mechanically. You hear Evan's frantic footsteps on the landing and the door to his room close. His door is always closed. Your dad walks into the kitchen, and you watch him from through the double doors. You're very far away from your own body and yet pressed up against its edges; you might just burst out.

'Want to help me make dinner?'

'Just give me a second!' You sound sing-songy and reedy, insubstantial. You can still see an after-image of the website, overlaid onto your father in the kitchen. You're projecting the woman into the room with him, and you feel sick. You want her to go away. You open your internet browser as nonchalantly as you can. You want to make sure that it doesn't tell anyone what you were looking at. But you don't know how.

You search it. You read page after page, until you figure out how to navigate to your search history. It's a list of the sites you've just been on, which have long names with capital letters. You click one of them and it brings you back to a video of two people in a bedroom.

You grab the speakers, knocking them over, before realising you already muted the sound. You close the page, the last frame of the video burned into your retinas. You whip your head round to the kitchen, but your dad doesn't react. You hear kitchen sounds, dishes being moved around and the fridge being opened. It's hard to believe what you saw was confined to the screen and not really present with you in the room. Maybe it's you that was transported inside the screen. Your dad is none the wiser; to him it's a box in a room. He likes that you use it.

You try again, determined. This time you manage to delete the site and feel relief. You go through your history with a fine-tooth comb, making sure to catch anything that might look suspicious.

You open up your instant message service and you have a message from Lorcan. You talk most days after school, mainly just strings of colourful words and pictures. This time when you open the message you feel a flash of fright. You always feel this way when you know you've done something you shouldn't have. You breathe deeply until the feeling of faintness dissipates and force yourself to reply to him. You chat for a while, the whole time your mind running through the things you've seen, unable to fully concentrate on what he's saying. The messages slowly fill up the chat window, just like the chatbot.

My dad is being soooo annoying today
Mine too!!!
He said he'd take me to football but he had to work
Mum is annoyed 2
Uggggghhhhhh

After a while, Lorcan tells you he has to log off for dinner. You haven't registered anything he's said anyway. When you're having your own dinner, you sit quietly with your family and listen to your parents talk. They ask you questions, and you give monosyllabic responses. Your mind is elsewhere, racing. You want a moment of privacy where you can fully comprehend everything. To go back to those websites and look at them again. You feel your family members move through the house like never before. You're aware of the moment your mother brushes her teeth, and you hear your father go downstairs when everyone else is asleep.

You know what sex is, or you thought you did. It was something your teachers had explained with black-and-white diagrams, that some of the girls had looked up in the dictionary. Laura had gone white as a sheet when someone read the definition aloud and had to excuse herself to the bathroom.

What you'd just seen was nothing like that. You want to know more.

And you get your opportunity. You develop a routine. You watch the videos using earphones, with only one in your ear, the other ear listening for someone approaching. You keep different tabs and windows open in case you have to change what's on your screen quickly, just like you did with your virtual pet website. Your parents don't suspect a thing.

Fiction and reality start to blend in your mind. In some of the videos you are the women, you can almost feel the things they feel. In other videos, you're the person behind the camera. It doesn't seem to matter to you who you are. What matters is that there's always a new video for you to watch. You're driven by a fierce need to keep consuming.

You learn the words of the website, and you learn the videos you like. You learn how you should look and the sounds you should make. You learn different uses for a hairbrush. You think it would be fascinating to have sex and even more fascinating to be filmed doing it. You want so badly to watch yourself having sex that, one night, you take the video camera from your parents' bedroom.

You film yourself taking your clothes off, mimicking the poses of the women you've seen. You watch the tape back hungrily, but when you see yourself framed by the screen you feel so revolted that you delete the video. Your body doesn't look real, or whole; there's too much texture to it. When that doesn't feel final enough, you take the memory card out and flush it down the toilet. Sometimes, when images from the recording swim before your eyes, you feel such a rush of shame that you nearly vomit. It takes years for the flashbacks to ease.

You're not sure how something could be so appealing in the abstract, but make you sick in reality.

You find, after a while, that the videos you'd found so fascinating start to bore you. You collect a lexicon of words that have no meaning to you beyond the search bar. You want to see photos and videos of people your own age; you're not interested in adults. You're just starting to develop crushes in school. But your searches bring up nothing, and you learn later that it's not something you should ever look for again. But at this time, you don't understand how it's different.

The chatbot grows boring for you as well; it's too predictable. You try to goad it into using the new terms you've learnt, but it just says:

Sorry, I don't understand.

Sorry, I am only one year old.

Maybe, with you.

54

You find a site that allows you to talk to other people instead. Every conversation starts off *A/S/L?* Allowing you to form a new identity with every click. The people on this website like the new words you know, and it's exciting to use them. Sometimes you pretend to be American and type words like sidewalk and quarterback. Sometimes you're a doctor. You get the best results when you pretend to be sixteen or seventeen, which feels ridiculously old.

Time contracts and releases. It doesn't take you long to develop an online identity; you feel like you've always had it. You start lying less. The men on this site don't seem to mind. You construct an identity you return to over and over again, until it feels like every time you sit at the computer you become that person.

Wow you're sooo good at dirty-talk!

They're always impressed. Whenever you start to feel that clawing sense of guilt again you leave the chatroom and the entire log disappears. And you start again.

For your next birthday, you ask your parents for a new iPod. It comes with a touch screen and internet capability. Later that year, you get wireless broadband. Now all of these things are in the palm of your hand and the privacy of your bedroom.

Five

You're standing at your locker, your phone in your hand. You rest your shoulder against the locker door, shielding yourself from anyone who might be walking by. You flip your phone open. Looking at the screen, it's easy to forget there's anyone else around, but you don't. You glance over your shoulder, just once, and make sure your phone is on silent. Your parents gave you it when you started school, for the new walk home, and it is the only thing that anchors you in this strange new space.

Your thumb moves across the keypad habitually, opening your texts. The bell rings, startling you. You flip the phone closed again, and the display on the outside flashes. The case is metallic pink, and you've decorated it with stickers. You run your fingers over them now, checking your phone is on silent once more before stowing it away on a shelf. You push your locker closed with your shoulder. The metal is cool against you, and you exhale.

The locker room is empty now, and you realise you're not entirely sure where your next class is. You walk through the door just as a group of boys are passing in the opposite direction. You see them jostling each other, pulling at one another's backpacks. You make eye contact with one of them. He nudges his friend and points at you.

'Dare you, Hugo.'

Hugo looks at you, you think he might be flirting with you; you don't know what flirting is yet. You're parallel to him now, and you can smell the acid of his body spray. Just as your body is an inch from his, he pretends to trip and catches himself on your chest, his hands squeezing firmly. 'Sorry,' he says, into your face, his hands still there.

They all laugh, someone high-fives him. It takes you a second to catch up with the situation, long enough that the sensation in your chest starts to fade before you've really had a chance to feel it. This is the first time a boy has touched you like this, and you missed it; it's like you aren't even here. He touched some sentient flesh that couldn't possibly have any connection to you.

You haven't done anything to warrant the shame that fills you, but you feel like you have. You've seen videos of men doing that kind of thing to girls, and the girls had enjoyed it. You don't understand why you feel this way and rationalise that it must be because you've done something wrong. You think it would be better if you weren't here; if you just vanished.

'Honestly, you're such a prick, Hugo,' Ella says from behind you. 'Get a life.'

The boys laugh again, except for Hugo. He goes quiet and keeps walking.

Ella turns to you and says, 'Can't believe you got lost again.'

'This place is a maze.'

You almost walk past the classroom door, before Ella pulls you back. Ella has an easy confidence you wish you could mimic. She always says the right things, and she has a way with people that you envy. She's settled into school life here easily and already has a group of friends. You look at her sideways now; you want so badly to be her friend. Her book isn't open in front of her, but Mr Fitzgerald doesn't say anything. She's drawing little hearts on the side of her pencil case.

The first thing you learnt about Ella was that she firmly believes she'll die before she's twenty-one. You wonder if that's something you should wish too. For some reason it sounds glamorous and self-assured, even though you don't actually want to die at all.

When it's time to fill out a worksheet, she writes notes to you in the margins. *This is so boring lol* she writes in red ink. Her handwriting is all loops and even spacing. When the bell rings for lunch, you walk with Ella back to the locker room. Walking with Ella is nice, it makes you feel like there's a place for you in this school after all. You take your lunchbox out, and Ella retrieves her own plastic bag.

'I kept losing my lunchbox,' she says by way of explanation.

You watch her slide her phone into it, and so you do the same.

The two of you sit by a beech tree in the yard. Your phone is cradled in your skirt, invisible to the casual observer. You take a bite of your cheese sandwich and don't notice that Ella doesn't touch hers.

'Why do you keep looking over to the field?' she asks you.

'Is that where the third years eat lunch?'

'Uh, yeah. Why?'

'I know one of them. He's my friend.'

59

'For real?'

'Yeah, he's like my . . .' You search for a suitable word. What comes out is 'brother' although your relationship with Lorcan is nothing like your relationship with Evan.

Ella's gaze is laser-focused on you now. Your sandwich is forgotten. 'What's his name?'

'Lorcan.'

'Oh shut up, he's on the rugby team.'

'Yeah, that's him.'

You can tell you've piqued Ella's interest, and you like having something she doesn't. It's nearly like she's interested in you. You tell her all about your family holidays with Lorcan. You know his dad lost his job, it's something your parents have talked about, thinking you wouldn't understand. You don't understand, not really, but you know what the individual words mean, so you say them now.

'That's so sad!' she says, and you agree with her. You show her Lorcan's text messages and you pore over them together. You like the attention she gives you. It feels like there is a lot to gamble and lose in this conversation, but you're not risking your own secrets: they're Lorcan's. You picture his face now, if he knew what you were telling her; maybe you've said too much.

'Listen, come back to mine later, I need to know more!'

You're embarrassed because you're excited. You've never been to Ella's house before, and it feels like a milestone. Your first new friend. You agree and text your mum asking if it's okay. After a minute, her reply comes through: *yes*. You hold your phone close.

You get through the afternoon with Ella, one class after another. Because you're with her, you don't get lost again.

When you look through the glass square into one class-room, you make eye contact with the boy from earlier. Hugo. He winks at you, and some part of you sinks inside yourself, leaving your body empty. You avoid looking at anyone else for the rest of the day. You're not even conscious you're doing it until Ella asks you about it.

'Why are you being so weird?'

'Am I?' you reply, keeping your face blank.

'Yeah? You're like looking over your shoulder every five seconds.'

'Oh. I'm just thinking about what happened earlier, with Hugo.'

'That's just so typical of boys,' she says. 'Honestly, they're sickos. I heard a story about some boy bringing his phone into the girls' bathroom and taking photos of everyone while they peed. I think he got expelled for it, but maybe that was a different school.'

You don't know what to do, so you laugh. Your conversation turns to urban legends, men with hooks for hands and murdered babysitters. You're both laughing as you walk down the corridor. It fades away into the ordinary.

The locker room is full of people again, talking on their phones even though they know they're not supposed to. Two girls are sitting on the window ledge and sending MP3s of songs to each other.

You flip your phone open, and then it vibrates. The girls look at you, and you shrug. You're about to dismiss it, when you realise someone is trying to send you something over Bluetooth. It's not from one of the girls. You see their phones go off with the same notification. You look around the locker room, trying to see who might have sent it.

61

From behind you, Ella says, 'Omg, don't open it, guys, it's from the lads upstairs.'

One of the boys' locker rooms is on the floor above. On Tuesday they'd thrown things out the window and your whole year had got into trouble for it. You've been inside it once, last week, when you thought you were on your floor. It's a mess.

You accept the notification. The whole room is in chaos around you; girls are laughing, yelping, grabbing phones. There's a charged energy that's palpable.

The photo is grainy and small in your hands. In it, a group of boys are standing around in a circle, all of them mooning the camera. Your pulse jumps in your throat, a thousand images appearing in your head. You swallow. This is the first time you've seen a naked image of someone you know, someone who's your age. You can see one of the boys' faces, and you recognise him: Hugo. Briefly, you wonder if this could have anything to do with you, if maybe he had actually been flirting with you earlier. It gives you a whole new lens to view the interaction through.

Ella nudges you, bringing you back to reality. 'Why did you open that?' she asks. Her words are innocent but her tone isn't. You already know how to answer it based on how she's phrased the question.

You shrug. 'It was an accident, I didn't mean to.'

You flip your phone closed, conscious that the next time you open it the image will still be there. You want Ella to like you, so you hold your phone down at your side, as if you don't even know it's there. You mimic her detached stance, her relaxed shoulders.

The window is open, and from upstairs you hear a boy

yell, 'Send one back!' and the girls around you laugh nervously.

Ella closes the window with a snap, putting a definitive end to the interaction, and the energy fades. But it doesn't leave your brain, not even when you leave the school. All the girls in your year are talking about it. A few of them are brandishing the photo, but you don't look over. The movements of the phones are like the arcs of meteors in the sky: appealing and fleeting. Instead of looking, you walk in step with Ella and joke about how pathetic it all is.

You see Lorcan waiting outside the gates, and you wave at him. Sometimes, when he doesn't have training or plans after school, he waits for you and the two of you walk home together. When he sees you with the other girls in your year, he gives you a thumbs up and starts walking in the opposite direction. You're happy he's seen this moment, that you can share it with him.

That is until Ella sees him as well, and something about her expression makes you deflate. She didn't seem happy, or curious. You know how to recognise jealousy; you've seen it in the mirror.

You're quiet as you wait for the bus, trying to figure out how you lost your footing in this interaction so suddenly. A few of the other girls get on this bus too, so you sit in a pack at the front upstairs. Ella tells everyone that she didn't pay for her bus fare, and the girls laugh and roll their eyes.

'I don't know how you get away with that,' one says.

'You just have to smile and make eye contact. Most people are too afraid to.'

One of the girls asks if you have any good songs on your phone, and you play one out loud.

'Send that to me,' she says. She reaches out and takes your phone, holding it next to hers. Someone had told you once that it makes the signal stronger. Although that might have been for a Nintendo DS. She types something into your phone and then hands it back.

'I put my number in,' she says.

You look through your contacts list. Her name is Kate. She hands you her phone, and you take it and input your own number. You didn't think it would be so easy, so casual, making friends in this new environment. Yet here you are, slotting into place. You think maybe your unease was misplaced, and it passes. Just another girl in a uniform, laughing. Maybe the bus does something, unlocks some temporary space where all the rules are blurred. You think next time you're on the bus you mightn't pay your fare either, just to see what might happen. If the other girls might laugh along with you.

The bus turns off the main road, past some public art, and then Ella presses the button. It dings pleasantly. Ella motions for you to stand up, and the two of you make your way shakily down the stairs. You're hurled around as it comes to a stop and nearly fall onto the floor. Ella laughs, and you laugh with her.

You thank the bus driver as you get off, and so does Ella.

'See ya, girls,' he says. You can't believe he hasn't noticed that Ella never paid. You wonder what else she gets for free.

Ella's house is two doors down from the bus stop. There is a large tree that's beginning to see the effects of autumn. A few horse chestnuts have fallen to the ground and split open. You pick one up and run your hand over the smooth brown nut before putting it into your pocket.

Ella retrieves her key from her school bag and leads you inside. You leave your shoes neatly next to the door. The hall is a mix of warm brown wood and white paint. Four different paintings of the sea hang from a picture rail. They remind you of the beach and summer, lit with the speckled light reflecting through the stained–glass door. In one of them you think you see a figure, outlined in curves of colour that move across the canvas. You walk over to it.

'Do you see the naked woman?'

'What?'

'The naked woman. In that picture, everyone sees a naked woman.'

'I guess.' You shrug, not wanting to appear too inter-ested. You wonder why Ella's family have a picture like that hanging in their hallway, and if she thinks it's indecent, or if you should. You think again of the image the boys sent you; you might excuse yourself to the bathroom to examine it more closely.

Ella's mum is in the kitchen, reading the paper. She's sitting at a long white marble counter, her legs crossed and her head balanced in her hand. She looks up when you walk in. You think there is something in her face that might remind you of the picture of the woman. Light is streaming in from a skylight, and everything is golden. She smiles and puts down her pen.

'Do you girls want anything to drink? A smoothie?'

She unfolds herself from the chair, revealing the pink dress she is wearing. She pulls the pouches out of a drawer in the fridge and hands them to you. The fridge is huge, the American kind with two doors and an ice dispenser. Stuck to one of the doors is an assortment of magnets and a calendar. From here you can't read anything on it, but you can see that it's full.

'Mum, can we have some chocolate?'

'No sugar before dinner, you know the rules.'

'Whatever.' Ella says it quietly, and you think her mother doesn't hear. You watch the two of them, fascinated, because their relationship is so unlike the one you have with your own mother. They move as though they are the same side of a magnet, repelling each other. You stick the straw into your smoothie, and Ella leads you out of the room.

She takes you to her family's office, which smells like wood varnish and is barely big enough to fit the two of you. It's warm inside, claustrophobic even. A big Mac computer takes up the entire desk. The mouse isn't attached to the computer by any cable. You pick it up and turn it over, flashing a red light around the room. The machine is sleek, an entirely different creature to the one you have at home.

'My mum's so annoying, isn't she?'

You're sucking your smoothie so you nod along to her.

'I mean, isn't she?'

Ella turns to you, looking for an answer. You swallow your mouthful and say, 'Um, yeah,' even though you don't think so.

'She just can't leave me alone.'

Ella sits in the large leather chair in front of the screen, and you hop up to sit on part of the L-shaped desk. You're above her, and slightly behind, so she can't see your face.

You and Ella spend the next half hour taking photos with the webcam of the computer. You don't know how to smile for the camera, or how to turn your head to get the best angles. But Ella does, and she shows you. She has this way of pressing her arms together that makes it look like she has cleavage. She tells you to unbutton your school shirt a little bit and you do. You turn the world negative, multi-colour, sepia. You mirror the image, duplicate it four ways. After a while, the image stops looking like you at all.

'Maybe we could send these to your friend. What's his name again?'

'Lorcan?'

'Yeah. It's just, I'd like a boyfriend. I'm ready for a boyfriend.'

Secretly you're not ready, but you know that's not the thing to say. So you say, 'Me too.'

Your phone is burning your pocket. You're aware of its weight. You've started to think about Lorcan differently. Now he slots into your life so nicely, so perfectly. You know what a soulmate is, and you think maybe he could be yours.

'Do you know what sex is?'

You do, but you can't tell her that. You think maybe she'd be impressed at your knowledge, but your desire to seem cool is outweighed by the certainty you have that what you do when no one else is home is wrong. You'd made a vow to never tell anyone, and you've been careful. You're not about to slip up now.

'Not really,' you say, grateful she can't see your face.

'Let me show you.'

The pictures she finds are academic, and you read long articles describing things that you still don't fully compre-hend. Ella gets creative in her googling, following blue hyperlinks, and you begin to get nervous. She hasn't turned the speakers off, and you're worried they'll come to life. But you feign ignorance. It's like she's never done this before.

Ella laughs the first time she sees a naked woman, and you say nothing at all. She clicks into the image, and you watch her, not wanting to look at the screen, but not wanting to look away either.

Now that you're with someone else, you realise that the women in the photos don't look real, and there's something grotesque and wrong about them. It seems unlikely your body will ever grow to mimic them, that you could one day possess such heaping masses of flesh. You begin to feel queasy, holding in your head all the images of today.

'Have you ever seen someone naked?' she asks you.

You take a moment to answer. 'Well, that photo today.'

'Oh yeah, gross. Do you have it?' She turns to look at you then. 'I deleted mine.'

Your hand goes to your phone. 'Yes.'

'Well, let's see.'

You're surprised by her demeanour, at how different she seems now. You hand her the phone, and she navigates to the image. You stare at it over her shoulder, the image tiny in Ella's hand. Now that it's here, in front of you, and you're being invited to look at it, you're disappointed. You can't really make anything out.

'I'd love to see someone naked,' she says to you, handing back your phone. 'But like real, not like this.'

Attention back on the computer, she searches 'naked men'. When the image results load, Ella screams and then blushes a deep shade of red. You don't react at all. She closes all the windows, and just in time. Her dad appears and asks what you've been up to, and shakes his head when Ella erupts into a fit of giggles. He rolls his eyes, completely unaware. You sense the danger here, it's a feeling of wrong-ness that spreads throughout your body; a warning. You feel you should be in trouble, and you don't know why. You wait, but her dad says nothing else, and when he leaves the room it's just you, and Ella, and the computer.

Ella moves to get out of the chair and you say, 'You have to delete your history.'

'What?'

'So they don't know what we've been looking at.'

'Aren't you full of surprises?'

You show her what to do, the whole time feeling on edge, like you're doing the wrong thing, even though you know you're not. You know you're helping her. She doesn't ask you anything, the unsaid thing hanging between the two of you. Ella leads you to her bedroom, and you're thinking about what just happened and what you've revealed about yourself.

'Do you think we're really going to get hair?' Ella asks you. 'Like, down there? And that much?'

You shrug, afraid to answer, to acknowledge this exchange as anything other than casual. You glance around her room, at the pink walls and velvet chair in the corner. You sit down on the end of her bedspread, feeling the fabric between your fingers.

'That's gross.'

'I don't know if I'd mind,' you venture, before you can think better of it.

'Then you're gross. I bet you're really hairy down there already.'

Ella's tone has changed again, the pendulum of power swinging back in her direction. You're on unsure ground, worried you're about to lose a friend.

'No, I'm not, I'm not gross.'

'Prove it then.' Ella's eyes are alive with mischief, and you're afraid of her. You sense that the mood in the room is shifting, and you don't know how to react.

'What do you mean?'

'Like, show me. Take off your skirt. I'll show you mine as well.'

You can taste hot blood in your mouth now, and you're panicking. You weigh your options. For all you know, this is something normal. Maybe Ella does it with all of her friends.

'Okay, but you first.'

'No way.'

You look at her once more; she doesn't seem to be taking any of this seriously, and so you know that you shouldn't either. It's just another one of Ella's games.

You swallow and then you get up off the bed and stand before Ella. In one quick movement you pull down your underwear and then lift up your school skirt. Ella giggles again, and you know you've done the right thing.

You drop your skirt and say, 'See? No hair.' You wait just a moment. 'Your turn.'

Ella laughs again. 'Not a chance, I'm not a pervert.'

Humiliation. It's a cold and hot wave that courses through your body. You pull your underwear back up and sit down beside Ella. She starts to tell you about the different boys she fancies and how she's going to get them to fall in love with her, but you're a million miles away. Your body sits obediently, laughing at whatever Ella says, but it may as well be the carcass of a dead animal, now vacant.

Things are different for you at school, and Ella doesn't seem to know why there's now this distance between the two of you. But the distance is real, and it's insurmount-able, and you never want to go to Ella's house again.

You find it difficult to look at what lies between your legs. Ella's laughter still rings in your ears. You spend more time watching porn. You study their bodies, and you compare them to your own. You can't do it without feeling disgust, but still a fascination inhabits you.

The discomfort moves from between your legs to the space around your belly button. You tell your parents and they think it's just a belly-ache. After two days of complaining they take you to the doctor. He pokes at you and asks you questions you don't know how to answer. He says maybe you should exercise more and lose weight. He sends you home telling you there's nothing wrong with you; perhaps he's right.

Six

You can't see your class group. The day is sunny for once, so you shade your eyes with your hand and look. The grass is full of people, groups lying out. To the untrained eye it might seem like one mass of teenagers, but over the last two weeks you've watched the social bubbles appear and burst and reform. You can see the careful delineations, the parts where people have their backs to each other, the places where they lie in packs like dogs.

You overhear a girl say 'Tá sé, like, so cringe,' and her friends laugh. You figure she must be talking about someone in the group beside them. One of the girls leans back and pointedly looks at a boy. He doesn't notice. It's possible his Irish isn't good enough to decode the message, even though that's the sole reason everyone has come here.

'I can't believe today is the last day,' Ella says when you finally make your way over to your friends. 'It doesn't feel like we've been here for two weeks.'

You know half of these girls from school; the other half you've picked up during the last few weeks. Ella's holding a digital camera in her hand. You're conscious of the way you move your body, the unflattering angles the camera could pick up, the way someone once said you looked like a dead person when you weren't smiling. She clicks back the lens cover and snaps a shot of you.

'Delete that.'

'You haven't even seen it yet.'

'Please.'

Ella rolls her eyes at you but complies. You watch her touch the bin button and relax. You sit down in the circle, people moving to the side to open up a new wedge of space. You put your bag down in front of you. Beside you, Jess is doodling with a Sharpie on Saoirse's school bag. She signs her name across the pink band at the front.

Ella is surveying the group with the camera, following everyone's movements on the screen in her hands. She moves the camera around casually, pointing it in different directions to see how things look. You position your body at its best angle, ready in case she wants to take another. You tuck your legs under you, twisting your torso and leaning on one arm to force a better perspective. You avoid making eye contact with the camera, but you know it's there. You hitch a half smile onto your face, trying to look candid.

'I don't feel like I've learnt any Irish at all,' you say, with a laugh for the benefit of the camera.

'That's not why you go to Irish College,' Ella says back to you. Across the green, she's eyeing a boy in another group. He has dark hair and freckles, and she's told you she fancies him. She shrugs her shoulders, looking over at him, and you see the moment he notices her.

'Why did you come to Irish College then?'

'Why does anyone?'

Ella abruptly stands up and says she's going to get a

drink from the machine inside. You watch the boy stand up a moment after her and then follow her over. If you hadn't been paying close attention, you might not have noticed anything happening at all.

There is a boy here you like, although you haven't told anyone yet. He's behind you and to the right now, you know, but you don't look. You wonder what would happen if you were to copy Ella and meet his eye. You can feel the potential string humming between the two of you. All you have to do is pull.

You allow your eyes to wander in his direction. He's clutching a can of Club Lemon, his red backpack resting against his legs. His head moves up, but Ella blocks your line of sight. She's back, holding a drink. You think maybe you've misjudged what just happened, but she gives you a knowing smile and you know you haven't. She sits down across from you.

'Can I borrow that camera?' you ask her.

'Sure, take a photo of me. I want to be in some of them.' She hands the camera over to you. It's warm from her touch, almost alive.

You slide the cover off and her face appears on the screen in front of you. You snap four or five pictures, then gesture at the ground beside you so you can take a photo with her. You hold your breath, sensitive that at any moment she might guess your agenda.

Ella squeezes in beside you and puts her arm around your shoulder. You hold still at her touch, as though a rod is going up your back. You exhale and allow yourself to lean into her, to appear natural. You force your body to work with you.

You hold the camera an arm's length away. You're not

very good at taking these kinds of photos. Without the screen to guide you, your aim is off, and you capture great lengths of your outstretched arm. The flash catches on some of your arm hair, and when you look at the pictures you're embarrassed.

'Hey, I'm barely in that picture,' Ella says.

'Sorry!'

You don't want a picture of Ella, though. You move a little bit to the left, a little bit down, and then you catch him. Framed between your two heads is Miles.

You turn the camera around to look at the pictures. The images are still, flat, lifeless somehow but perfect because of it. Anyone looking at them would think the two of you are friends. You flick through them, the two of you moving like stop-motion characters, the poses rehearsed. Miles is perfectly centred, his hand moving as though he's saying something. Then, he lifts his eyes and his bland expression starts to shift. In the next photo he's smiling; in the one after that he's flashing a peace sign. Heat rises in your face.

'Omg that's so funny, Miles is right between us.' Ella calls over her shoulder, moving faster than you can process: 'Stop photobombing.'

You're afraid to look, so it takes you a full four seconds to turn around. You meet Miles' gaze and say, 'Yeah, you're ruining our photos.' Your voice sounds like Ella's, and it rings in your ears. You'd spent the last two weeks trying to pluck up the courage to talk to him, so you have no idea why you suddenly sound aloof.

'Whatever,' he calls back, his attention already back on the group around him. You hadn't managed to give him the look Ella had given the boy, you're embarrassed you said anything at all. You stare at the side of his face, hoping he'll turn around again, but he doesn't. The camera in your hand feels significant, as though by capturing the two of you on the same surface, you're solidifying your bond.

Ella says she's going to go back to the room to start getting ready, and everyone moves. You get up, slowly, hoping Miles is looking at you. You want him to notice you, but only when you're doing something not deliberately done to make him notice you. Miles doesn't say anything or follow you, but you walk like he might be looking your way.

As soon as you get back to your dorm, the girls start buzzing with excitement. Music is playing from a phone, and everyone is laughing. Your makeup from that morning has started to collect in your pores, and your mascara is running down your eyes. You have a heavy hand and blue eye shadow. You only just mastered foundation and eye makeup, and you know nothing else.

'Do you want some bronzer?' Jess asks you.

There is a sour tang in the air, which you recognise as fake tan. The smell of it mingles with the burning coming from Saoirse straightening her hair. 'You have to wait until it smokes just a little bit,' she assures you.

You don't tell them this is the first disco you've ever got ready for, but you feel like they can read it on your face. You do your best to study them, to copy them, to learn from them. You hate feeling out of place, not knowing what to do. You've read about experiences like this in books and seen internet posts describing what to do.

One of the girls does your makeup for you, and the person who stares at you from the mirror is a stranger. You've never seen your face like this. Your eyes are rimmed in a dark brown eye shadow and your lips are red. You look older, and everyone tells you you look great. When you smile for the photos all of your faces light up white from the amount of pressed powder you've used.

'No flash!' Kate says when the camera is pointed her way.

'No, no, I need the flash,' says Ella.

Jess asks if you're really going to wear your runners, but you haven't brought anything else. Looking around, all of the girls are wearing clothes with frills and layers and strategic cut-outs. You smooth out the t-shirt that you're wearing; your mum bought it for you the last time she'd taken you shopping.

You feel light-headed. Someone lends you their shoes, and when you stand up you're four inches taller. Your ankles hurt. Time catches up to you: it's nearly time to head down.

Ella says, 'I've been saving this.'

She pulls a water bottle with a sports cap out of the recesses of her bag. 'I stole it from my parents.'

You look at it, confused. A hush falls over the room.

'Is that . . .?'

'It's vodka.'

She passes the bottle around the circle and you all take a sip. You pause when it comes to you, then take a gulp. It's thick and warm and bitter. The other girls had been hesitant, chaste even, and you sense an opportunity to prove yourself.

'Save some for the rest of us, god.'

Ella takes photos of each of you as you drink, and you don't think about asking her not to, or blocking your face. You don't know about consequences yet, or a digital footprint. The more photos she takes, the funnier it becomes to you.

'So what's the plan for tonight?' Saoirse asks.

'The what?'

'You know.' She wiggles her eyebrows. 'No one is leaving here a fridget. It's our last night.'

'Oh,' you say.

'Who does everyone fancy?' Ella asks, then quickly follows up with, 'I bagsie Michael.'

The question whips around the room like a boomerang, everyone rushing to answer it and pretend they don't care. You're worried what will happen if someone has the same answer as you.

'Miles,' leaves your lips casually and Ella says, 'Really? Him? Okay.'

The alcohol dulls the sting of her words, so you just shrug and nod, as though you're confused about it too. Your confession is immediately followed by someone else's, and you feel lighter for sharing it. You think it could be funny to show them all the doodles you've done of his name, the loops you've made between his name and yours; at the back of your brain, however, a danger light goes off and you remain silent.

The bottle comes back around to you, and you drink, and it's time to go down to the disco.

The corridor is cold – someone's left a window open. You run your fingers along the smooth yellow wall. The staircase is funny, amusing to you somehow. You grip the faded wooden handrail for dear life and laugh as the girls push and shove each other on the way down. You feel ready for what might happen, for what you think is going to happen. The camera flashes, and you no longer care how you present yourself to it. You've never felt more alive.

The air is full of expectation now, thick with it. It makes you feel nervous and sickly, like something is settling in your belly. You breathe it down into your lungs. You're ready, or at least you think you are.

You smile for the picture Jess is taking. You raise your hand in the air. Around you, the room has been decorated with streamers and balloons. A pop song is playing, and you move with it. You want this weight lifted off your shoulders, you can almost feel it disappearing around you.

There are people at school who've bragged that they kissed someone when they were ten, and with every passing day it feels more and more shameful to not have done it. On this trip, boys have approached groups of girls and asked them if they're a fridget or not. You'd laughed and pretended the question was preposterous, even though everyone knew it wasn't.

You have some lip balm in the pocket of your jeans, and you apply it nervously all night. You hold eye contact with anyone who looks your way, and you don't blink nearly enough. You try to dance to the music, but you're so preoccupied with what's to come that you can't find the right rhythm.

Jess reaches for your hand and suddenly you're dancing with her.

'Boys like it when girls dance with each other,' she says in your ear. 'I read about it online.' She twirls you around and then pulls you close and pecks you on the lips in front of everyone. You don't react, not really. You just think in your head, This isn't it, this isn't my first kiss. She spins you around and then she's dancing with Ella. They're getting closer and suddenly they're kissing. Not the peck you had, but full-on kissing. You look away as the lights flash from green to blue to red overhead. They break apart.

You keep dancing, this time alone. You're adrift in the crowd; around you groups move to a rhythm and you can't get inside them. No one seems to notice that you're there, and no one lets you in. You think maybe you should go and get some air. Some air will reset the night for you, let it start again. Your shoes are heavy now, they feel like hooves. You unstrap them and walk barefoot outside.

Ella and the others are here. You squint into the darkness and think you see figures meshed together there. Ella produces the plastic bottle from her bag and you take it off her, swigging deeply. You cough and splutter and take another sip. By the door, some of the supervisors are watching you, but they're eighteen and don't care enough to stop you. One of them laughs.

Ella takes you by the hand and leads you back inside. All around you, people are kissing. At the back of the hall, someone has their hand up a girl's skirt. You remember that day in Ella's room now with a shudder. Sensations begin to meld and mingle, and you connect this moment to that one, a chain that will stretch out into the future as well.

Then, at just the right moment, someone taps you on the shoulder. It's him. Your heart flutters in your chest. Your mouth is dry. You haven't applied any lip balm in at least twenty minutes. Your hand goes to the pocket of your jeans now. He leans his head down next to your ear, and as he does you grasp his arm. The sleeve of his shirt is soft in your hand.

He looks at you with his blue eyes, the same eyes you've

been drawing in your notebook all week. At night, you've tried to decide their exact colour. You want him to know that you don't only like him for superficial reasons, that you've seen him and thought about him and want him. You nearly say this out loud.

'Will your mate score me?'

You hold on to him for just a second longer, the smell of him imprinting itself somewhere in your brain. You close your eyes, once, then twice. There is an impossible dryness in your mouth. Your tongue feels thick, clumsy. You see the moment for a split second from the outside, you see the stillness on your face, the way his thoughts shift gear and start wondering if you're okay. You think you might faint. The lights continue to flash behind you.

You know what this means; of course it was obvious. No one ever asks someone to kiss them, you need at least one, if not two, buffers for rejection. You nod slowly. The muscles in your face start to move, warmth goes back into them and you're hot. You turn to Ella and say, 'He wants to score you,' and point over your shoulder. You do this mechanically, fulfilling your role. Jess is holding the camera. You've never wanted to die before, never wished you didn't exist, but you do now, for the first time. It won't be the last.

Ella smiles at you. You'd told her you liked him, so you expect her to shake her head in rejection. Instead, she goes over to him. You see her move in slow motion, as though through water. She is fluid and graceful and unashamed. She walks past you, and you smell the body spray she used earlier. You think you must smell like sweat, that must be the problem.

She's past you now, and you pivot slightly on your foot to watch her progression across the rest of the space. The song has a heavy bass, each beat resounding in your ears. You're not sure how you feel, if you're feeling anything at all. You want to know how to feel. You want to find something to tell you how to feel.

You swear she looks at you when she does it. You swear, as she is devouring his face in front of you, her eyes open to see if you're watching her, and you are. Inside, you are burning. The different-coloured disco lights bounce across their writhing forms in a way that is nearly beautiful. She puts her arms around his neck, the way you've seen people do on TV, the way you're supposed to kiss someone.

They break apart, and Ella sees you looking at her, and she winks at you. You exist at the very centre of space, the very point where the entire universe turns. The world is being sucked into it.

No one in the room has a face any more, they're all just shifting forms and masses. A few people try to dance next to or with you, you're not sure, but you don't react to them. Someone taps your shoulder again, and you startle and move away. You can't make yourself believe that this is real, that any of this could be real. Your lip balm falls out of your pocket, and you're glad when you notice it's gone.

You take yourself to bed early, and no one comes to get you. You crumple your discarded outfit into a ball and stuff it into your suitcase. You never want to wear it again. You scrub your face with water, and the makeup runs down your cheeks. Your hands are stained with mascara and brown eye shadow, so you scrub them too.

You spill water on the floor in front of the sink in the bathroom, and when you look at yourself in the mirror you realise you're crying. You breathe in great sobs, each one a rattling in your chest. You can still hear the music from downstairs, the laughter.

Your sadness turns into anger, and that anger is undirected and chaotic. You cover your head with your hands and press yourself into as small a shape as possible until the pain of it starts to crystallise. You rage against the whole world and everything that brought you here. It burns a hole in your belly. You're shocked at the emotion that comes pouring out of you, unable to meet your own eyes in the bathroom mirror, some part of you too filled with shame to witness this moment. You bite down on your finger so hard it bleeds.

When the anger fades, you are exhausted; depleted of something vital. You think that this must be how it feels to die, that you must be some kind of dead thing, and that is why you are so disgusting and wrong. You close your eyes and lock the bathroom door even though you know no one will be in the room for a while yet. You push the emotion away, as you always have, until you feel nothing any more.

You put the lid down over the toilet and take a seat, heavily. You feel faint again, and a low throb is echoing through your abdomen. When you lift your top up to look at it, you see a hole the size of a euro coin in your belly. It goes straight through you, as though your rage has burned away the flesh. In the mirror, you can see the porcelain behind you. Slowly, you reach your index finger inside, and it sinks all the way to the knuckle. There is no texture to it, no feeling; you're aware of it only in its absence.

A tremor goes through your whole body, the only thing you feel; the quiet drop of certainty, of knowing you are defective. You get up, unlock the door and sink into bed.

In the dark, you think about Miles. Silent tears roll down your face, and you curl up into a ball. Your stomach-ache gets worse, and you sink your finger deeper into the hole, reaching for what isn't there, trying to coax yourself into feeling anything at all.

You don't stir when the other girls come in. You don't hear them talk about their night, or the people they kissed, or what else happened. You are barely a presence.

The next day, you wake early. Your hand instantly goes to your stomach, feeling for the part of you that no longer exists, the part you lost last night. A single sob hiccups through you when you touch it, which you stifle before anyone can hear. You stuff all of your things into your suitcase and try to erase your presence from the room.

When you change in the bathroom, you don't look down at yourself at all. You avoid looking in the cracked mirror above the sink. You don't even look into it as you brush your teeth. You're not sure what you're afraid of seeing; perhaps some warped version of yourself, or some nightmare figure from a horror movie. Perhaps you would see yourself as you really are, and that would be worse. So you opt to sit on the toilet and stare at the wall, the energy having gone out of your legs.

You'd packed extra vests with you. At the time, you didn't know why. Your brain had said just in case, and you'd obeyed. Now you put as many layers of clothing between you and the outside world as possible.

The girls wake up slowly. They don't say anything but

you can feel the weight of their gazes as they flick over you. They begin to pack up their things too. When Ella wakes up you pretend nothing is wrong. You sense some discomfort from her. She doesn't try to apologise, but it's clear that she's expecting you to be mad at her. And she'd find it funny if you were.

As you're leaving the dorm, suitcase in hand, she says, 'Hey, are we okay?'

With blank eyes you respond, 'Yeah, why?'

She seems surprised, confused even, and you enjoy it.

Ella smiles, 'Good! I'd hate if we fell out over a boy.'

You look at her with a question in your eyes, daring her to read into it, daring her to think she's rattled you. But you don't react, and neither does she, and so she moves on. You watch her walk down the corridor, the yellow light bouncing off her hair. You breathe again, your hand unconsciously on your navel, grabbing at the meat of your belly.

The buses are waiting in the car park when you get there. The girls are all chatting, and you think perhaps they're a little bit quieter when you join them. You just smile at them blandly and don't react. They realise you're not going to say anything, and the volume is turned back up.

You're very tired. You want to get on the bus and go to sleep. You don't want to talk to anyone here. You think about Lorcan; you wish he was here now. There is a rightness to the world when Lorcan is in it, a wholeness, a feeling so divorced from what you feel now. You picture him on the beach and feel unbelievably lonely. You can't believe you had to leave the holiday early for *this*.

On the bus, Ella and Miles hold hands the whole way

home. You sit next to someone you don't really know, and they fall asleep almost immediately. There's nothing to do but stare out the window and look at your phone. You put in earphones and play music. You want to call someone, to text someone, to talk to someone. But then you realise that everyone will be talking about what a great time they had at Irish College, how amazing it was. You realise that if you lie and say that it was also a great time for you, no one will be able to prove otherwise.

You've experimented with fake identities online, but you never thought that they could carry over into real life. You're resolute. It seems obvious. You will say you had a great time, you will tell the same stories everyone else does, you will print out pictures and stick them to your wall. And in a few years, when you look back, all you will remember are the good bits you decide to keep. The ache in your stomach starts to fade.

The bus pulls into Dublin and the scenery outside the window becomes familiar. The girl beside you wakes up and looks sheepish, and you tell her she's drooled on her shoulder. She wipes at it, going red. You wonder what stories she'll tell about this bus ride, if she'll make up ones about singalongs and games.

Off the bus now, and everyone says tearful goodbyes, promising to stay in touch, to add each other on various messaging and email services, and you know you will never talk to these people again.

You spend the next few weeks reading posts online telling you how to behave, so you don't have to feel like an outsider ever again. You do your hair like they tell you to and dress in the unofficial uniform they pick out for you. You buy the same brown eye shadow the girl had used on you, and you wear it every day. After a while, you forget that you started all this by pretending. You're no longer putting on an act, wearing a shield. You are just the girl they all think you are.

Seven

You're sitting at the desk in your room. Kate is sitting on the floor beside you, her back against the radiator. Last year you'd painted over the fleshy-rose walls with a vibrant lime green. You're in the liminal space between child and teen-ager, where everything is painful and confusing. The faces of countless celebrities and teen idols stare down at you from the walls, observing the scene. Their bodies are perfect; unblemished; desirable. When you look at them, a hollow pang goes through the place you can't feel any more, but you don't know how to look away yet. The window is open, letting a faint breeze disturb the stagnant air.

In front of you is an open maths book, but you're not paying attention to it. Instead, you hold your new phone in the palm of your hand. Your thumb flicks across the touch screen. A crack spiders across the top corner. Your other hand rests casually against your navel, as though by accident, holding yourself together. It's a new habit, one that you'll have for the rest of your life. You're not thinking about that now, though, not with your phone in your hand.

You navigate through your apps, flicking past rows of free games. A new one came out last week, and you'd spent two evenings alone in your room playing it.

You open the browser and type in the address of a new social media site. It autofills after a couple of letters. Everyone was talking about it in school earlier, and you're excited. You and Kate are supposed to be doing homework, that's what you told your parents, anyway, and they'd believed you. Lying to them is easy and mostly by omission; they don't know the right questions to ask. Kate holds her own phone in her hand, going through the same process as you.

'Ready?' you ask her.

The screen prompts you to create an account. Kate's screen mirrors your own: the two of you looking through different windows into the same world.

'Are you sure we're supposed to use our real names?'

'Yeah,' you say, 'how else will people find us?'

'But what about the people we don't want to find us? Like our parents? Or teachers? I would die if Mr Fitzgerald found my profile.'

'All of them are way too old.'

'Are you sure?'

'Definitely.'

Your voice is full of surprising confidence. You have no idea if what you just said is true, but you know it's the thing Kate needs to hear. Truth is a strange concept to you. You don't understand why it matters. The website wants you to add your personal details to your account, so you do. You don't have a job so you leave that part blank. It asks you a few questions you don't have answers for yet, but you don't let that stop you.

'But what if someone finds the picture and it stops us getting a job?'

'I'm, like, ages away from ever needing a job.'

'My mum said never ever post anything about yourself online. Someone could show up to your house and kill you.'

'If you're not going to post anything about yourself, why did you make a profile?'

She doesn't answer you. You're not sure why you're being standoffish with Kate; it's just the way the words are forming on your tongue. It's how you feel you should be treating her, just following along with the script. You know that you're the reason she made a profile, but you don't want to acknowledge it.

You scroll through the photos on your phone. The memory isn't very large, so there aren't that many. The first one is of you and Kate and Ella on the bus. You're smiling, and Ella is pursing her lips to emphasise her cheekbones. Kate is slightly out of frame. You flick to the next one quickly; you don't want Ella to be in your profile picture. The sight of her sends a flash through your gut.

You open your phone's camera and turn it around, pointing the lens at you. In the reflection of the window, you can see the little screen and how you're framed by it. When you turn the camera around, you're not happy with the photo. Your body isn't doing the things you want it to; it never does.

'Let me do it.' Kate stands up and holds her hand out for your phone. You pass it over and get into position. You read online once that you should have photos taken from above and turn one shoulder towards the camera. You mimic the pose now, willing your body to look like the posters behind you. You make eye contact with one of the singers over Kate's left shoulder, the curly-haired boy, your mouth dry.

91

'Aren't you afraid people are going to leave nasty comments?'

Kate's anxiety almost amuses you. You're not worried; you are entirely in control of how you are perceived online. It's real life you have no control over, where you're never sure which parts of you people are looking at, or what they might be thinking about. In a flattened picture on a screen, your body looks like anyone else's: just flesh. You don't know how to express this to her, you're not even fully aware of the thought, so you roll your eyes at her and say, 'No.'

Kate hands your phone back to you, and you post the image. You don't have any friends yet, so no one comments, but they will later. You send Kate a friend request and she accepts. You think the fact she's chosen a Disney princess makes her seem immature, but you don't say anything. Your phone is starting to grow hot in your hands, and the low battery alert flashes. You plug it in, then place it on top of the book on your desk. You continue scrolling with your index finger.

You start sending friend requests to people. When you click on someone's profile you find lists of people you might know. Acceptance notifications are pinging almost as fast as you can send them. Everyone must be online, doing the same things you are, existing in this same shared space. The time between getting home from school and dinner. This site feels different to every other one you've used. It's like the virtual pet website, only real life as well. You feel its potential, the way you could use it. The rest of the world falls away around you, and all there is is the screen in your hand and the life you could live in it.

You search for Lorcan's profile and show it to Kate. He has had three profile pictures. The last one was taken on the beach. You'd recognise the rocks anywhere. In the bottom left corner you can see one arm of a blue folding chair and a single hand. You know it's yours. You don't remember the photo being taken, but you feel connected to it now. It seems significant that Lorcan chose this picture. You know Kate has a crush on Lorcan, even though she's never said anything to you. Everyone has a crush on Lorcan. You send him a request and watch Kate's face.

'Are you going to send him one too?' you ask.

'Should I? No, I don't think so.'

'You could.'

'Do you think?'

'Yeah.'

With your approval, and a promise that you'll tell Lorcan it was your suggestion, she sends a request. Her eyes dart around the room and her index finger worries the skin around her thumb. You like predicting how people will act, and when they follow through on it; even better when you've nudged them to do so. A few minutes later he accepts both of you, and Kate begins to flick through the rest of his photos, which have just become accessible.

You glance at the photos over Kate's shoulder. She stops on one of him playing rugby and uses two fingers to enlarge it. He's covered in mud, and his face is screwed up in a grimace. Sixty people have liked the photo. Most of them are people you don't know. There's something voyeuristic about seeing his profile on Kate's phone, almost like you're spying on something intimate.

You laugh a little bit and say, 'It's such a shame I'm probably going to end up marrying Lorcan.'

Kate looks over at you jealously, and you like it. It's easy to pretend to her that you don't know exactly what you're doing; you think she believes it. You watch her over the top of your phone: the makeup stains around the collar of her shirt, the way she picks at the skin of her fingers, her slightly too large nose. You see these things without judgement, but you know it would be easy to judge her for them. If you wanted to. It's a bit silly, everyone having a crush on Lorcan. You're not sure if what you said is true, but you want it to be because you love how the other girls' eyes shine when you say it.

'You're so lucky your family knows his.'

'Yeah—' You don't have to lie about it '—but I just wish my soulmate was a bit cooler.'

Kate continues to look through the photos, but she's self-conscious about it now. You know you've made her uncomfortable, which means she can't make you uncomfortable. You exit Lorcan's profile. You don't want Kate to catch you on it. You'd be mortified if Lorcan ever found out you said this kind of stuff, of course. But maybe he's said the same thing about you. You banish the thought from your head before you can analyse it any further.

You click through the different functions of the site, searching for a distraction. There's an option to poke someone, and so you poke Kate. You look over at her, waiting for the notification to come through on her phone. She laughs, looks up and pokes you back. The two of you press the same button every few seconds until you get bored. It's like a challenge, waiting to see who breaks first. Eventually it's you, but you wait until a moment where it feels like a power move. You catch Kate just as she pushes the button to send a notification over to you, but you don't look at it.

You stretch and yawn, exaggerating your movements. But careful, always careful, to make sure that your shirt doesn't come untucked from your skirt. You wear a vest every day and never take off your jumper in school. You put your phone on the desk so you can control the movement of your clothes as you stand and readjust them as soon as you're upright. You go to the bathroom and pretend everything is normal.

Luna is sitting in the laundry basket. When you close the door she startles and runs into the hot press. The thick green paint on the doors has made the hinges stiff, and they creak as she pushes them open. Her tail flicks inside.

'Sorry,' you say, but it doesn't make a difference. Her reflexive eyes stare out at you, her dark fur blending with the shadow.

You're on your period: not for the first time, but you're still new to the sensation. You sit on the toilet for a few minutes longer than you have to, clutching your belly. One of the girls in school told you period pains are worse than heart attacks, and now every time one comes you're afraid it's a heart attack and you just haven't realised it yet.

Your belly aches, but the hole hasn't grown any bigger. Slowly, you pull your t-shirt up. You shut your eyes tight, screwing up your whole face, until you work up the courage to look. The sight of it always rips through you. Your finger runs around the edge of it, and your revulsion turns into something more physical. There are days when you convince yourself it's not there, and days when it's all you think about. You've thought about showing it to someone, maybe Kate, but thinking about that fills you with a deep shame. You pull your top back down and breathe out.

The pain is still there, but it's easier to not think about it when it's covered up. You wonder if anyone has noticed the way the fabric morphs a little bit around the hole. You want your phone in your hand, something to drown out these thoughts.

You remember Kate waiting in your room. You jolt with panic a little bit, and you're not sure why. You clean yourself up, and as you wipe away the blood a sensation goes through you that echoes in your stomach. You are disgusted by how much blood there is and how much toilet paper it takes before it comes away clean. The dark-brown strands of mucous. You wash your hands and leave the bathroom. Luna is still hiding in the hot press, the sole witness.

When you return to your room, Kate is holding back laughter. She keeps looking at you and then at your phone on your desk. For one horrifying moment you think she must somehow suspect what you were doing in the bathroom, that your constant fear of surveillance has finally manifested in reality. Then you realise your phone is in a slightly different position than where you left it.

'What did you do?'

'Nothing,' she says, but the word comes out staggered, on the cusp of a laugh.

You clutch at the thing you're hiding in your belly, although you're not aware you do so. Your fingers claw at the fabric; later, you'll find five scratches making a star around the hole. You cross the room and scoop your phone up in your hands, gently.

You have a notification: Lorcan's poked you.

You look over at Kate, and she finally lets the laugh out. You realise that she's poked him and most of the boys in your year. Notifications start piling up. You pretend you're furious, but you're secretly delighted. You love the attention, the validation. The fear pours out of you, evaporating into the room. Your phone is a whole ecosystem in your hand, and you want to dive into it.

People start updating their statuses about the poke wars they're involved in and you can't hide the smile that breaks out across your face. Kate's phone doesn't have nearly the same amount of notifications lighting it up. You see her disappointment and maybe a touch of resentment. You pretend not to notice.

In your hand, everything is chaos. People are typing comments to each other in all caps. You leave laughing faces and *lol* in the comments of the posts, strings of *hahahas*. Kate leaves her phone face up and unlocked when she goes to the bathroom, but you don't touch it. When she comes back, you act like you've done her a favour.

At dinner, your parents ask you what's going on at school. You look at Kate over your mashed potatoes and both of you say, 'Nothing.' Evan rolls his eyes at you, but he doesn't say anything. Lately, he's not been saying much at all.

Your parents are doing their best; this is something you are aware of. But they don't have the language or reference points to understand your world, and you're tired of explaining it. They think you were really doing your maths homework and that you just use your phone for games. Sometimes they ask you about cyber-bullying, which only frustrates you further. Your mum once asked you if you'd spent all your phone credit on ringtones, and you'd had to tell her that everyone keeps their phone on silent now.

Your grandmother's breathing rattles across the table, breaking the silence, the smell of smoke hanging in the air. She's been coming over for dinner more and more; it's something you've been meaning to ask about, but it's never seemed like the right time. You've come to expect her presence at every family meal, but each day you feel you are more at a loss for what to say.

After dinner, you and Kate go into the sitting room to use the family desktop computer. Your mum is driving your grandmother home, and your dad is watching TV upstairs, so you're unsupervised. Kate logs into her profile and the two of you start scrolling. It's so much more satisfying on the big screen.

Eventually Kate's mum comes to collect her, and you're alone. You take your phone upstairs with you. You update your status with whatever you're doing: homework, showering, getting ready for bed. You get notifications and scroll through the profiles of the people you know, liking whatever they post. You feel connected to them, like what they're saying is important and so what you're saying might be important too.

The next morning you're excited to log on, and when you do you see a whole new selection of things to read. You prop your phone against the sink as you brush your teeth, and it nearly falls in several times. You wipe splatters of water off the screen with the sleeve of your pyjamas and leave a smear of toothpaste on one side.

In school you are eager to talk about the site with people. At break time the locker room is buzzing with chatter. People want to know who's friends with which boys in the year and who they should be adding as a friend. Saoirse has already had her phone confiscated, but that doesn't stop people from brazenly using them in the corridors. Kate asks you jokingly if you've stopped getting notifications yet; she wants people to know she was part of what happened last night.

Ella doesn't say anything. She's been making a point of ignoring you lately. You've noticed her watching you, but when you smile her eyes go hazy, as though she's deliberately looking through you. She's standing nearby, close enough that her refusal to acknowledge you feels cold rather than unintentional.

You don't know how to act around her, not since last summer. The fact she's acting like you've done something wrong unsettles you. You feel the need to make up for something, or apologise, and you don't like it. You've been thinking of asking Kate about it. She's sitting beside you now, scrolling through her phone. You haven't thought about Miles in months, but you suddenly wonder what would happen if you sent him a friend request.

'Hi, Kate,' Ella says.

She stands in such a way that her body comes between you and Kate, and her back is to you. You're staring at her grey school jumper, a wall erected between you and Kate. You lean around her and see Kate look up. She holds her phone limply now, but face down, as though she doesn't want Ella to know what's on her screen.

'What's up?'

'Did you get the message I sent you last night?'

There's a frost in the air. Kate hadn't shown you any message from Ella, but maybe she sent it after Kate went home. She still hasn't accepted your friend request. You run your thumb over the crack in your screen. A little piece of glass detaches itself and sticks into the meat of your thumb.

Ella turns to you, her movement quick as a whip. 'Something wrong?' There is aggression in her stance, but below the surface, so you question if you can even sense it.

'No,' you say lightly, with a shrug. You flick the piece of glass out of your thumb with your forefinger.

'You can get your screen repaired in town.'

Your face is burning then. The embarrassment makes its way through your entire body, always settling in your stomach. You clutch at it now and stare deeply into your phone until the feeling goes away. You don't catch what happens next, you're too lost in the screen, and when you resurface you're sitting on the windowsill alone and Kate is gone. You look from side to side and then stand up coolly, as though everything you do is intentional.

You spend the rest of the day thinking about your interactions with the two girls. You wonder if Ella is trying to turn Kate against you, if you did something to deserve it. You pick apart everything that's happened in the last few weeks and still come up empty. You speculate, wildly, if Kate noticed something about your body and told Ella about it.

You pack your bag quickly at the end of the day and set off out of the school gates before anyone else. You don't want to have to walk home with any of the girls, and you know Lorcan has rugby training today. You want to talk to him more than anything, but he's been so busy. It's been weeks since you've seen him. His parents don't come to dinner any more, so neither does he. Sometimes his dad watches the rugby with your dad, but you avoid joining them if you can help it.

You sit down at the computer. No one else is home. You run your hands over the armrests of the chair, your fingers finding the familiar grooves you carved into them so many years ago.

You navigate to the social media site, and when you do it's already logged on. But it's not your account: it's Kate's. She forgot to log out when she left last night. You know you shouldn't do it, but at the same time there's no stopping you. You tell yourself it's just innocent curiosity, you want to see if her page is different to yours. You're excited, ecstatic even.

You scroll for a minute. She knows all the same people you do; it might as well be your account. Some of your posts from last night pop up in her feed so you like them. You think about poking some people, to repay her the favour from last night, but everyone might be tired of that. Then a red notification catches your eye.

You click the button, more out of habit than intent, and the start of the message appears. It's from Ella:

And I know I shouldn't be annoyed but I really . . .

The message trails off too soon. You know you can't click into it. If you click into it Kate will be able to tell someone was reading her messages. You clutch the armrest with your left hand, your right hand holding the mouse over the message. You close your eyes and breathe out, then open them and left click. You aren't thinking any thoughts as you do this.

The message is about you.

And I know I shouldn't be annoyed but I really don't want to have to spend any more time with her. She's so fake. You and I were friends before her, and she's ruining it. I want it to go back to how it was, when it was me, and you, and we were like sisters. It's not the same with her, she's not like our sister. But I have to spend sooooo much time with her because she's part of our group. I think we should kick her out.

Your whole body is full of rushing emotion. You read the message over and over again. Each time is like a hot knife to the gut. You think you might be sick with the pain, or you might faint. Then you start to cry, the heat escaping through your head. You don't know why Ella's turned against you; you can't imagine it. You've gone out of your way to never antagonise her, no matter what she'd done to you.

You let go of your gut, and you stop thinking about it. A feeling of knowing settles over you, dark and terrifying. You stop thinking about anything and become pure action; you want to lash out. If you cannot restore what you've lost, maybe you can at least take something from someone else. It feels like an equal exchange.

You text Kate. You tell her that you saw her account. You say you're sorry and you know you shouldn't have done it, but the much greater problem is the fact that she'd been bitching about you behind your back with Ella. You'd thought both of them were your friends. You type the message at the speed of speech, and it doesn't feel like writing. It feels like pure, condensed emotion.

Kate sees the message. Her replies come in staggered blocks, full of spelling mistakes. Somehow it feels like she's already lost. She's furious you read her messages, and she's even more furious because she has had to tell Ella and now Ella is annoyed at her too. She says she doesn't want to be in the middle of it any more.

You forget where you are, you forget what you're doing. You're only aware you're sitting at the computer screen when Evan comes home and slams the door. It jolts you back to reality. You hear his footsteps as he walks into the kitchen. He grunts when he sees you through the double doors, and you hear him run the tap. You don't see any of this, because your head is cradled in your hands.

The tap turns off and there are more footsteps. Then they stop.

'Are you okay?'

The world is thick and exerting too much pressure on you, as though all dimensions are closing in on you, compressing you, turning your body into mush.

Your voice comes out reedy and sharp. 'Oh, now you want to talk to me, is it? *Now*?' You look up at him. His legs are muddy and he's wearing his football kit.

'Jesus Christ, sorry I asked.'

He leaves then, and you're alone. Your thoughts become louder, so loud that you cease to be able to hear anything else.

It no longer feels like you read a private conversation between the two of them, it feels like they said those things to your face. By immortalising them in print, it felt like you were part of the conversation too. A mute observer.

The computer screen flashes, prompting you to log in again. Kate changed her password; she no longer trusts you. The bridge of your friendship has been burnt to a crisp, just as you were finally fitting into school.

You call Lorcan to tell him what happened. You crave his easy company. His house is only a few minutes away, and in a wild, desperate moment you think of running over to him. He must be home by now. You already have one shoe on when he answers, one arm inside the sleeve of your coat.

'Lorcan?'

There's a muffled sound on the other end of the line and he says, 'Hi, yeah, I'm just with some of the guys now. Oh, and Aisling.'

'Okay?'

'And I kinda have to go.'

You're still crying, so you wipe furiously at your eyes. 'I need someone to talk to.'

He stays on the phone with you for another few minutes before saying he really has to go. The whole conversation feels wrong, hashed out somehow, as though there was too much being unsaid to really understand. You kick your shoe off and leave your coat crumpled in a pile on the floor.

You retreat into your room and get into bed. You're so exhausted you take off all your clothes and throw them in your laundry basket. When your mind quietens, you look down. Your belly is folded into itself, forming three distinct rolls. You run your fingers over the flesh now, feeling it, delaying the inevitable. You imagine yourself as some frightened prey animal, about to be slaughtered. You know what those folds hide and how much you hate them for it.

You flop back onto your pillows, freeing your head from the covers and breathing in fresh air. You arch your back, far enough that you're staring at the wall behind you. Your stomach stretches back out. Then you return to looking at your belly, one hand moving the covers away from your naked body.

You insert one finger into it and then another, shuddering as you do it. It's bigger now. You lie there for a while, head empty, hand inside yourself, thinking absolutely nothing. You're not sure there will ever exist a moment beyond this one. You don't think the world could possibly move on from what's just happened.

But it does. The next few days are difficult, with Kate and Ella eyeing you in the corridors and refusing to speak with you. Whispers seem to follow you everywhere. You spend your evenings scrolling through the profiles of people you're in school with, occasionally messaging a few of them. And you have Lorcan. You message him most of the time, with whatever thoughts you're having, and he responds.

Then, two weeks later, Kate sits next to you at lunch and tells you Ella's being annoying, and you get invited to Ella's birthday party, and it all impossibly blows over.

You never forget the feeling of reading those words, as though doing so had chipped away some part of yourself. You feel it as a kind of emptiness, a hunger, deep inside you. You think about them all the time. They haunt you. You read everything your friends post, searching for some double meaning, and shiver every time you get a notification. You read and reread every sentence you type, because these interactions don't only exist online; they bleed into real life too.

Eight

You walk along the corridor of the house your family are renting this summer, holding your phone high in the air. The bars in the top right corner waver between zero and one. You refresh your most-used apps, hoping to load something, but you're met with greyed-out boxes and blank screens. You flick airplane mode on and off, but nothing changes. Your entire attention is focused on the screen, the world around it a blur on your periphery.

You have a creeping anxiety, a fear that you are missing out on something. At this point in your life, it's very hard to live in the present. It's like your consciousness is floating somewhere above you, made up of invisible strings of data. Your friend group is a hive mind; nothing is real if they don't know about it. Summer is in full swing, and everyone is off on holidays or working; your phone is the only tether to them.

You lean against the wall, pressing yourself into the cold stability of it. Your hand plays with the hem of your t-shirt, unconsciously. There's a loose thread, and you're tempted to pull it. This year, you're staying in a new house. It's modern, with chrome finishings and purple cushions. You miss the pale green bath and cracked taps in the old house. You feel out of place in this space; you feel out of place in a lot of spaces.

You're not excited to be here. You'd thought it would hit you when you crossed the Galway border, or when the church and row of multicoloured shops came into view, but it didn't. You had been texting Kate at the time, and it failed to register. You hadn't felt any different, not with your phone in your hand. You used to love the change in landscape, but all it's done this year is drive a wedge between you and your online life, shifting you from a participant to an observer, trying to look in through the cracks.

'There's no signal,' you call out, to no one in particular. Your parents are in the kitchen unpacking the food, and Evan has already retreated into one of the rooms. They're talking about your grandmother, although they're not using any nouns. You know your dad doesn't like spending time with her, even though he's never said it out loud. It's a feeling he emits that pervades the entire room, the way men's feelings do.

You open doors at random, trying to find somewhere your phone has reception.

Your grandmother is staying with you this year, a shift in dynamics of the family. Her presence has become quieter, somehow, older. You can see her now, sitting on a chair just outside the front door, smoking. In the kitchen: whispers.

You have a nose for conflict, a way of sniffing out the things people are trying to hide from you. But you are also good at ignoring the obvious and keeping yourself in blissful ignorance.

You get two bars in the corner of one room and perch

yourself on the windowsill. Outside, the sun is peeking through the clouds, and two cows are lying on a patch of grass. You don't see any of this, you don't bother pulling back the curtain. Your eyes are fixed on the screen in your hand as it fails to load your friends' latest posts.

Your dad comes in to you, pulling your suitcase behind him.

'Is this going to be your room?'

You nod, not looking at him. His voice is cheerful, jovial even. It's a tone he puts on for you and Evan, and one that he never uses when talking to your mother any more. You understand, though: she annoys you too. At this age, you're easily influenced. Your thumb pulls the page down, trying to get it to load again. The room has twin beds, and your dad puts your suitcase down on the one furthest from the window. The bedclothes are white with purple accents. He looks at you. You feel his gaze and don't move in case it provokes yet another conversation you don't want to have.

'We're going to head down to the beach in about half an hour if you're ready.'

'It doesn't really seem like beach weather.'

When your friends go on beach holidays they post pictures of white sand and paddle boats, sun loungers and huge ice creams. There's never any grey, not like there is here. Your impression of this place has become overshadowed with storm clouds; you hate thinking about how you used to act on the beach, all tank tops and laughter, and how you can't act that way any more. You can't even begin to imagine how you're going to post about it.

He laughs, 'Well, it's not raining.'

You pull back the curtain an inch and peer out. The

day is overcast. On your phone the weather app says it won't clear up for another three hours, and after that it might rain.

'Your phone doesn't know everything,' your dad says when you tell him.

He's been saying things like this more frequently. Of course, you know your phone doesn't know everything. It just has more to offer you than being in this house. Being around your parents makes you feel as though you're some kind of sea creature who has outgrown its shell; pressed up against the constraints of your life. It's like you don't even speak the same language.

Your dad leaves the room, and you unpack. Your friends are sending pictures of the dresses they'll be wearing at Ella's party later, and you look at each one jealously. You hear raised voices from the kitchen, your father yelling. Suddenly, holding your phone doesn't offer you comfort any more. You are aware of it as an object, and this panics you. These little moments of recognition, where you peek behind the curtain and briefly brush against the things that structure your reality unsettle you. You want the wide open space of the beach.

You fix your makeup, adding more pressed powder and eyeliner where you need it, and grab a bag for the beach. You think of all the things you cannot pack, of how different you are now. You picture it as a mass of swirling shadow eroding your stomach. You stare at the bag until your thoughts quieten into nothing and change into your new dress. It's red and made for warmer climates.

Before you leave your room, you smooth the fabric over your belly. The corridor is too wide, the space too unfamiliar. You find your mum in the kitchen, although you don't feel as though it's you standing there. It's someone else, some imposter who is wearing your skin as a costume, forcing your body to move through space and time. She is making rolls, the way she always does, packing them into the blue cooler. When things are unsettled, she cooks. It's something you're not even sure she's aware of, a habit you'll revert to later.

'Will you go ask Evan if he's coming?'

Silently, you walk along the corridor until you get to the one closed door in the house. 'Are you coming down to the beach?' you say after you knock. There are gunshot and laser sounds coming from within, and you're not sure he hears you. You knock again.

'No!'

Your dad comes out of the master bedroom, just in time to hear. Neither of you know what to say. Evan used to love the beach. A quiet thought says: *So did you.* You're uncomfortable, compressed, pushing at the edges of this holiday, mourning the fact there isn't space for you any more.

You don't pay attention to the car ride down to the beach. Your grandmother says something, but you don't feel the need to respond. Your parents exchange glances in the rear-view mirror. You're holding your phone. Drama is brewing. Kate had accepted a friend request from a boy, and everyone is commenting on the post. An argument is bubbling away; you'd been drawn into it by the last comment, the first one you read, which was some boy calling Ella fat. You don't like the comment, but it makes you smile.

One hundred comments in, and it's like you're sitting

in a room with these people, listening. You don't look out the window, or notice as your body moves to open the car door and get out. Kate is messaging you privately, and a group chat you're in is being flooded with messages:

Like my next comment, okay?

Yeah that's good!!!

Maybe change the wording a bit . . .

You like the posts you've been instructed to. You're behind everyone else, though, because you still can't get good signal. Messages ping in all at once, or not at all, and when you click into the profile pictures of the boys commenting they don't load.

You only look up when your foot catches on a rock in the laneway and your phone hits the ground. You're surprised to find yourself here. The sun has burst through the sky, and you can see the ocean. You pick up your phone and check to make sure the screen isn't cracked, and then put it into your pocket, the group chat suddenly feeling very distant.

The air smells like turf and gorse and salt. More than that, though, a kind of nostalgia is wafting over you. When you breathe in, you feel a connection to each time you've walked this laneway before. You walk faster now, without realising it, leaving your parents behind.

When you emerge onto the beach, you feel present and excited. You kick your sandals off and dig your toes into the sand, gazing out over the water. It hasn't changed, not really. There are more rocks and fewer clumps of seaweed than last year, but the essence of the beach is unchanged. You recognise it, and it recognises you.

You see Lorcan before he sees you. He's sitting on the sand with some of the younger cousins, building sand-castles. You can't hear what he's saying, but the way he moves his arms and the giggles coming from the children tell you everything you need to know. Lorcan's good with people: all people. You haven't seen him in what feels like a long time: he's been busy, and so have you. You've been looking forward to seeing him, to sharing this place with him again.

You walk over, carrying your shoes in one hand. That feeling of time happening all at once persists, the presence of the children making you feel off-kilter. That used to be you, but it's not any more. The beach may be the same, but you aren't. Something has burrowed away at you, changed you. You feel out of place now, as though all the previous versions of yourself that have existed in this place are standing around you, forcing you to acknowledge that you are different.

Lorcan sees you and smiles. 'Hey.'

You open your mouth to say something, maybe to ask him a question, but no words come. They're drowned out by something overwhelming. You let out a wisp of air, but the noise is covered by two of the kids laughing. They're hanging onto his arms, giggling, asking him to spin them around again.

'I'll catch you in a second,' he says to you.

You could sit down with him, one of your little cousins even asks you to, and maybe you could reclaim a place for you on this beach. But you're not ready to admit that time has moved on, even though you've outgrown playing with sandcastles and running across the rocks. In your mind's eye, you are still a little girl, and these children aren't born yet.

You walk away, hoping it's the right thing to do. Part of you thinks you might be impressing Lorcan, by showing him how mature you are. You fold out your chair and sit reading your phone, peering over the top of the screen every so often to see if anyone is looking at you. You adopt an air of detachment, as though this place holds no interest for you; it's not a difficult role to play.

After a while, Lorcan comes over to you and your parents.

'On your phone?'

You shrug, 'Yeah.'

'Want to come in for a swim?'

You're upset at the impossibility of the question, at the fact that Lorcan doesn't know better than to ask it. But, of course, he couldn't. Your insides are knotted up, and you're angry both at yourself and the world. You can't go for a swim. You don't trust the fabric, the way your skin morphs and bulges in all the wrong places now.

You don't know how to tell him this, how to communicate your regret. So you keep a hold of that apathy and say, 'No, thanks.'

'You won't miss anything.'

'How would you know?' You're defensive now and terrified. You clutch at your stomach and fight to keep your expression neutral. You're not used to fighting with Lorcan, not about anything substantial. His tone of voice, his judgement of you and your phone, only makes it more apparent how much you've changed.

'It's a huge waste of time, really.'

'You just don't understand.' And he doesn't. There is

so much about you he will never understand and even more that you will never tell him. You think he's being childish, so you act childish in return. Something about this space is returning you to some younger version of yourself, but not in the way you hope. You're surprised at your attitude; you're watching your actions from somewhere other than inside your body.

'Okay, whatever.' He says it in a jokey way, but he might as well have sworn at you. You flash back to the first time you swore at him, and that same rage fills you now. You let none of it show on your face as you watch him walk away from you.

He enters the water determinedly. When he is waist-deep, he shrieks at the cold once and then dunks his head under. You count the seconds he's underwater. He emerges laughing, his body red, and says, 'It's actually nice, once you're in!'

The gulf between you has never felt so cavernous. You feel it as a physical thing, a void space that calls out to you. You could be floating.

You wrap a towel around your shoulders and take a selfie. When you post it later, anyone would think you'd been in the water. Your fingers shake as you pull at the edge of the towel, wrapping it tighter and tighter around yourself, until you're almost entirely obscured.

Watching Lorcan in the water holds no joy for you. The beach has no joy either. You sit with your eyes closed, willing time to go faster so you can finally leave this place. You think Evan had the right idea when he stayed up at the house.

You get up and walk to the rock at the end of the beach, to the place you like to go. Climbing it is more

115

difficult than you remember, and you're less confident about where to place your feet. They no longer fit into some of the grooves. Around the other side, with your back against something solid and no one else around, you feel safe. You dip your toes into the water and breathe out. You take a picture of your feet in the sea and post it. It feels more authentic than anything you've posted in weeks. Kate immediately likes it.

You spend a while sitting on the rock. The tide is on the way out, and eventually you can't touch the water any more. A deep sadness crashes over you, one that you don't have a name for. It beats in time with the waves. You hate that you don't like this place any more, you hate that it doesn't feel right for you. You hate that you've been morphed into a new, distant object. You hate your body, this dying thing that you are trapped inside. Your flesh feels like meat, like something cold and dead and on display in plastic packaging.

You're crying now, silently. You post another picture, one of the horizon, and caption it with a song lyric. No one on the other side of the internet has any idea of the truth behind it, which you enjoy. If things are falling apart, at least you can perform for this audience. Saoirse messages you, and you reply: *lol.*

Lorcan finds you here, after your tears have subsided into quiet contemplation. He asks you about your day; he asks you a lot of things. It's obvious he knows something is wrong. You're connected by a string, like the telephones you used to make with two cans and a wire. Sometimes you can feel it.

You remember the next moment very clearly; it's one of those still images that's burned into your mind. The sun is just peeking out from behind a cloud, but in the distance you can see rain. The day is unsettled, confused, about to change.

You're about to ask him something, or share some joke. You don't really know. You know he will understand, meaning will flow between all of the things you've left unsaid. You want him to know how you're feeling; you want him, or anyone, to understand. Your hand leaves your stomach.

Except he's not even looking at you when he says, 'I've a girlfriend now.'

'What?' You don't understand. The words don't connect themselves to any meaning. They're just sounds.

'Yeah—' He does look over at you now, and he seems embarrassed '—from my football club. Aisling.'

You knew they were spending a lot of time together, but Lorcan spends a lot of time with a lot of girls, and none of them ever seem to stick around. You're not sure why she's different. He's never had a girlfriend before.

'Oh.'

'Yeah.'

You smile then, your hand unconsciously clutching your stomach again, at the hole you know is growing, stretching out, eating you. You don't feel it; you don't feel anything. All that welcomes you is the apathy that's always lying there waiting to swallow you.

'Great,' you laugh, and the sound resounds inside you. 'I'm sure all the girls will be disappointed.'

'I doubt that.'

'Are you kidding? Everyone I know is obsessed with you.'

'But not you,' he said.

'No,' you agree. 'Your charms don't work on me.'

'And that's the real tragedy here.'

You laugh, and he laughs too, but you think you're laughing for different reasons. It reminds you of how you used to laugh as a child when you didn't know what was going on.

'Anyway, I wanted to tell you first. No one else knows, I haven't told my parents.'

'Your mum would probably cook a lasagne for her.'

'Oh god, she loves making a lasagne for people.'

You ask questions about the girl, mining for information and teasing him. It's easy, this. You've seen her social media profile and flicked through her pictures after she commented on something Lorcan posted. Now there is new weight to the times that Lorcan has thrown her name into conversation, as though testing the waters.

The two of you laugh, and then Lorcan stops. Suddenly he's serious.

'Aisling's said, well, she's said that she doesn't want me to talk to you as much. Or, she doesn't want me to talk to you more than her. She said me having a girl as a friend gives her panic attacks.'

'Oh,' you say again.

'That doesn't mean we have to stop being friends, or anything, but just she needs to be my priority.'

You smile. 'Of course.'

And then you walk away, back down to the beach. The sand is wet and sticks to your feet. You hear the sound of the ocean and nothing else. White static, inside and out.

Nine

You are sitting on the floor in front of the mirror in your bedroom, your laptop open in front of you. Long gone are the green walls and boyband posters. Now they're painted a soft purple and covered in movie memorabilia and photos of your friends. You're at that stage of life when you're feeling uneasy in all spaces, and so you change them to reflect the growing pains you feel. And so they look better in the background of your posts.

You are waiting for a video to buffer, the wheel spiralling on the screen. Your head is resting on one hand, and with the other you are holding your phone and scrolling. You put it down when the video loads, trading one screen for another.

The video is a makeup tutorial, but that's only half the reason you watch it. You pick up your eyeliner pencil and follow the motions the woman makes. In between teaching moments, she tells you about her life, her friends and what she's been up to. You know all the people she references. You've watched their videos. You know these people better than you know your own friends. You can't get your makeup right, so you wipe it off and wait for the next video to play.

In it, a boy with a swoop of black hair appears wearing a brightly coloured t-shirt. You nod along as he speaks and laugh. It feels like a conversation, like you are both the observer and the observed, letting these people into your life as you enter into theirs.

There are things they talk about that you don't understand, but that doesn't bother you. There are things that you've experienced that they couldn't hope to understand, either. For all the answers you've come across, you've yet to find a video that explains to you what's happening to your body. It's something you search in the middle of the night, after everyone in your house has gone to bed.

You close your eyes until the thoughts leave your brain entirely, until all you can hear is the boy's voice as he describes his first kiss. You ignore the creeping sensation, you don't dare to give it a name. Nothing you've done has stopped it. You don't look at your body any more, it disgusts you so much. When you don't look, it's like it's not there. In the dark, though, you feel it.

You shut the laptop when the video ends. In the silence, your thoughts start to wander. You find yourself remembering your unblemished prepubescent body. You were thinner then, and your skin was better. You were more like the people you see online, more attractive somehow. Now, fat gathers in pockets under your skin, and stretch marks have begun to stripe your body; imperfections that feel like death sentences. You gather your stuff from the floor and pack it in your backpack before going downstairs.

Your parents are in the kitchen. Your mother is sitting at the dining table and your father is chopping up some vegetables at the counter. They are talking quietly when you walk in, not so much whispering as arguing in hushed tones. Your dad spends his evenings at the pub with Lorcan's dad and always comes home in a bad temper. Frequently it's been just you, your mother and your grandmother for dinner: three generations of women deliberately not talking about the men in their lives.

In your memory, they are happy; but memories aren't reality. You can paint whatever golden meaning you want onto them, warp them to your own bidding. Maybe you were too young to see the truth of it.

Evan is nowhere to be seen, but that doesn't surprise you. He spends as little time as possible in the communal areas of the house. Sometimes you hear him late at night, playing a game or creeping downstairs for sustenance. You've begun to notice the way your parents look at him and gently ask him what he's up to. You've noticed them arguing about that too, when they're in the other room and the sounds trickle towards you. You're not sure exactly at what point your family started coming apart at the seams; maybe at the same point you did.

You let your bag drop to the floor and walk over to your mum. There's an awkwardness in the room, a feeling of things not addressed.

'I'm ready to leave now.'

She puts down the pen she's holding. An unnatural moment of silence passes, where your mum looks at you, and then your dad, and then back to you.

'Right,' she says as she stands up, 'let me get my keys.'

You pick your bag back up, swinging it over one shoulder, and follow her out of the room. Your dad yells goodbye, and you hear him pick up the knife and continue chopping.

There's a chill in the air as you step outside, and the sky is heavy with rain. You say as much, but your mum doesn't react. You click your tongue in your mouth, just for some answering noise. She doesn't say anything until you're in the car. The locks click. She pulls out of the parking space and says, 'You know, I made a lot of mistakes when I was your age.'

You have the urge to groan, but you suppress it. This conversation has been lying in wait for some time now. You'd thought you'd managed to evade it. You glance down at the door lock and for one wild second imagine throwing yourself out into traffic.

'Right.'

You let the word hang there, although you know she wants you to say more. You can feel her intent so vividly it fills the car. You ignore it. Instead you stare out the window and play with the zipper of your backpack. You think about the videos you watched earlier. Maybe if you waited until she slowed down to take a corner you wouldn't even get hurt.

'Nothing surprises me.'

Again, silence.

'I know what these discos are like, and I know you know all of this because you have the internet and you're so grown up, or you think you are, but that doesn't mean you're not vulnerable.'

You close your eyes. She has taken an interest in your life lately, and it's grating. You don't have the words to tell her that she has nothing to worry about, that you're way behind the rest of your friends and terrified for someone to even touch you. That maybe, just maybe, if you did kiss someone at the disco tonight it wouldn't be the worst thing. It might even be normal; it might make you normal. Your hand is on your gut now, searching for comfort, or an answer. All you feel is sick.

You sit in silence as she tells you all kinds of stories that obliquely reference mistakes she made as a teenager, with morals all loosely along the lines of 'Respect yourself.' You say 'I know' in as many ways as possible, really testing out how tonal the English language can be. She wants to understand, and you know that, but the world she grew up in is not the one you're living in now. She couldn't hope to understand you. She doesn't even know how to copy and paste.

At last the car pulls into Ella's driveway. You say nothing and reach for the handle.

'Aren't you going to say thank you for the lift?'

'Don't you mean the ambush opportunity?'

'Don't be ridiculous.'

'Thanks for the lift, Mum.'

You're glad to leave the car behind. Your mother always acts as though she has no motives, but you've been able to read her for as long as you could think for yourself. You notice things a lot lately, and you're quick to jump to your own conclusions. It will take you years before you realise that your parents had entire lives before you were born. You approach Ella's door, hopping across the stone path. You think about who you were the last time you crossed the threshold to this house and shudder when you remember how you felt when you left it: a past life of your own you're doing your best to forget.

Some distant part of your brain keeps a hold of your mother's words, replaying them slowly in the back of your mind. She is a tiny voice in your head.

Ella's dad answers the door and tells you the girls are all upstairs. You know where her room is, although you haven't been inside this house in what feels like a long time. Feelings that are only echoes pass through you, jumping at your throat.

Ella always invites the girls over for these kinds of things, and they always upload an album of the night onto Facebook. Over the last few months you've scrolled through each one, trying to piece together some idea of the experiences they've had. They talk about them in the locker room on Mondays in school, and they make it all seem so glamorous. You've practised keeping your face still, impassive, and when they ask you why they never see you out, you lie and tell them you have no interest in it. This is the first time you've been allowed to come.

Ella's room has been painted since you were last in it. Gone are the pink walls; instead a geometric wallpaper with gold accents has been put up. But it feels the same. The bed is unmade, and two girls are sitting on it. Music is playing from a speaker on the window. Ella stands beside it, wearing a robe, scrolling through the pink iPod Nano connected to it.

The room is thick with movement, arms and legs everywhere, and it feels like invisible walls divide it. You're not sure how to cross them and become part of one of the conversations, or if you'd even be able to stand next to the mirror trying on something from the discarded piles of dresses on the floor.

You loudly say hello to everyone, moving your arms in the empty space of the room, asserting yourself. Ella looks at you over the iPod in her hands and smiles, just a little bit. The tension cracks like an egg, and you dump your bag on the floor before rummaging through it.

You bought a dress similar to one you've seen Ella wear on Facebook. Not the same one, no, but similar enough that no one comments on it being out of the ordinary. A few of them even say it's nice. Saoirse says she could never wear a dress like that, but there is a hint of envy and self-deprecation in her voice, so you take it as a compliment.

Ella steps out of her robe then, in just her bra and underwear. They're a matching black set. You're drawn in by her navel, which is flat and completely whole. It makes you go dry-mouthed and nervous. She steps into her dress, but you can't shake the image from your head, or the afterglow of her confidence hitting you like a slap.

All around the room the other girls are doing the same. They're completely unashamed of their bodies; their bodies are perfect. Breathing is a little bit more difficult for you now, a weight has been placed inside your chest. It's like you're sinking through the floor and also about to float away.

Ella is in the process of gluing her eyelashes on. You can see into her ensuite bathroom and the girls crowding around the mirror inside it. You feel exposed. You'll always feel exposed, no matter how much clothing you wear. You hold the fabric of the dress against your stomach like a shield, crumpling it against you.

'Where's your bathroom?' The words come out reedy, like a gasp, so you swallow.

One of Ella's eyelashes is dangling precariously. You hold up the dress you're clutching in both hands now, your palms sweating onto the fabric.

'Just get changed here.'

'I can't,' you say, before you have time to think about your words.

Ella's eyes narrow. 'You on your period or something?'

You blush deeply, not able to think of anything to say. She rolls her eyes at you and then breaks the silence. Her voice crackles with an energy only you are attuned to. 'Go down the corridor, second door on your left.'

You nod at her, then leave the room. The corridor is expansive, rolling out beneath your feet. You trail one hand along the wall to keep you grounded, until you reach the bathroom.

When you close the door, you realise it doesn't have a lock. This panics you even more. You go to the sink and splash water on your face. It does nothing to calm you. You're not sure why you did it; you think you've seen it before in movies and TV shows. You're aware, maybe for the first time, that what you see on screen is a reality that looks like your own, but functions in a very different way. It's something you only realise when that conception of reality fails you, and you become aware of how badly you misunderstand everything. You wipe your face with the hand towel.

You sit with your back against the door. You search for calm, for control over this situation. You want to be here. Being here is important. You repeat the same sentences over and over in your head. You convince yourself that all your feelings of inadequacy hinge on this night.

You brace yourself against the door with all your weight and clumsily remove your clothes. You contort yourself into unfathomable shapes, your elbows bent, your legs in the air. You don't look at yourself in the mirror opposite before hiking up your dress. When you're fully clothed, you step away from the door.

Just as you do, the handle turns and it creaks open. You jump back and scream. Your foot catches on the bath mat, and you end up sprawled on the floor.

'Oh Jesus, sorry!'

It's Kate. She's wearing a skirt and a crop top, flaunting unblemished skin. You wonder if she has anything she's hiding from the world. She reaches down and helps you to your feet. You smooth out your dress across your belly, carefully checking it hasn't snagged anywhere.

'Ella told me you were in here? She said you were on your period. I have painkillers with me, if you want.'

'Thanks, but it's okay,' is all you say.

You follow Kate back into Ella's room, the corridor a normal length this time. You shove your discarded clothing into your backpack and take out your makeup bag. Ella looks at you with her eyebrows raised, and you force yourself to smile at her. She's curling her long hair into delicate ringlets. You clutch the cracked plastic of your makeup bag tightly. The rest of the girls are sitting on the bed, so you join them.

Kate offers to do your eye shadow and you accept. Your fingers are caked in foundation, so you rub them off on the underside of Ella's duvet. You feel a secret satisfaction in doing so, and part of you hopes she knows it was you.

You try to imagine a world where it's not 'you' and 'the girls', but one where you exist in harmony, melding together. You want what they seem to have, the ease at which they navigate these situations. It always feels like you're performing, and it always feels like you're being watched.

As Kate leans forward to do your eye shadow, you stop yourself from staring at the rolls of her stomach you can see under her crop top. You're fascinated by them, by the way the skin folds and bends. There's a fullness to her, a completeness, that you yearn for. You want to be as unselfconscious.

'Do we know anyone who'll be there tonight?' You throw the question out as something to fill the silence. You're pretty sure you'll know no one; you're hoping that'll change.

'I hope Daniel's not there,' one girl says, 'because I'd like to get with Alex but if Daniel's there I'm going to have to get with him.'

'Why?' you ask, your eyes closed as Kate applies a thick coating of brown to them.

'Because he'll expect it.' She's sipping from a 7UP bottle, but you've gathered from the situation that she's actually drinking vodka that her sister bought for her. You wish you had an older sister who'd buy you alcohol, and you miss Lorcan. You haven't spoken to him in months. He waved at you across the school car park once, but you pretended you couldn't see him.

Kate sees you eyeing the bottle and hops off the bed to retrieve her own from her bag. She offers you some. You're afraid, tasting the memory of the last time you'd had alcohol. In your head, you connect it to your vanishing in a way that nearly makes you physically sick. You gag ever so slightly, and one of the girls laughs. You take another swig; what happened last time won't happen again, you're going to make sure of it. It's mixed with Coke, whatever it is, and almost tastes spicy.

'I have a naggin in my bag we can share,' Kate says. You close your eyes and let her resume her work.

'I got with Alex last time, he's a bad score,' someone says, 'and he made me give him head after.'

'That's so gross.'

'He just unzipped his pants and kinda forced my head down, and I just wanted to get back to you guys.'

'Where?'

'In the park.'

'Before or after the disco?'

'Before.'

'So that's where you went off to.'

Someone giggles; your eyes are still closed so you don't know who. You listen to the silence, before asking, 'What was it like?'

'Like, fine, I guess.'

The girls laugh again, and you smile. You're in on the joke now, part of it. It doesn't matter that you don't know which park they're talking about, that you've never been there. You listen to them talk, aware of what their words mean individually, but not exactly what they're describing.

'I wish I had your eyelashes,' Kate says to you.

One of the other girls says, 'I wish I had her tits.'

You laugh, because you don't know what else to do. You're self-conscious about the dress now. The neckline is like nothing you've ever owned, and the other girls are talking about your body in a way that they never have before. You feel outside yourself, as though the body they're talking about could not possibly be yours.

You'd do anything to hold on to this feeling. When Kate finishes your eyelashes you open your eyes and smile. You play the part you've been practising. You help the

129

other girls choose shades of lipstick as though you know what you're talking about, though it doesn't matter to you. Being detached, being uncaring, is a way to insulate yourself from harm. You hold your arms across your body in a way that emphasises your chest and covers up your stomach. They all say you look great as you stand there in your green dress. You return their compliments to them twofold. Kate hands you her bottle, and you drink again.

Once everyone has a full face of makeup on, Kate takes out her digital camera. It's metallic silver. The lens cover slides back and the screen flashes on. The girls pose against one wall, their hands at their sides. You know how to pose now, how best to position your body. You stand with one foot behind the other, your body twisted contrapposto, your hand on your hip, a smile on your face.

Ella's parents pay for a bus to take you to the disco, and in it the girls produce more bottles of alcohol from places you weren't even sure it was possible to hide them. Saoirse has one hidden by her ponytail, Jess takes one out from the small of her back. The motion of the bus is making you feel sick. The lights are flashing. You take the drink that is offered to you and drink half of it in one. Someone stands up and starts dancing. Music is blaring. The camera flashes once, then twice.

You're aware of the eye of the camera; it's a beam of light focused entirely on you. You move with the lens, thinking to yourself you must look perfectly candid. You want a good photo to be uploaded tomorrow so you can have a new profile picture.

The bus pulls up to the disco, and the girls all chatter

and laugh. You leave behind a graveyard of plastic bottles, but no one is worried about them being evidence of anything now. The driver tells you to have a good night.

The night is cold, but you don't feel it. Kate is standing beside you and links her arm in yours. You're grateful to her, because it makes you feel stronger. You've spent a long time imagining what this night will be like, and you're about to find out. You can taste the anticipation: it tastes like vodka.

You join the queue to the door. A girl leans over the railings in front of you and vomits onto the pavement. It's mostly liquid and a few chunks of what might be noodles. Someone in a yellow vest ushers her out of the line, and you don't see where she goes. Behind you, some lads are jostling at each other. You hadn't expected it to be like this, but at the same time there's a normalcy in the delinquency that makes you feel like you fit in. These are the experiences your parents have tried to protect you from, but they're not here now. You smile.

In the disco, the walls are damp. The combined condensation created by two hundred teenagers drips down the walls. Somewhere, a fog machine is going off. You recognise the song, but only barely. You are uncomfortable, so you chase the feeling you had outside. You're not sure when you're taught how to behave in places like this; perhaps now is the time to learn.

You want to go dance, but someone says that no one dances this early. You accept this logic, and later on you'll find yourself repeating it to someone else. They'll nod as though it's sage advice and you'll feel pleased.

The disco is being held in the bar of a rugby club, with the smoking area facing out across the pitch. You hadn't been aware that your friends smoked until now. You're not even sure why an underage disco provides a smoking area. The smell of it reminds you of your grandmother, her frailness and her hacking cough. Groups of people are milling about. Some of them have actual cigarettes. The air is freezing but no one wants to go inside.

Someone offers you a cigarette, and you shrug and take it. You don't know how to smoke, but you don't want them to know that. They light the cigarette for you and you watch it burn. Occasionally you hold it to your mouth and pretend you're inhaling. You know how to stand with it because you've seen movies. You feel like your grandmother, and you don't like it. Ash falls onto your leg.

The night thumps on around you. You're beginning to get into the swing of it. People are chatting. You lean into conversations like a tree bending to the wind, and the moment people look at you strangely you float into another. You recognise some of the people around you. You think you've seen their photos on your friends' profiles. But no one seems to recognise you.

You're starting to panic, just a little. You'd thought it would be more like Irish College, that there would be dancing and the movement of bodies around you. Instead you're milling around outside and cold.

At last Ella tells the group she wants to dance, and you filter inside. After the chill of the smoking area, the dance floor is humid. The moisture in the air hits you like you've stepped into a sauna.

The music is loud, and you start to relax into it. You scan the crowd, waiting to see if someone will approach you. You see some of the guys you were talking to outside follow your group in, but they stay on the other side of the room. You're aware of every single person in this room and how little you matter to them.

Then it happens. Someone taps Kate on the shoulder and points at you. You know what he's saying, even though you can't hear him. Context is a powerful mode of communication. You hardly register what he looks like, it doesn't matter. You might recognise him from school, but he's not in any of your classes. You nod at him, and suddenly he's upon you.

His tongue flicks around your mouth. An image swims before your eyes: trying to get the last bit of yogurt out of the pot. The image is so powerful it overrides the physical sensation, and you almost feel nothing.

You are triumphant. You've taken something away from the world, some weapon that could have been used against you, and now you're normal. You're not sure why you'd been so worried about it in the first place; now that it's over it feels like nothing. You feel, for a moment, whole.

As he pulls away, you register a bright persistent light. You blink and see Ella. She's pointing her camera at you, and the flash is on. She's laughing. Behind the light, you see a crowd has gathered.

Dread. You wipe at your mouth and rearrange your hair. You are at the centre of an impromptu circle, which might as well be a spotlight.

'Ella?'

She's not paying attention to you. Instead she turns to the girls around her and says, 'Oh my god, guys, I got her first kiss on camera. This is history-making.' The camera is still on, and she points it to each person in turn, recording their reactions; some of them are laughing, some are clapping, some are observing you in silence.

You freeze, and everything happens very slowly. It's like you're stabbed, that little moment of victory ripped from you. It doesn't matter that you've done it, in fact it's wrong that you did. You pull at the skirt of your dress, which feels much too tight. There is an emptiness in your stomach, a lack of substance. You are above this scene and beneath it; you are anywhere but inside your own body, which is on fire. A hot film of sweat coats you, making everything feel slick.

You wait for a minute, for the camera flash to go off. Ella tells you it's a joke and you just look at her in silence. You keep your face neutral. You wait for the crowd to disperse, for you to vanish back into it, for the audience to melt away, before leaving the dance floor. You stumble, and your vision blurs.

Out in the smoking area, someone offers you another cigarette and you take it. Someone offers you the bottle they're drinking from, and you take that too. Anything to fill the hollowness inside you. You're terrified of your own body; of the way it betrays you.

You're dizzy; the world is starting to lose focus. Your brain isn't recording things properly. There's a metallic taste in your mouth and a looseness to your limbs. You want to leave. The night doesn't have any texture to it any more. Nothing has substance, least of all you.

You walk back inside, past the dance floor, to get your coat from the cloakroom. On your way there, you're stopped by the boy from earlier.

'Are you okay?'

You shrug at him and say something, although you're not entirely sure what.

'Hey, come in here.'

He grabs you by the arm, tightly. You lean into him, into his warmth. You're in the bathroom now, and it stinks of piss. There's no one else here, it's just you and the boy. You are a world away from everyone else.

In a stall, he motions for you to sit down. You do it, but you don't have to pee. He unzips his jeans and suddenly there's a penis in your face. It's so absurd you laugh, which makes him angry. He grabs the back of your head and pushes it forward, until the thing is in your mouth. There's a rhythmic motion to his hand, the way he bobs your head in waves; it fascinates you.

You spit it out. The boy still has his hands around your head, so you say, 'Let me go.'

His face is shadowed over. You're confused and just want to leave. You've watched videos where this happened, but you'd always been in some kind of silent fugue state. So you sink back into yourself. You know how you're supposed to act, so you do.

This experience is nothing like porn. Whenever you've watched porn, you've felt some amount of stirring desire. Now you feel nothing except the pounding in your head and the feeling of the boy's hands on you. It's just like when you would sit in bed and message random men and feel nothing at all. You don't make any noises; it's silent in the stall. This is nothing like you imagined it would be.

You're not entirely sure what happens next, only that the boy lets you go, and you leave the bathroom. The taste in your mouth is bad, so you wipe at your tongue with the back of your hand. You're looking for someone you know, but you can't see anyone. You check your phone and realise it's almost time to meet your mum. You're not sure where the time went.

You make your way to the cloakroom. The door beside it is open, and inside you see the drunk tank. Kate is in there, her head between her knees and a silver emergency blanket draped over her shoulders. You wonder where Ella is.

Tears are flowing from your eyes. They well along your waterline before falling. A headache is starting to set in, one deep in your skull. It thumps along with your heart-beat. You wipe your eyes before walking to the pick-up spot, the chill of the night knocking some of the drunk-enness out of you.

You clutch your coat tightly around you, and ten minutes later your mother drives up to the pavement and you get into the car. She asks about your night and you shrug at her, which seems enough. She's used to your moody silences; this is no different. The fact you were at the pick-up location on time is proof enough that nothing bad happened to you; she doesn't know any better. She drives you to the chipper and lets you go inside and get yourself something.

You eat the chips in the car, the vinegary heat of the bag comforting against your abdomen. You picture the journey each chip makes as you eat them, down your throat and then lost somewhere in the black hole of your insides. You close your eyes and try not to think about it.

Your mum says goodnight to you, and you put the half bag of chips on the counter before washing your hands in the sink. Evan comes into the kitchen, his hair messy and his eyes bleary from playing games on the computer in the dark. He takes the bag of chips and retreats back into his room.

Your feet are heavy as they carry you to your room. You know what's waiting for you; you always feel it before you see it. Or don't see it. You undress entirely before turning to look at the mirror. There are red lines across your body from the places your clothing was too tight. You still have the imprint of your bra across your back.

On your stomach you see it's grown. When you touch it, you feel hot and light-headed, like you might faint. You fall onto your bed heavily. You push the flesh of your stomach this way and that, wondering if the hole will close up somehow. You are detached from your body as a concept. Three fingers fit inside now.

You pull your nightdress on, and the hole is gone, like there is nothing wrong in the world. The pain has subsided too. Instead, you feel nothing. In that nothingness, you begin to unpick the night, to figure out exactly what happened. And to understand how you can make sure it never happens again.

You don't dream that night, or you don't think you do. You fall asleep watching a video on your laptop, so you wake every so often to the sound of someone talking.

The next morning, you log on to Facebook. No one has texted you asking where you went, so you're surprised when you see you have several notifications. Ella has posted a video on her wall, and people are commenting. You've been tagged multiple times. It's you and the boy from last night, kissing on the dance floor.

Your body belongs to someone else; it's angled in ways you've never seen before. The boy has his hand on your ass, and the video zooms in on it. You hadn't even felt it at the time. A flash of horror goes through you as you imagine what else he might have felt.

You click into his profile and scroll through his pictures, but his face is already embedded in your mind. You have a name to put to a face now: Jack. Maybe you should comment about what happened in the bathroom, make some kind of joke about it. You start typing something out, but your fingers stop. If kissing him had been wrong, you're not sure what the other thing was. The memory already sits hazily in your mind, as though you're not sure it actually happened. You remember the girls talking on Ella's bed; perhaps it had been nothing.

You start to cry, the type of quiet crying where tears leak from your eyes.

Kate comments: *We all know you wanted to score him . . . Jealous much?*

You wonder if she's right, if Ella is shaming you now because you've done the one thing that she'd wanted to. If somehow by virtue of it being you, the action is now tainted. Maybe she feels the way you did at Irish College, but you doubt it. You watch people argue in a thread under the video. Most of them don't know you, you're just some faceless girl they can use to slag the boy about. Someone comments: *Nice, another notch in the belt.* And Jack replies: *Oh god, don't even remember this.*

People tag other people in the video; some of them have strange names, and when you click into one profile it's full of pictures of girls around your age. They're all dressed up for discos, wearing heels and short dresses. You see Ella in one of them, at the last disco. The page is called 'Hot Young Dubs' and she's commented underneath *Omg tnx sooo much xx.* You return to the video.

You cover your face in your hands, but the world keeps turning around you. People keep commenting, and you have no option but to read. You'd wanted to be included, you'd wanted to be part of the photos they upload online, and now you're the star of the show.

Ten

Jack's name sits on the bar at the bottom of your screen. You like making him wait, seeing if he's willing to message you again or not. It makes you feel powerful in a way you seldom do in person. When you're at a party or sitting in the park with your friends, you can feel his gaze on you; that imperceptible way you know someone is thinking about you, trying to inch themselves just a little bit closer. You can almost see the attention he is paying you. It amuses you to make him think that you can't.

You share a screenshot of the notification into the group chat now and say *lol another one.* The responses file in:

Lol

So eager

Treat 'em mean keep 'em keen.

You smile, because there is jealousy behind those messages. Ever since you made the group chat, the girls have been sending in snapshots of their lives. They want to have a boyfriend, they want to have someone to message, they want what you have. Or they want what you're refusing to acknowledge you have, which is even better.

I wonder if he'll message me again tonight?

Obviously!

You're not sure who you're leading on more: him or them. But at this stage you're not aware of that. You're just aware of the feeling of safety this power gives you and how it insulates you from all of your previous anxieties. Your hand hangs around your belly as you read the messages, but you're not aware of that either.

You feel very detached from it all. You're replying to messages out of habit and liking posts without fully reading them. For you, being bored on the internet is a dangerous thing. You're just learning about all the taboo things in the world, and you're curious. But you don't know the difference between swears and slurs, and your school friends use both with abandon in the chat. You don't understand why they shouldn't.

You also don't know the difference between good sex and bad sex, you don't really understand any of it. To you, it's all this exciting and developing thing. The more you see, the more you want to see.

And the internet provides.

You open up a private browsing window, even though this is your personal laptop. You scroll past images of naked people and feel nothing about them. At one time they would have made you blush. Last year there had been a leak of celebrity nudes that boys in your class had joked about, and you'd pretended to not know what they were talking about. You don't know about consent yet, and you won't learn for some time. Looking back, you'll realise why it took you so long to pick it up.

The videos you like to watch are pretty hardcore. The first time you'd seen a blow job, it had made you gag. The image had been so jarring, so disgusting, and you'd pictured the man pissing on the woman's face. Last week you'd seen a video of a man actually pissing on a woman, and it had felt normal.

You put your headphones in and click into some of the videos now, fast-forwarding to the middle. In this one, a woman's arms have been bound behind her back, her legs held open with a bar. In the next one, the woman's mouth is held open with a gag.

The taboo makes it exciting: the idea you'll see something you haven't become desensitised to. You're not sure if you want to be those women, or if you just like seeing them powerless. There's an allure in losing control like that completely, and a total fear. By choosing to take pleasure in it, it makes you feel better about the way boys treat you, even if you refuse to think about it that way.

You're feeling hot now, all over. You close your laptop and take off your top. You look at yourself in the mirror and see the hole. You cover it with your hands, and it's like it's not there. You imagine you can hear the sound of waves coming from it, like when you hold a shell against your ear: something giving life to the emptiness. You use your phone to take photos. You're posing just so, so that you can't see anything is wrong with your body. Your chest is more pronounced, your flesh more shapely, your waist impossibly curved by the way you hold your body. The tension is a rod that runs up your back, an ache that spreads like a seized muscle.

You sit back down on your bed and put your top back on. You crawl under the covers. In the private window, you open up a chat site. It takes two refreshes before you find a man who immediately asks if you want to sext. You pretend to be reluctant, because you know that they like to convince you. It's all part of the game. You tell them you're seventeen, even though you're not yet, and they don't have a problem with that. Every one of these conversations is the same, and each one makes you feel simultaneously in control and tiny.

When you send the picture on, they tell you your body is beautiful. Each time this happens you close your eyes and relish it. They tell you that they've finished, that you helped them, and sometimes they thank you. You always close the window before they ask you for an email address or social handle.

You repeat the same lines over and over again, to the point where you copy and paste some of them from a file you have. In a way, you're using these men as much as they are using you. Or at least that's how you see it. It will take a long time for you to not see it this way.

You see so many dicks, so many stubby fingers, so many faces full of acne, that they all meld together for you. One thing becomes associated with the other in your mind, transforming your perspective. Things that you once found disgusting you now find funny. Things that you once found degrading become normal. One man asks you to spit on yourself, and you tell him you do, even though you don't move out of bed. He tells you you're sexy and then attaches a photo of his flaccid penis. You

144

have all the information in the world available to you, ideas that have started wars and divided countries, but this is what you use the internet for.

When you get bored, you close the window. You get a fright when you see your Facebook profile, a reminder of reality. You delete the photos from your phone, and it's like they never existed, like you hadn't spent the last half hour doing what you were doing. These parts of yourself, separated by different windows on a laptop screen, feel like separate identities. You slip back into your normal register now and engage in the social internet.

You have a message from Kate. She's talking about a boy and asking for dating advice. She says dating, but you know that isn't all she means. People made fun of you for weeks, but now treat you like you have some kind of secret knowledge. Maybe that's part of the reason you lean into it.

There's a rumour going around about you, about what really happened that night. Part of you suspects it's Jack spreading it, except in the story being told, you don't have a name.

You cling to the anonymity of the story, reacting with a knowing wink when people bring it up. The fact that it may or may not be true adds power to the story, and mystery: almost respect. You've noticed more people talking to you in school and commenting on your posts. It seems like a fair trade. Now, when Ella makes jokes about you, you make them back, and everyone laughs. If they're going to be talking about you, you might as well make it worth it.

You reply to Kate, sending her links to websites and videos to watch, which she will never mention to you in person, at least not sober. Once she told you she was afraid to orgasm. You'd laughed. You close your laptop when your dad yells up to you that dinner is ready, and you are cool when your parents ask what you've been up to.

'Just homework.'

You take a plate from the counter and spoon some pasta from the pot on the hob onto it. Your father fills a jug with water from the tap and puts it on the table. You sit down at the same seat you've been sitting in your entire life, one leg bent under you. You spear a piece of fusilli with your fork and eat it.

Your parents chat about their days for a few minutes, and Evan wolfs down his plate. There is a formality to this dinner, something humming in the subtext. You can sense your parents trying to be normal, to act as though you're one big happy family, as they so often do. You don't know why they bother when there's no one to see it. Your grandmother isn't even here; she hasn't been coming since she went into the nursing home. She hasn't been able. You sensed the relief in your dad's posture the day she was checked in, and you resented him even if you felt the same way.

Just as Evan's moving to stand up, your mother says, 'Wait just a second, both of you.'

'We want to talk to you two about internet safety,' your father elaborates.

You make eye contact with Evan and share one millisecond of exasperation. This is the one thing you still have in common these days: your parents.

Your parents tell you that a letter was sent home from the school, advising parents against certain viral videos.

Last week, someone in the sixth-year physics class had played one on the projector when the teacher was out of the room. You don't tell them the boys in your year had done the same thing yesterday, only they hadn't been caught. They made fun of anyone who covered their eyes, so you had stared at the screen and pretended to be disgusted.

Everyone has seen all of those videos. It's like a contest, who can watch the worst one, who can come in the next day and tell everyone about one they hadn't seen before. One girl. Two girls. Three girls. More. Every video is more extreme, with more people, more gore, more shit. Some of the videos are supposed to be grotesque, some are clearly fetish content. The line between sex and horror becomes more blurred with every one.

Evan sinks in his seat, guilty, and won't meet anyone's eyes. You see your parents notice, the glances they exchange. This is the only thing they've been united on for years. You're much more convincing when you tell them that you have no idea what the video is about, and you don't correct them when they say the name of it wrong.

You go upstairs after dinner, bored again, and open a private browsing window on your laptop. You have one headphone in, the other ear listening to the activities of the house. You're always careful.

Later that night, Jack messages you *Goodnight x* and you take a screenshot of it to send into the girls' group chat. People reply saying how cute he is.

In two weeks he'll ask you out, you'll update your relationship status and watch the likes roll in.

Eleven

This isn't the first time you have sex. That time was in the hazy light of a sunbeam coming through his attic bedroom window. You had lain there in warmth and let it happen, and it was over before you'd experienced it. But it was enough to count. Enough to message your friends about later. Enough that now, when you read those posts about sex positions and tips, you feel like you're in the know. He hadn't asked you to take your top off, he's never questioned why he can't touch you in some places. He's confessed to you his own body insecurities, told you about forums he reads. That time, you'd felt like you'd got away with something.

No, this is the sixteenth time you have sex. You mark them off on the calendar of your phone, just in case that's something you ever want to know. Each time, he wants to try something new. He's asked you what you like, but you've spent so many years hiding that side of you that you find you can't quite vocalise it. So, you let him decide. The first time he performed oral sex on you, he'd told you afterwards you were just lying there like a dead fish. It had embarrassed you so fully, so completely, that it's all you think about. You'd got it wrong, which is the worst thing; you'd been acting like you were still sitting at a computer screen, with your parents in the next room. Now, each time, you make sure you're responding to what he does, expressing yourself in the way he expects you to. You can barely feel what happens to your body, and that fascinates you. Desire has become a mercurial thing that you interact with as object, not subject. He calls you a bitch, puts his hand against your throat, asks you if you want it harder. Each time you say yes, because you haven't learnt to say no.

This time it starts like this: you're lying next to Jack, a discarded Domino's box on the floor beside his bed. His parents are home, but they let you two go upstairs by yourselves. They normally sit in the dining room, drinking a bottle of wine, and don't disturb you when you're over. His father had bought him a box of condoms, something he told you as though it was funny and not mortifying. You wonder if his parents still have sex, if that is where this attitude comes from. You wonder if they love each other.

You're full, in a pleasant way. The air in the room is hot and smells like dough. Jack is running his fingers up and down your arm as you scroll through your phone.

'Look at this photo of Ella,' you say, and show it to him. She's wearing a neon-pink dress. You zoom into her leg and see a streak in her fake tan. 'She's so fake. I think she photoshops them as well. Does the wall look weird to you?'

His mind is elsewhere, and he doesn't look at the image. He never cares when you talk about this. He uses the internet in a way that is very different to you, that makes him seem mature and knowledgeable. He says it's silly to care about what Ella does, and you agree, but that doesn't stop you. Last week, Jack had shown you a subreddit where the photos are all blacked out. When you click into one, it's either a cute image or something awful. He'd laughed when he showed it to you, and laughed again when the image revealed itself to be someone's degloved hand.

He slides down in the bed until he's next to you. You roll onto your side so he can spoon you and keep scrolling on your phone. You're looking at photos from the school trip last week. In one, you're caught in your side profile and your chin is weak. You message Kate and ask her to delete it. She replies immediately, and the photo is gone.

Jack's hand moves from your arm to your waist and you tense up. Without thinking, you move his hand away from your torso. Your body is hot; his fingers got too close. Sometimes it's easy to forget about it when you're not thinking, and you have Jack to reassure you that you're wanted by someone. That doesn't stop the hole from eating away at you. Now your entire fist fits inside. If Jack were to see you without your top on, you're sure he'd break up with you. This is not a rational thought, or one you're able to fully articulate, but it comes to you with a punch of dread.

'What's wrong?' he asks.

'You know I don't like to be touched there.'

'Even by me?'

He's kissing the side of your neck now, moving your hair out of the way so he has easier access. You clutch the phone tightly in your hand.

'Yes.'

'Why?'

He moves his hips against you, and you feel his erection. His breath is in your ear, and it smells like pepperoni. You can tell he thinks he's being sexy. He's always found convincing you to do something you're hesitant to do sexy. He's told you so.

'Not now.'

'Why?'

'I don't want to.'

'Come on!'

He rolls you on top of him, and your phone goes flying. It lands on the carpet with a thud, and you push yourself off Jack. You get off the bed and walk over to the pizza box, opening it for another slice.

'I'm serious, I'm not in the mood.'

You pick up your phone again. He follows you over to the box and takes the slice out of your hand. Then he bends you forward so you're lying across the bed and stands behind your ass. Your arm is bent beneath you, and your phone is digging into your chest.

'Please?'

You turn around to face him, your face now level with his crotch. You can smell it. Nothing has ever been less sexy to you. His hands move from your face to his zipper, and now you're looking at his dick.

Somewhere, in the back of your mind, you flash back to that night in the disco. You are living it again, even though it was over a year ago. You feel the same way, and it gnaws at you. It makes you feel sick. As the memory rises up in front of your eyes, it merges with now, and the two moments become impossible to separate. You close your eyes. You don't think about that night; part of you is sure you'd imagined it.

Maybe, you think, this is just how it is. You relent to Jack and let him fuck you. It's intense, and over soon enough. You feel a little bit sore afterwards, and he cuddles you in bed. His hands still move around your body, so you hold them, directing them away from that central point. It's all you can see in your head as he holds you. You imagine your entire self vanishing into that point, just gone.

You waddle to the bathroom and sit on the toilet, disgusted with yourself. This isn't the first time you've felt this way with Jack, but you're not yet sure it's him that brings this feeling about. As you sit there, greasy and hot, you think it could be your fault.

When you sit back on the bed with Jack, you're afraid. Not of him, but of losing him. Of losing what he represents. These thoughts are consuming you when he says, 'Sorry, I don't know what came over me.' He pets your hair and kisses the side of your face.

'You're so annoying,' you say, on an exhale of air.

'Isn't that why you love me?'

You laugh and tease him, because that's just what you do, but you don't answer him. You've trained him to read compliments into your ambiguous statements, so you're sure he hasn't picked up on any of your legitimate hesitation. And that suits you.

Later, his parents come in and offer you a lift home. You're worried they can smell the sex in the air, that they see the evidence on the sheets. That it's written on your face, or your body. You tell them you're getting the bus home, and they leave you.

Jack walks you to the door and kisses you goodbye, and then you're out in the open air. You clutch the sleeves of your cardigan as you walk. Rain is threatening. You are feeling nothing at all, waiting at the bus stop.

On the bus ride home, you scroll through your phone.

You're reading posts about sex, about how sex is supposed to feel, and when you should be having it. You don't know it, but you're searching for an answer to an unasked question. Sex never feels like anything to you; it's an absence. You had built it up in your head for so long, but the truth is you can barely feel Jack when he's inside you. Your mind is too present, too full, your body too focused on looking right that the sensation of it is entirely secondary.

Every post is written from the point of view of the man. They tell you that men have uncontrollable urges, that it's easier for everyone if you just give in. You read about the practice of free use, where the woman is supposed to be always available for fucking. Users link their favourite porn videos to the discussion, where men play video games while disinterested women spread their legs for them. You put your earphones in and flick through them.

There is some relief, you think, in finding out what had just happened is common. The more you read, the more you rationalise it. You tell yourself that it had been okay, that Jack hadn't hurt you. He's told you he's insecure, that he needs you.

You don't want him to feel the way you feel, you want to protect him from that. You're not sure why you feel uneasy, or why as soon as the bus doors closed behind you you began to cry. What happened is a secret you'll never tell anyone. You look at everyone around you, again wondering what is written on your face. You stare at your reflection in the window and then stare back at your phone.

The more posts you read, the worse the feeling becomes.

You know it now; it's familiar. You clutch your insides to yourself and sit quietly for the entire ride home. Your underwear is a cold and soggy presence, not allowing you to leave this moment.

Twelve

The beach looks more idyllic in photos than it does in real life. You're scrolling through your phone, trying to decide which ones to post. You have three options that feature the laneway. In the first one the colour balance is off and the sky is grey. The clouds are washed out and the light is watery. It's like a horror movie, or the way some Irish poets talk about cities. You play around with the exposure and saturation settings, but there's no saving it. In the third one, you'd held your phone low to the ground and used an outcropping of grass to frame the one patch of blue sky. You zoom in with your thumbs and examine each blade of grass.

You want to include the sea, so you pick a photo of you taken from the highest part of the laneway, just before it dips. Evan is giving the finger to the camera in the background, which you decide to leave in as an unairbrushed touch. It's unintentional in its intention.

The last picture you select is one of your name and Jack's written in the sand. In it, you can see your shadows and the spade you used to write it. You're doing a peace sign. A bump in the sand changes the nature of the light around your navel, and you panic. But you're wearing a hoodie, and there's no way anyone could see right through you.

You scroll through filter options until you find one that warms up the landscape. You add a vignette and a colour overlay, and caption your post with *Same place, new year.* You flick through the carousel, satisfied.

You post the images and wait for the notifications to filter in. Someone's liked it after just fifty-four seconds. You wonder if anyone will comment on the fact that Jack is here with you, if they know how he changes the feeling of this space.

Your phone has grown hot in your hands, so you put it away.

'Have you seen my post?'

'Not yet.' Jack is sitting beside you, his phone in his hand. You see the tag notification on his screen but he doesn't open it.

'You've already posted?' Evan asks. 'Get a life.'

'I have one, thanks.'

You refresh your notifications until Jack's comes up.

'Thanks,' you say to him.

'Yeah.'

'You guys are so weird.'

Evan puts his bag down on the ground next to you and walks away across the beach. You watch his back as he goes. Evan's so tall now, but he gives the impression he isn't. It's like some part of him is sinking away. You haven't really spoken in months; you have nothing to speak about. Something about this beach gives rise to ghosts; impressions of who you used to be when you last walked this sand. For one second, you picture Evan as a little boy, yellow bucket in hand. The image is jarring.

Evan doesn't like Jack, he never has. He didn't come out of his room the first time you had him over for dinner. Once, Evan had asked if you knew who the girl in the video that was circulating around school was, and you'd lied and said probably Ella. Evan and Jack are on the same football team, but neither of them talk about each other.

It's too difficult talking to Evan now, it's like he's an entirely different person. His blue t-shirt disappears behind a rock and he's out of sight. You fidget with your bag before rooting around inside it and pulling out your sunglasses.

You don't like how Jack looks on the beach, how he adds a new dimension to it. He's merely eating a bag of crisps, but the simple act annoys you. It's wrong somehow. You hadn't thought that you'd mind him being here, but you're embarrassed now. Having him here makes your relationship too real. It was easy to go along with it, hemmed in by the school gates, but now that it's bleeding out into your real life, you feel like you can't control it.

And, of course, you're not sure how Lorcan will react. You're not close any more, not since he got serious with Aisling. Part of you thinks you brought Jack here just to provoke him. He's never invited Aisling. This is a thought that is so far back into your mind that you don't know it exists, but you can feel it all the same.

'Look at this,' Jack says, leaning over to you. Watching him teeter in the chair makes you cringe, so you've been gazing out over the ocean, reflexively. The tide is just starting to turn. He passes you his phone. It's open on a thread of comments.

'What?' you ask.

'It's this story on Reddit, someone pretending to their

159

girlfriend they've never seen a potato before, and her parents believe him. It's amazing.'

You're glad it's just a text post and not some horrible image. You don't know it yet, but the things Jack shows you will burrow themselves inside you. The thread you read and scroll through now will stay with you. You're just beginning to realise this, but not enough to do anything about it. You haven't yet learnt to recognise the red flags, but you will.

Your dad looks over your shoulder at the phone; you can sense it more than see it. You're not sure what he sees when he looks at the screen, if he can connect it to a wider network or culture. Your mum certainly couldn't, but she's not here now. She's with your grandmother up at the house, making the lunch.

You're not waiting for Lorcan on the beach, but you're aware when he arrives. The entire landscape pauses and takes a breath. You feel the current that pulls you to him, and you smile. Lately you've been thinking about Lorcan more, although you've been pretending you haven't. You miss him, terribly. You miss him when you're alone, and sometimes when you're with Jack.

You watch his progress across the beach, the easy way he moves. He's carrying a picnic cooler and his mother's folding chair. His dad isn't here, but you knew he wouldn't be. Not since the separation he's been raging against when he sits in the kitchen with your dad, the two of them talking late into the night. A pile of glass bottles still there the next morning. You watch Lorcan set everything up in the sand. Lorcan's strong, you know that. But you're still surprised. Part of you imagines you're both still children. But he's in college now, and you will be soon too.

You're not sure if he knows you got in. You think your mum must have told his during one of the conversations they've had, but you can't be sure. Both of your parents had made it clear to you they weren't taking sides, in the way that they sat you down and said those words aloud. Their actions have demonstrated otherwise. You'd meant to message him, casually, but had never managed to work up the courage. You never knew what to say.

He's impossible to keep track of online, because he has almost no presence. Aisling never accepted the follow request you sent when you felt you had a reason to. You've caught glimpses of him in the backgrounds of other people's posts, but he's been disappearing from them too. You know nothing about him any more. Sometimes you open his profile, imagining you are seeing it through his eyes, and it makes you feel closer to him.

As though your thoughts have called out to him, he looks up and sees you. You freeze, like you've been caught, and then return his smile. Something passes between the two of you, and you're embarrassed. You look down quickly and then over at Jack. He hasn't noticed anything. In your mind's eye, you're a child again, and your relationship with Lorcan is as it always has been. You're not sure how you know this, but it feels like everything's about to change.

You don't want him to talk to Jack. You're upset at yourself for bringing Jack here at all. It feels stupid and childish. You'd asked your parents if he could come almost as a challenge, willing them to have something they could mutually disagree with, deliberately placing yourself in the firing line. But they've both been trying to win you over, even if they don't know it. Looking at Jack, scrolling through his phone, makes you feel sick.

Lorcan had once messaged you, asking why you were with Jack. You didn't see how it was any of his business. At the time, you'd replied something about how he'd changed since he started dating Aisling. But you're not sure if it's possible for him to change and become unrecognisable to you.

'I'm going for a swim.'

You know Jack didn't pack any togs, you'd had an argument last week about whether or not the Atlantic was too cold to swim in. That's why you ask, 'Want to come?'

'No, thanks.'

You jump out of your chair and go around to the other side of the rocks. There's more coverage here. You take off your t-shirt and pants. You're already wearing your togs underneath: a one-piece. You meticulously smooth out the fabric, making sure it hasn't caught anywhere. The hole is something you've learnt to live with; you've resigned yourself to the idea that one day you will disappear. You understand your destruction so completely that the slow recession of your flesh means nothing to you.

The water is icy and unwelcoming, and it stings. You wade out until it's almost to your waist and then dunk your head under. You burst up to the surface in a splash of water and chattering of teeth. It takes several minutes before you grow used to the temperature and start to enjoy being in the water.

You swim a few metres out into the bay, avoiding patches of seaweed. You float for a minute, looking out at the headland across from you, and behind at everyone on the beach. This is your entire world. When the feeling gets too much, you go around the big rock to the little shelf, hidden from view, that you used to go to with Lorcan sometimes.

You pull yourself up onto the rock and lie there. It's warmed from the sun and does enough to keep the chill out of your bones now you're not in the water any more. You run your hands over the cracks and bumps in it and stare at the sky.

This, you think, is happiness. To be visible, but totally unobserved. You feel as though you're whole for the first time in a long time, like you might just belong to this place. There is something special about this beach, about this patch of rock in particular. It's almost like you can finally be yourself.

And it's here that he finds you. It was always going to be here.

You're not aware of anyone approaching at first. The sound of footsteps merge with the crashing of the waves. A shadow falls across your vision, and when you look up to see what caused it, you see Lorcan.

'I thought I might find you here,' he says.

'Did you?'

'It's where you used to come when you were thinking something secret.'

'You're making that up.'

'I can always tell.'

He sits down beside you, finding the groove in the rock where it's comfortable. You notice he has a graze on his ankle. His body is longer than you remember it, more toned. You watch him move his hands to balance himself and see the veins along his tendons. You see all of this because you're not looking at his face.

'Jack seems lonely back there.'

'Oh?'

'Can I ask you something?' he says.

'You just did.'

'You know what I mean.'

You lie back down on the rock. From this angle, all you can see is his back. It's been so long since you've spoken properly, you need a barrier between the two of you to make sense of it. You know you can't hide from him, not on this beach, not here. You feel so much like time is moving in reverse and things are resetting.

'Go ahead.'

'Why are you with him?' When you don't react immediately, he says, 'Jack.'

You look away from his back, unsure of how to answer. The name sounds wrong when Lorcan says it, comical even. Sunlight is glinting off the surface of the ocean, and a ferry is going by, causing a ripple of waves in an otherwise calm ocean. You prop yourself up on the rock. The pose is so rehearsed, it almost comes naturally to you. It flattens out your stomach. It's a defensive move, one that you'll think about and unpick later, and maybe feel ashamed of. Before, you'd always felt comfortable letting Lorcan see you as you are. But things have changed now.

'I'm sorry about your parents.' It's not an answer to his question, but it has the feeling of one.

'I'm not.'

'Really?'

He shrugs. 'They've been unhappy for a long time. Dad is dad, you know?'

'I do.'

You stare at a rock just breaching the water's surface,

thinking it might be a seal. You wonder if Lorcan can see what's happening to your parents' relationship, if it's obvious to anyone except you.

'I broke up with Aisling.'

You sit up fully, your shoulder brushing his. You see the profile of his face, the strong line of his nose. He's watching the water as well.

'What?'

'Last month.'

'I'm sorry.'

'No, you're not.' Lorcan has always been able to see right through you. 'It's okay, I'm not either. I've just been thinking a lot about what a happy relationship should look like, and I don't think we had one.' Your eyes meet then, but Lorcan loses his nerve and returns his gaze to the sea. 'I know it's my fault we stopped talking.'

You find it difficult to believe he's saying these words. These words you so badly wanted to hear, that give voice to all the delusional thoughts you've had over the years.

'Well . . . good.'

The air tastes like salt and sunlight. There is a perfection to this moment, a presentness, that fills you up. It's like something from a dream. The words aren't even your own, they feel as though they're being fed to you by some higher power. It all feels easy.

He turns to you. 'So, why are you with him?'

'Oh, I don't know, I just am.'

'Cause he's a bit of a tool, like, I'm just saying.' You say nothing, so he says, 'And you don't even seem to like him. I was watching you, earlier, and you basically ran away from him.'

'You were watching me?'

165

Now you do look at him, and it's his turn to look away. It seems impossible the two of you could be looking at each other at the same time, inhabiting the same plane.

'Don't be weird,' he says.

'You're the one who was watching me.' You let a moment of silence pass and then say, 'You're right, though, he is a bit of a tool.'

Saying it out loud is freeing; it's almost like you've been given permission. You hadn't been aware of how much the pressure of pretending you're happy has been weighing on you. You almost tell him everything, but something stops you. And you realise you no longer have to tell him anything; it's like he already knows.

Lorcan breathes a sigh of relief. 'I really thought I'd pissed you off there.'

'Oh, you piss me off all the time, but not this time. I just . . .' You pause. 'I don't know what to do. I don't know what to say to Jack, but I don't know if I want to lose him.'

'What's there to lose? Like, we agree. He's a tool.'

'I don't know how to find another boyfriend. This one was hard enough to get.'

You want to pull the words back inside you. It's a thought you're not sure you've ever fully formed, but it's true. You worry that Lorcan will judge you, but your relationship is beyond that now. You smile at him. Your hand brushes his, and so you take it in yours.

'There will be other boys.'

Again, you can sense the unspoken words, as though they hang around you and you can taste them in the air. You know what this moment means, and you know how to take it. Previously you've let each one go by, but not this time.

You lean forward and kiss Lorcan. He seems surprised, he exhales a small breath of air, and then he is kissing you back. Lorcan is a good kisser, even better than Jack, and you'd spent a significant amount of time training him up. Lorcan's skin is damp and he smells of seawater. He tastes like the beach.

His hands are on your back, pulling you closer. It feels different than when you've kissed Jack, like maybe for the first time you're actually enjoying it for what it is, not what it could represent.

Somewhere overhead a seagull cries. Your body is pressed against his now, and you can feel every inch of him. Your body responds of its own accord, moving the way you know you're supposed to move, the way Jack likes you to move. Memories come flooding back to you, and you see them in your mind like comets shooting across the sky: Jack telling you he loves you and you laughing at him, kissing Jack in the disco, telling Kate that you thought Lorcan was your soulmate, the non-existent feeling of Jack inside you. You take a back seat in your mind, and suddenly you are empty.

Thoughts of the hole enter your head, obliterating everything else. Lorcan's hands continue to move, but now you're worried about what they might touch; about what they definitely won't. Your thoughts keep spiralling out of control, and you picture your life with Lorcan. You can't lie to him. You imagine him seeing you as you are, and hating it. Nothing is more terrifying. The future turns to ashes in your mouth, and you pull away.

'Sorry,' you say, 'I probably shouldn't have done that.'

'No,' he says, 'it's my fault.'

'I should go back.'

'No, wait.'

'This was a mistake.'

The words hang between you, irrevocable. And he lets you go.

You walk back over the rock, retracing the path you've worn into the stones over many years. You stumble just before you reach the sand and stub your toe. Correcting your balance is not as easy as it once was; you've never really adjusted to having a new centre of gravity. You've been so many people around Lorcan, he's seen so many sides of you, but this one you will take with you to the grave. Nothing would be worse than having Lorcan touch you and then go straight through you. You would immediately fade away into nothing.

When you return to the beach, you pretend nothing happened. You say your swim had been nice, thank you for asking. You retrieve your clothes from the rock and sit with a towel wrapped tightly around you. When Lorcan appears on the beach again you make aggressive eye contact with him, as though you're trying to prove to him that nothing happened. You don't go swimming again.

At the end of the week, you break up with Jack before he heads back to Dublin. He doesn't take it well, but you hadn't been expecting him to.

Moments after waving goodbye to him, he updates his status to single. Messages start flooding in, people asking what happened, and you watch them start to form their own narrative. The next day you see a photo Jack is tagged in of him shifting another girl, his hands inside her jeans.

Three days later, on a rainy day when you're in bed, you get a message from Kate.

Hey, I think you should see this.

Your phone is already in your hand, so you see her message in a banner at the top of the screen. You open your chat with Kate. She's sent you a screenshot from a chat between Mark and Jack. It's clear they're talking about you. Your name isn't mentioned, but the context is enough. Or at least Jack's calling someone a bitch.

You're unmoved by this. He's been venting about you on Facebook and Twitter for the last few days and posting mopey posts on Instagram. You think probably in an attempt to get you to talk to him, but you haven't given in. You're considering blocking him, but you don't want him to think that you care. You haven't been removed from the group chat you were in with all of his friends, but it's gone suspiciously quiet.

Another message comes through. You swipe across to open it, flicking from one screenshot to another. The photo is a naked woman, not just any woman. *You.*

Her face isn't visible. But you know it's you. You're wearing a particular bracelet, and the colour of the wall behind you is the same as your bedroom. And, of course, your hand is splayed out across your belly: hiding.

You'd felt good when you'd sent that picture. Photos are the only way you're comfortable showing your body, and Jack had started asking you why you were never fully naked around him. This had felt like a pacifying measure.

You zoom into the photo. It's so strange. At once you, at once not.

Kate messages you again: *Jack is saying this is you. Is it?*

A video comes in now. You recognise the bed-sheets as the ones on Jack's bed and the comic-book poster on the wall. The girl is wearing a tank top, but no under-wear, and she's being penetrated. You blink once, then twice.

The girl has the same hair colour as you, though you can't see her face. The girl is wearing the same top you're wearing right now. You don't remember Jack taking this video, but it's obviously you.

The girl dips out of frame, and you hear the sound of a slap, and then another. You stare, astonished, your hand against your own face. You remember it now. He'd been in a foul mood, and you'd just wanted it to be over. You live it all again. As Jack fucks you, he tells you to ask him to do it again, so you do, and he spits on you.

You stare out the window, out into the darkened sky beyond. It is very difficult for you to imagine time moving forward from this moment, or you continuing to exist. The cows in the next field over have nothing to say either.

You return to the screen. Your face isn't visible for any of it, and neither is Jack's. It's just two people, and the video is so low quality you can't distinguish any of the things you're remembering. There are noises, but they're indistinct, with no real meaning.

You don't know what to say to Kate. If you tell her the truth, perhaps she'd be disgusted with Jack. Perhaps she'd be disgusted with you. If you deny it, then the whole situation could be brushed under the carpet.

Lol
I don't look like that
Nice try

Oh thank god
That's what I said!

You close your eyes. Behind your eyelids, you can still see the screen. It's like the light is boring straight into your brain. No matter what you do, you'll never be free from it.

You lie in bed, powerless. You'd thought it made sense to say it wasn't you, but now Jack is free to share that image around without repercussion. It's better this way, though, and you know it. If no one knows it's you, it'll become just another image of a naked woman on the internet: so commonplace as to be entirely boring.

Your phone vibrates again. You crack open an eye and hold the phone an arm's length above your head. Your lockscreen is a photo of your class in school on your graduation day. Jack has sent two images into your group chat. The one that had been so obviously killed. A violent and uncontrollable shudder goes through you.

It's the picture again. The second image is a photo you had used as a profile picture the month previous. You have a hand in your hair, pushing it out of your eyes as the wind blows it. Jack's put a red circle on it, around your bracelet. He follows it up with a message:

Liar

Anarchy breaks out in the group chat. Kate is frantically sending in strings of letters, trying to flood the chat so

171

people can't see the image. She messages you privately as well.

Messages are coming in faster than you can read them, and the world becomes alerts and banner notifications. Your perspective shrinks entirely. You forget about yourself, you forget about your physical form, you forget about the fields outside. All you have, and all that matters to you, is exploding in your hands.

The messages keep coming.

Kate tries to call you.

Your dad asks if you want anything from the shops, and your voice is a strangled thing. You hear him ask if you're okay, and your grandmother's rasping voice echoes him. None of it is real. You're not sure how you've managed to mess things up this badly. You want to talk to Lorcan, but you've been avoiding him. He's a five-minute walk down the road, but it feels a million miles away.

You are tired at this point. And these people are nothing to you any more. Their messages all meld together, becoming one single voice attacking you.

You are fine if they hate you. You are fine leaving bridges burnt. You are fine with them seeing the photo, which you've carefully crafted anyway. You leave the group chat. You block half of them. You have a feeling of being forged, nearly, of being made stronger. You can move forward with no past, and have a life free from the expectations of these people and the person you are to them.

Focusing on the future is the only thing that stops your belly from aching.

Thirteen

You check the name of the lecture hall against the one in your email three times before entering it. You're wearing a new outfit; new jumper, new shoes, new you. You wonder if anyone will be able to sense how much you're performing, or if they're all performing as well. You take a seat at the end of a row, leaving one seat fallow between you and the next person. Being in a crowd of strangers induces anxiety. Ireland is so small, Dublin even smaller; you can't be sure what they might have heard about you. Who they might know. What they might have seen.

The ice-breakers you are forced to play are pained. You study the reactions of the other students as the roll of toilet paper is passed around. Some of them are indifferent, some of them put on an air of detached irony, but loudly so everyone can tell they are very much attached to it. When you're told you have to say a fact about yourself for every square you took, you hide half your pieces in your pocket. An urge comes over you to lie, to say you have a twin or were born in Switzerland.

You're so nervous that you don't remember what anyone else says, except for one girl who says she has a dog. After, you approach her and ask what breed it is.

'A poodle,' she says, before leaving the lecture hall.

You stand and watch her go, curious about where she's going. You look around the room, which feels much too big now. The last few weeks have been quiet. You've convinced yourself you're better off without your friends, more stable. You've ignored a few messages from Kate; you almost feel bad that she's become collateral damage in this whole thing. But you need a fresh start. The hole inside you has stopped growing, as though in stasis. But you're lonely. You'd watched a video on YouTube that said the first day is the easiest day to make friends, and you're determined to make one.

Still sitting in one of the seats is a girl on her phone. Her head is bent, so you can't see her face. She's typing away furiously in her notes app. You see her delete the whole thing and start typing again, trying to look busy. This encourages you.

'I'm just about to get a coffee,' you say to her, 'want to come?'

'Oh, thank god,' she says, 'yes.'

She tells you her name is Fiona. You learn all kinds of things about her, including that she cannot stop talking. You let her go off for a bit, finding the rhythms in her speech and identifying the breaks in her monologue. It's easy to talk to people who never shut up, and comforting somehow. You just need to make the appropriate noises to keep her momentum going forward.

As you walk through campus together, you see Lorcan. He's dressed in a blue t-shirt with a society logo on it, handing out flyers for some night out. You notice him immediately, as though he has a glow that radiates through the crowd. It's always funny seeing Lorcan when he doesn't know you're watching; he's the same, but different. You wonder what he's doing; the distance between the two of you has only grown, and you have no idea what society he's part of. You have no idea if he's seen the video or not, and the idea that he has is terrifying to you. You've received messages from guys you don't know, so you know Jack has been spreading it around. Every time you watch porn, you expect your video to show up in the sidebar. *Amateur teen barely legal fucked from behind XXX*. You stop in your tracks and Fiona looks over at you.

'What?'

'It's nothing.'

'Okay, well, come on—' She pulls at you, linking her arm with yours '—I think I might actually want to sign up to tag rugby.'

You can't make yourself move, which feels unbelievably foolish. You're still staring at him, imagining him seeing the video. Imagining his reaction. You see it all at once. The crowds, the cobblestones, the grey stone buildings around you make no impression on you. You shake yourself and kick into gear. Your head is filled with the hollowness inside you, as if Lorcan will be able to sense it across the square. If anyone could, he could. With your spare hand, you push your palm against your navel, willing the disgust away. He sees you then, and his gaze anchors you in place. You scan his face for any sense of what he might be thinking, but he's as calm as ever, and you feel tiny.

Fiona nudges you. 'Do you know him?'

'Uh, yeah, very well actually.'

'Oh good, so he's not a creep.'

Fiona directs you towards him and you're powerless

175

to stop her. It's too late to explain your much-too-complicated history. You breathe in deeply, steeling yourself. You're good at summoning calm from nothing, at making sure you're totally unaffected, at borrowing strength from some alternate version of yourself. You see the video in your head now, it's like a film over your vision. It's impossible to be emotionally present in more than one place, so you find yourself shunted back through time.

'I see you finally made it.' Lorcan sounds the same as he always does. He looks the same as he always does. His solidity makes you feel as though you're melting away.

'Just about,' you say. 'This is Fiona.'

'Making friends already? I'm impressed.'

'We're both just desperate.' You like how Fiona is self-aware and unapologetic about it. It's not clear if it's natural for her, or if it's something she consciously does. Maybe it's a tactic you could steal.

Lorcan leads you over to the society desk and you hand over the requisite amount of money in order to receive a tote bag and a badly printed membership card. You clutch the card so tightly it digs into your skin. You pay very close attention to the blue plastic table, which has a gash cut into one side, probably from an easily distracted student with a box-cutter. There are flyers for guest speakers and sign-up sheets on it, and you deduce it's a debating society.

'Oh, my sister said I had to sign up,' Fiona says, picking up a flyer. You keep sneaking glances at Lorcan, trying to catch a flash of panic or regret crossing his face. He remains unreadable, and you miss the days when you knew him better than anyone else.

'We're having a wine-and-cheese night later. You guys should totally come. The wine will be bad, but it'll be free.'

'We're there,' Fiona says, and when you raise your eyebrows at her, 'Well, I don't have any better plans.'

'No, me neither.' It's so tempting to fall back into the normalcy of it all. But you still remember what it felt like to kiss Lorcan, you still remember the feeling of his hands on you. You get goosebumps thinking about how close they had strayed to your centre, how stupid you had been. How he might see you now: tainted, used.

'Great! Always good to be someone's last resort!'

Lorcan gets called away by a guy holding a bucket, and you watch him go. He doesn't look back. Fiona turns to you and says, 'So, is he like your boyfriend?'

You laugh, and then hesitate, and then laugh again; the question feels ridiculous. It's nice to be around someone who hasn't known you for years and who doesn't know Lorcan. It's freeing, even. You like who you have the potential to be around Fiona, and that relaxes you. You want to share something with her, to give her some insight into your life. You want it to be the right insight.

'Don't even go there. No, absolutely not, we've just known each other for ever.'

'Ah, so it's like a childhood soulmates thing?' Fiona is light and breezy, interested but not pressing. You think confiding in her wouldn't be a big deal. You're starting to really like her. It's so different to Ella, and even Kate, where there had always been some element of risk involved.

'Not even.'

'I don't believe you.'

'Okay, well, I kissed him this summer but that was a big mistake.'

'I knew it!' Fiona is triumphant. 'I can always sense these things.'

'But there's absolutely nothing going on there at all.'

'Okay, cool, just testing you. He's cute, and I may have just fallen in love with him there.'

You gesture with your hands. 'Be my guest.' The sooner Lorcan starts to see someone new, the easier it will be to get past this thing. You're used to your female friends acting this way around Lorcan. It reminds you, in a way, of the before times. The times you were whole. You've talked about it with Lorcan before, but not recently. Not since you'd told him his charms didn't work on you.

You've carried that conversation around with you for a while, and you think of it now as you and Fiona walk through campus together and she tells you more about her life. She's from a big family, all sisters, where they interrupt each other at the dinner table and steal each other's clothes. By the time you sit down for coffee, you've forgotten all of their names, but it doesn't seem to matter.

'Sorry, I know I'm insufferable,' she says as she drinks her coffee. The café is packed with what you presume are students, and it's loud. You settle into your chair and check your schedule on your phone as Fiona talks. You don't have a taste for coffee yet, it's still bitter and dry, so you dump three packets of sugar into it.

The afternoon passes quickly, and you find Fiona easy company. You talk little about yourself, afraid of playing your cards too early. The two of you walk through town, window-shopping, discussing all the things that feel consequential but really amount to small talk. You're on autopilot. You want Fiona to like you, and you want things to be normal between you and Lorcan. The gap between wanting and reality has never seemed so wide, and you arrive at the society room before you've had a chance to prepare yourself. It's in one of the older buildings on campus, past a brass door knocker of a lion and up a flight of stairs.

You push open the door and people are still setting up inside. The room has maroon walls and sofas held together with duct tape. The windows face out onto the square beyond.

'Are you here for the event?' someone in a suit asks you.

'Yeah,' you say.

'You're early, can you come back in like twenty minutes?'

You click the side of your phone. You're on time, not early. Your phone opens onto the Facebook event page; you'd been keeping an eye on it to make sure to avoid this exact situation. 'The event says it started one minute ago?'

The guy looks like he might argue with you, but just then Lorcan comes into the room. He is so at ease here, so natural. His shirt is crumpled, but it suits him. You watch him move across the room, and you watch Fiona watch him too. It feels so much like you're transported back in time, to back before things became complicated. You're elated, nearly.

'Don't worry, Brian, I know them.'

Lorcan hands you a plastic cup filled with wine. You don't know a lot about wine, but you know this is particularly bad stuff. It tastes like warm vinegar and goes straight up your nose when you drink it. Fiona swipes two more from the table when no one is paying attention and pours an extra one into your cup.

'Just in case they run out,' she winks.

The room slowly fills with people, and you slowly fill with alcohol. Lorcan introduces you to a lot of people, and you smile at them across the room when they make eye contact with you after. Being with Lorcan makes you feel important. You've given yourself over entirely to the potential of who you could be.

Fiona has started to hit it off with another first year she's just met, and you've lost sight of her. All you see is a sea of heads. You're not used to being in crowds this dense, and so everyone looks almost like someone you know. The idea that they might be fills you with a pooling sense of dread you fight to ignore. You're adrift in the room, trying to decide what your next move should be. You stare up at a portrait of an old man, wondering if he's a president of Ireland, or just some guy. Then Lorcan is by your side.

'Lonely?'

'Always,' you say. 'No, I've just lost Fiona.'

'Well you've already made one friend, why not make some more?'

Lorcan smiles down at you then, and you roll your eyes at him. A memory flashes. Lorcan is teaching you how to ride a bike, and you see the moment he lets go of the handlebars and you hurtle down the road alone. The memory fades, and you're back in the present, disorientated. You step away from him, putting the crowd between the two of you.

Fiona finds you, and she's holding more wine. 'Sorry about that,' she says. 'I might just be in love.'

'That's the second time you've said that today.'

'And it probably won't be the last.'

There's a funny edge to the evening, which you think might be because of the wine. You down your glass in two big gulps. You shake your head with the acidic taste of it. Fiona tips her glass against your empty one and knocks it back. She gags, but gets it down. You hold your phone out and take selfies with her. They're blurry, the lights catching on the angles of your face. You look very grown-up. You know you'll post them later.

'So his name is Matt,' Fiona says, 'and he's not even fit in a nerdy way, but in like an actually fit way. You know what my type is.'

At this point, you do. You know Fiona's entire life story. She pulls up Matt's Facebook page and hands it to you. You scroll through the pictures. There's even a video of him doing squats at the gym.

'He has a brother?'

'I think so.'

'Well, who's this?' You hold the phone out to her and show her the picture. Matt's standing next to a boy who looks just like him and an older couple who must be his parents. You think it's his graduation picture.

You glance around the room then, trying to spot him. Fiona nudges your arm.

'Stop being so obvious. Besides, I saw him go down to the bathroom a few minutes ago.'

'Should I add him?'

'Couldn't hurt.'

'Boys are so stupid he probably wouldn't even know what it means.'

You feel like you already know this guy. You've become accustomed to the internet providing you with answers to unasked social questions. It's not an invasion of privacy or an act of voyeurism; it's essential to the functioning of society. You take your own phone out and send him a request. You have a number of mutual friends. You see Ella is one of them, and some distant part of you recoils. You feel like you need to get to him and find out what Ella might have told him about you, if she's told him anything at all. You wonder if the video found its way into some group chat he's in. You remind yourself your face isn't in it, it's just another amateur porn video amongst a million others online. No one would think twice about it.

You're afraid that these people are not strangers any more; you're afraid they know all about you. Being anonymous in a crowd affords you a kind of privacy, and the privilege to sculpt your own image. The idea that that might not be possible fills the night with threat and makes you clutch at your stomach. But you're not thinking about it; you don't want to think about it. The thought goes away, chased by images you don't want to acknowledge. Even if he'd seen the video, he'd have no way of knowing it was you. You'd thrown out that top.

You hold your phone tightly in your hand. Someone's turned off the overhead light, and now loud music is playing. You take photos. They're all blurry, just smudges of people's faces lit up by coloured lights. It mirrors exactly what you're seeing.

Later, as the night begins to take hold of you, you see Fiona and Matt. And then, after a while, you see neither of them. Fiona sends you a message and says she's okay. She also sends a winky face.

Lorcan pulls you aside. His face crystallises in front of

you, and you hug him. Now the world is resolved. For the first time in months, you are truly carefree.

'Want to come to an afters? We're getting kicked out of here now.'

Things are happening on fast-forward. Suddenly you have your coat, and you're out on the street. The walk through town is chilly. You pass several people vomiting on the side of the road, their friends gathered around them. You're disorientated. Dublin City exists to you as a network of disconnected streets. You talk, but you're not sure about what. Someone behind you is singing. You feel like you belong here, in this moment.

'Good night?' Lorcan asks you.

'The best.'

You link arms with him, using him for support and body heat, like you had with Fiona. He talks to you about something, but you're not really listening. His body is beside you, the only solid thing in the world. You're looking out over the quays, seeing the River Liffey as though through new eyes, the city transformed. Lorcan squeezes your shoulder and pulls you into him as you ricochet off a lamppost.

The afters is in a tiny flat on Tara Street. You walk past the door initially, and Lorcan has to drag you back to it. You laugh and lean against the wall as you wait for someone to buzz you in. The corridor that leads to the front door is winding. Lorcan keeps cracking bad jokes. You hear the party before you see the open door.

You feel no trepidation as you walk across the threshold. It feels like you can't do anything wrong, like you're finally fitting into a space that was made for you. For the longest time, you've been stretching yourself to fit into the world, and you feel delight at the idea that this place may accept you for who you are.

None of the doors can open fully without banging into furniture or other doors. You're through the hallway before you even realise it's there. Every surface of the apartment is covered in debris: society newsletters, empty packets of soup, envelopes torn open. A frying pan is hanging from a hook on the wall.

Lorcan goes to the fridge and takes out a bottle of white wine. It's half empty.

'This is mine from last night,' he says, 'four euro a bottle.'

He grabs some glasses from a cupboard in the kitchen and pours you one. You're grateful it's at least cold. You're not used to being out this late, and your mouth is dry, so you drink it in three gulps and then hold the empty glass close to your chest so Lorcan doesn't know what you've just done.

Back in the hall and into the sitting room, you see the rest of the party. You recognise a few from the night, but you don't know their names any more. They have playing cards out on the table, some kind of drinking game. You sit down next to them.

'You're Lorcan's friend?' they ask you and you nod. You take off your coat. Losing the layer makes you feel exposed, but you lean into the feeling, as though you're the type of person who doesn't mind, for the first time in your life. One of them notices your empty glass and fills it. 'You'll need it for the game,' she tells you.

People ask you how you're finding Freshers Week. You tell them you haven't decided yet. For some reason they find this funny, and you settle into the night. These people are nice; it feels nice to be here. They all add you on Facebook, and you wait a while before you accept. You pretend there's an option for you not to.

You watch Lorcan across the tiny room. Maybe for the first time in your life you're going to be equals with him. For as long as you can remember, you've felt the age difference between you; or for as long as it has mattered. It would be nice to feel as though there was no power difference. You wonder what that feeling might do to your relationship.

Lorcan is talking to someone. The conversation is animated, with a lot of hand gestures, but even when you listen in you're not entirely sure what they're talking about. Someone scolds them for arguing – again, apparently – and calls the other guy Ross.

You open his Facebook profile and scroll through it while he bangs a bottle of vodka on the table in front of you. He studies history. He's graduating this year. You glean all of this information in a matter of seconds, and then put your phone away because he leans over to you. Lorcan has left the room. You're not sure where he's gone, or who he's with.

Ross is tall, or maybe it's the smallness of the apartment making him seem like a giant.

'Hello,' you say.

'Hi,' he replies.

He asks you if you have enough to drink. You nod and shake your glass in your hand. He misinterprets this as you asking for more, or maybe you didn't hear him properly, so he pours vodka into your cup. Not wanting to seem rude, you drink it. It's warm, and there's nothing to mix it with except for the last of the wine in your cup. You swallow incorrectly and it nearly comes out your nose.

He tells you this is his flat, and you listen. He says how nice it is to live close to campus, how cheap the rent is. When he flirts with you, you let him. He tells you you're beautiful and touches your leg with his fingertips. When he invites you back to his room with him, you go. It's dark in here, and you stop him turning on the lights. In the darkness, it doesn't matter what you look like.

You feel free, for the first time in a long time. In the dark, in this new setting, with this new boy, you have nothing to hide. It doesn't matter if he sees you, or doesn't, because he is nothing to you. The thought is empowering: the idea that this could all be meaningless.

You keep your top on the entire time, even when he motions for you to lift your arms above your head. He shrugs and doesn't ask you any more questions. He doesn't care, and that thrills you. It's different to being with Jack; Ross is gentle in a way that almost disturbs you because it gives you a comparison point. The things Jack used to say to you during sex are a radio frequency you are tuned to, constantly playing in your head. You will carry them with you always, baggage you can never fully unpack.

Your bodies don't quite fit together, but you find this amusing instead of horrifying. You're laughing, you're not sure at what. His body is so different to yours he might as well be another species. You feel yourself as flesh, but not in a bad way. In a way that is almost forgivable.

Afterwards, when he rolls over, you lie with your back to him. In the darkness of the room, you snake your hand up under your top, reaching inside. You hadn't felt any pain, but it's an old habit. You breathe out into the dark room, feeling no change, and listen to Ross snoring. It doesn't have to be like it was with Jack, not any more. You had thought, somewhere at the back of your mind, that the next time you had sex it would rip you apart. You're confused, almost, that it didn't.

You gather your discarded items of clothing from the floor and pull them on. It's chilly now, and goosebumps rise on your damp skin. You emerge from the room, bleary-eyed and still drunk. Everything looks a bit different, a bit shabbier. Without people to fill the rooms you can see the dust. Everything smells like cigarettes and beer. The party has long since dissipated. When you check your phone, it's after four in the morning.

You search for your coat in the sitting room. Rubbish from the afters is scattered all around, making the shapes of things hard to distinguish in the half light. You put your hand on something and it comes away damp. You wipe your fingers off on your jeans.

There's a large pile of coats on the couch, and when you rummage through them you dislodge someone sleeping there. Both of you yelp in surprise, and then you're face to face.

After a moment, your brain too confused to process faces, you realise it's Lorcan. His familiar features arrange themselves in the gloom. You're close enough to smell the alcohol on his breath.

'You're still here?' he asks you. 'I thought you left?'

'No—' A pause '—I didn't.'

Embarrassment begins to creep in. Lorcan sits up and groans, stretching his long limbs. His hair falls over his eyes, and he pushes it back. A coat tumbles off him and falls to join other discarded items on the floor.

'Don't tell me you were just with Ross.'

You shrug at him. Yellow light from the streetlights outside filters through the blinds. Now that your eyes are adjusting you can see the individual stripes across Lorcan's face. Outside, a Garda car drives by with its lights on, siren blaring.

'Careful, maybe they're coming for you.'

You gesture at the light in the room, but he sidesteps your joke. You straighten your shoulders and lean back, putting distance between yourself and Lorcan again.

'Well?' he says.

'You told me not to tell you.'

'For fuck's sake, were you actually?'

He's sitting up now, staring at you fully alert, all sense of groggy sleep shedding off him. You start to feel bad, you don't know why he's being so mean to you. His behaviour is making you re-evaluate your own. Maybe it was wrong, maybe the hole inside you should have expanded. Maybe it should expand out entirely and erase you from the world.

'I didn't bring you here so you could fuck the first guy who shows interest in you.'

You pull your coat out from under him, jerking it three times before it comes. You think you hear a seam rip, but you're not sure. Your heartbeat is now thumping in your ears and you're beginning to feel dizzy. You're losing control. This directionless rage is eating away at you, so you decide to give it a direction. You look him in the eyes this time.

'You know what? Fuck you, Lorcan.'

You remember the first time you ever swore at him. You remember how he'd made you feel stupid then too. He'd taken something from you then, but you don't want to let him take this too.

'He's just like Jack. You clearly have a type.'

The siren fades. You don't react; you have nothing to say. In your mind, the video is playing again. You feel it all at once and not at all.

'No,' you say, 'he's not.'

You see something change in his eyes, some little shift, and he softens.

'No, wait, I didn't mean that.'

This, somehow, is worse. You know that he's seen the video, and that he knows it was you. You hate uncertainty, but you hate certainty more. There is no room for you to delude yourself into reading some new, shinier meaning. You can feel the domino effect of his words, how one by one all of your fears are confirmed.

You leave the apartment before you start to cry properly and hail a taxi out on the street. The driver is kind to you, he asks you what's wrong, and you don't know how to tell him. The streets of Dublin flash by, with your cheek pressed against the window. Your head is pounding; everything aches. When you pull up outside your house the driver tells you to take care.

You let yourself into the house making as little noise as possible. You don't want to wake your parents. You have messages on your phone from Fiona. You stagger up the stairs, clutching at your belly. There's a light coming from under Evan's door, and you can hear him laughing inside.

You vomit into the toilet, throwing up the taste of the evening. You think you hear Evan's door open, and maybe sense him standing in the hallway, but you don't say anything. Maybe he's on the landing hovering at the edge of speech, but you don't know.

You fall into bed, sore all over. You don't need a mirror to know what's happening to you. You can feel it without touching. You'd thought you were getting better, but that had been a mistake. You sink into the sheets, unable to comprehend the night.

Fourteen

You're sitting on your favourite bench with Fiona. The two of you are drinking coffees and chatting, optimistic about the change in weather. Fiona is wearing huge sunglasses and has ditched her winter coat. You shade your eyes with your hands when you look over at her, wondering how she isn't cold. When winter started to set in, she told you that she doesn't believe in dressing sensibly, and that had proved to be true. You still wear your coat, and you're grateful for the extra layer of fabric.

You don't feel at ease here, despite the routine you now have with Fiona. Everything has some uncanny quality just by virtue of the fact it's you doing it. You do all the readings you're assigned, terrified that your TA might call on you and you won't know the answer. You get okay results. Days pass and turn into weeks before you have time to acknowledge them.

There's a hollowness to it. The hole hasn't expanded. You've spent the last few months shying away from anything that might provoke that feeling in you again, and you've been successful. There is a wall an inch thick between you and the outside world. If ever you're sitting for too long and your mind is allowed to wander, thoughts come crashing in like waves on a storm beach. So you avoid silences, filling every void with your phone in your hand.

You don't know how Fiona fits in so well. She's telling you about her latest date with Matt now, and it's getting serious. You nod along at the right moments, gasp when her eyes go wide, laugh when she shakes her head. She no longer calls it a situationship: she says situationships can't last for more than six months. You've come to rely upon her, her easy conversation and the way she makes you laugh. You message each other every day, even when you're in the same room. The flow of conversation never ends.

'You should let me set you up with someone,' she says, then, 'Maybe one of Matt's friends?'

You recoil a little bit when she says it, unconsciously. Part of you would love that, but another part of you is terrified of the idea. Sex never seems to work out for you; not with the body you have and all that's wrong with it. This isn't a thought that consciously comes to you, but more of a feeling that washes through you.

'No, thanks,' you say, instead of anything else.

'Why not?'

'No offence, but Matt's friends are all weird.'

'Not all of them. You're exaggerating.'

'Am I?'

She looks at you sideways. 'He's friends with Lorcan, you know.'

'I do.' You don't move. You know she expects you to react. She's been slipping his name into conversation more and more lately, and you've been doing your best to ignore it and act natural. You've spent years teaching yourself to remain impassive, and that stands to you now. Your body takes over, autopilot, your emotions sitting somewhere around your navel, distant.

'Apparently he's always asking about you.'

'I can't imagine why.'

'Hmm.'

You say nothing, the sound of the ocean in your ears.

'Are you really going to keep ignoring him for ever?'

'I'm not ignoring him.'

'Oh yeah?'

'I see him all the time. He was over at the house last month with his dad.'

'Right.'

She doesn't believe you; you don't believe you. Lorcan had been over at the house for your dad's birthday. You'd seen the strained expression on your mother's face every time Pat had laughed; you both prefer it when Lorcan comes over with Mary. Pat brings out all of Lorcan's worst qualities, and you know he knows it too. Happiness, it seems to you at this stage, is something no one ever really has. It's one great delusion.

Then the adults had adjourned to the sitting room and you'd been left alone with Lorcan and Evan. The atmosphere had been so thick and stilted that it might as well have been preserved in resin. You don't know how to talk to either of them any more. Lorcan likes some of your posts occasionally, and you imagine it's like him catching your gaze across a room; you don't know how to avoid it. You'd spent the evening looking through your phone, trying to emit an aura of indifference while your insides were screaming.

Fiona continues to push you, but you don't want to

talk about this any more. Something is curdling inside you. Fiona would never understand. You put your hand on your belly and press gently. When you don't respond, Fiona changes the angle and says, 'Well, I think you should get Tinder, anyway.' Fiona is persistent, but she knows when to move on from a topic that is going nowhere.

You breathe out. 'Oh yeah? Why?'

'Because I can't, and I want to see what the boys are like out there.'

'It's hard being taken.'

'It really is.' She tosses her head back as she says it. 'Anyway, I want to go on a double date.'

You don't resent how well things are going between her and Matt. You like how much gossip there is to talk about and how easy it makes having a conversation with Fiona. You've probably become closer friends because of it. But it's hard not to be reminded of how deficient you are, how much you lack. Fiona's dress has a belt of lace at the waist, revealing small patches of skin. You're not made for the type of happiness she has now, and you never will be. You know she can't be perfectly happy, however, because you've decided that no one is. This makes it easier to bear.

You don't explain this to her. Instead you shrug and take your phone out. Dating apps aren't real to you, they're a game. It takes a minute or two for the app to download without Wi-Fi. While you wait, you update your story with a picture of the grass, and then one of the two of you. You're hoping some other people will see it and come join you, or reply to it. Kevin has been reacting to every other thing you post. He doesn't talk to you in lectures, not really, but you can feel the way his presence brushes up against yours. You're afraid of what he might do next; you're afraid he won't do anything at all. Sometimes you change your privacy settings so he's the only one who can see your posts, which creates a thrilling intimacy, even if he doesn't know it.

The app downloads, and you open it. Fiona is on her own phone, and you can tell she's messaging Matt.

'Which photos should I pick?'

She returns her attention to you. 'Good question, let me have a look.'

She exits her messages and starts flicking through your tagged photos. You do the same. 'What about one of the photos from the ball last month?'

'Is that not a bit too formal?'

'Maybe you're right. There's this photo with Lorcan, but you don't want anyone to think that you're using photos from a date or something.'

Maybe she doesn't know how to drop things. You think you look good in the photo. Happy, even. Happier than you've felt in weeks. It's a photo from Freshers Week, and you're laughing. That happiness feels tainted now that you know how that night ended; everything feels tainted. Sometimes, when you walk through campus, you feel like bursting into tears. Nothing prompts it, but the feeling is always accompanied by a stabbing in your gut.

'Do people really think like that?'

'I do,' Fiona says.

'But you're not "people".'

'Watch yourself.'

You come across a photo from a night out. It's slightly blurry, but you think in maybe a sexy way. You show it to Fiona and she agrees you should use it. You don't quite remember the night it was taken, but the photo is filled with some residual joy. You want to crawl through your screen and be in that moment again.

'You'll want a photo that'll show off your tits as well.'

'You're so crude.'

'I'm not wrong though.'

You don't argue. You know now that objectification is wrong. But it feels different when you do it to yourself. You can't connect the abstract concept to the reality, especially when it comes to things like this. The two of you spend the next while finding photos and then coming up with a bio.

'Nothing too sexual,' you say.

'Don't worry, I don't think of you as a sexual person.'

'Hey,' you say, but you can't disagree with her. She's seen you flinch when guys touch you and heard your excuses for why you can't go home with anyone. She probably thinks you're a virgin, which you're okay with her thinking; you don't want to tell her about Jack. You're ashamed of it now. You think if you told her, she'd look at you differently, perhaps with pity. Sometimes, when the light hits you a certain way or a smell evokes a certain memory, you are back with Jack. You feel his hands on you, you hear his words. Things long buried rise to the surface with a violence that shudders through you. There was Ross, but that night had torn something out of you, and you can't think of it without feeling sick.

'How about something like, "Looking for a rich husband because I'm doing an arts degree?"'

You weigh it as an option. 'It doesn't really have much personality.'

'Neither do you.' She peers over her sunglasses at you, watching the joke land.

'It's true, I'll be anyone you want me to be.'

'Oh, that's good actually. Go with that.'

'Definitely sounds too sexual.'

You trade options back and forth, but you end up picking the third option on a list you find online. It's too difficult to sum up your personality in an appealing way. And if you can't be yourself, you might as well be someone pre-approved by Google's algorithm.

For the first few boys, you give them the attention they deserve. You read out their bios to Fiona, and you have a good look at each picture. She asks you questions about your type and the future you see for yourself. You quickly grow bored, however, and start making snap decisions. Fiona wants to see as well, and she's pickier than you are. This game is familiar. You let Fiona message them from your phone, impersonating you. She does a good job of it, right down to the punctuation, and for some reason it's eerie to you.

All of the boys' faces become the same to you. Instead of swiping on individuals, you're judging Tinder for the quality of men it presents to you, and you're unimpressed. You start making decisions for the pettiest of reasons: one boy's profile picture is too posed, another not posed enough. You think it could make a good drinking game. Drink every time a guy is playing a sport. Drink every time there's a picture of a car. Down your drink if he's holding a fish.

You come across Lorcan's profile. The photo stops you; it's one you took. You'd shoved your phone in Lorcan's face, and he hadn't wanted to stay still. It's from the beach, on one of the days last year when you'd been trying to pretend everything was normal between the two of you, as though each moment wasn't supercharged. You'd looked at the photo and said, 'It's so annoying how photogenic you are when you aren't even trying.'

You don't allow yourself to speculate how many matches that photo has got him, or if he thinks about you when he looks at it, or the girls who message him because of it. You wonder if he thinks about you at all any more. Or if he thinks about that day on the beach, which now feels hazy and dreamlike.

Reading Lorcan's bio is strange. You're not sure how you'd sum him up in a few sentences. He's gone for an Irish flag, his height and a pick-up line.

Is it okay if I tie your shoes for you?
I don't want you to trip and fall in love with
anyone else.

'Okay, match with him,' Fiona says.

'What? No. Why?'

'You know why.'

'I definitely don't.' Your face is hot now, your insides squirming under her watchful eye.

'Well, then you're an idiot. I'm tired of seeing him moping around campus.'

You know what she sees in this situation, you're not stupid, but she also doesn't know what you're protecting yourself from. You're thinking about Lorcan now, about that day on the beach and that night in Ross's apartment. Something strange happens, the two memories merging, and you see disgust on Lorcan's face as you kiss him. Fiona slides her hand over and flicks your screen.

'It's a match,' you say, looking at your two photos together on the screen.

'Of course it is.' Fiona shakes her head. 'Honestly, you're so frustrating.'

'Just what I want to hear on a Friday.'

'Someone had to tell you,' she shrugs, 'might as well be me.'

She checks her phone and slaps her legs, announcing she has a class to get to. She leaves, and you stay sitting for a while. You miss her when she's gone, which makes you think she's probably the best friend you've ever had.

When she's out of sight, you unlock your phone again. You look through Lorcan's profile and remember all of the times you'd told your friends in school that you were soulmates. It's funny now, in a childlike way.

You find a photo of Lorcan and Matt. You click into Matt's profile, thinking about Fiona and her new-found happiness. You can see why she likes him. There's an easiness to him, as though he's genuinely a good person. You think that maybe if you had met him first, it would be you and him dating. You could see yourself holding his hand, touching him. Your mind draws up the images now, and you blink them away. It's just an idle fantasy anyway, one born out of the toxic bitterness you can never seem to escape.

You spend a while looking at photos of Matt on his social media pages, just thinking about things. You're careful that your thumb doesn't slip and accidentally like any of them. You keep glancing over your shoulder, wary of anyone sneaking up behind you and seeing what you're doing. You're used to being constantly contactable, to messages pinging in group chats and notifications, so you never feel alone any more.

You think of a funny joke, something self-deprecating about you always wanting what you can't have. But you have no one to tell it to: certainly not Fiona. You crave the quiet intimacy of being around someone who really knows you. You think of Lorcan and how much you miss him.

Every day, now, you think about him, even without Fiona's prompting. You think about reaching out to him. Fiona could probably sense it. You think of all the reasons that would be a bad idea. He's the only person who could get close enough to realise how broken you are. You can't admit it, but that's what you're really afraid of. Maybe matching with him will help to normalise your friendship; you repeat it over and over in your head, and tell yourself that's the reason you can't stop thinking about it. There's nothing that makes subtext vanish more quickly than acknowledging it. You struggle to feel anything at all about it. At this point, your feelings are vast and unquantifiable, so large as to dwarf you entirely.

You stand up shakily, your phone making the feeling of uncanniness worse. You leave campus through the back gate and get a coffee at the DART station. Your shoulder is sore from carrying your bag, and you're in a bad mood. That familiar hollow ache is beginning to set in again, that storm at the edge of your vision that always threatens tears. You have no words to describe it; you have no way to escape it.

You see him just after you swipe your travel card. He's close, sitting on a bench by the vending machines. You jerk, splashing some coffee out of your cup. You swear, and put the cup onto a nearby wall, fishing in your bag for a tissue. When you find one, you wipe the edges of the cup.

'Hey.'

Lorcan's here, right at your shoulder. You know it's him before you turn around. You always know it's him. It still startles you, and you drop the cup. By some miracle of physics it lands squarely on its base and doesn't tip over.

'Jesus Christ.'

In your surprise, you forget to be mad at him. A hint of a smile rises to your mouth before you get it under control, lost again into the void that consumes you.

'What?' Your voice is flat, toneless. Some spark in him dims when you say it, as though he too had sensed your lapse in judgement.

You look at him, neither of you knowing what to say. His t-shirt is new, but somehow still classic him. He might have got his hair cut, or maybe it's longer. You only register the change: you've always tracked changes in yourself through him, as if he's reflecting something vital back at you. You cock your head to the side, almost daring him to say something. A moment passes, and he falls into a relaxed stance. You sense a challenge in his eyes, as though he's looking deep within you. You wonder what he might be seeing.

'I don't like this.' He stuffs his hands into his pockets, taking a step back. 'I don't like this at all.'

'Well, tough.'

'No, that's not good enough. You've been ignoring me for months.'

'No, I haven't, I'm talking to you right now.'

He shakes his head. 'You know what I mean.'

You look away then, down the platform and out to the sky beyond. The clouds are pink, and the sun is just beginning to approach setting. A seagull the size of a cat lands on the platform and begins to pick at a discarded sandwich wrapper.

Lorcan's still standing beside you, showing no sign of moving. His form is solid; you can feel the space he's taking up. Unconsciously, you mimic the way he is standing.

'I don't know what you want me to say.'

'I want you to say, "Oh, Lorcan, I've missed you terribly, let's never fight again," and then fall into my arms.' You're unimpressed, and he meets your gaze, smiling. 'Sorry, that doesn't sound like you. Maybe more "You're an idiot, Lorcan, but I know you'd be lost without me, so let's be friends again."'

'Your impression of me isn't good.'

'I thought it was pretty good.'

'It's a two out of ten from me.'

Despite yourself, the familiarity of the banter is lowering your guard. Lorcan senses it too. He comes around to the front of you, so you have nowhere to look but at him.

'Look, I'm sorry, okay? I shouldn't have said what I did at Ross's, even if I do think he's a bit of a prick sometimes. But you can do what you want. And in my defence, I was still drunk.'

'What's your excuse for the other times you've put your foot in your mouth?'

He smiles. 'I blame it all on the alcohol.'

You stare at each other for a moment, neither of you breaking eye contact. Between the two of you is an invisible barrier so strong that you're sure people on the platform can see it. He steps close to you now, his hand on your arm.

'I'm sorry about Jack,' he says. 'I should have said that from the start. You deserved so much better than him.'

The subtext has been acknowledged, and yet it doesn't all melt away. You know he's seen the video of you; everyone has. But he hasn't judged you for it. You don't see reflected in his face the shame that you carry around with you, and you don't know what to do with that feeling; it's a new one. So you allow the barrier to drop, and it's like nothing ever happened between the two of you. Almost nothing. And you won't let anything ever happen.

'Next time,' you say, 'it'll be much worse for you.'

He holds his hands up. 'I don't doubt it.'

The train arrives, and you board the same carriage.

'So how are you finding college, really? You haven't responded to any of my messages.'

'It's been nice,' you say, and then your voice falters. You catch the concern in his eyes, and confess to him a fraction of the way you've been feeling. He always used to make you feel better about yourself, and maybe, just maybe, you can trust him with this.

'It's actually kind of horrible,' you say, 'but in a totally mundane way.'

'Oh yeah, welcome to adulthood.'

You don't know why confessing things to him is so easy. Confessing all but one thing. You want to tell him, you really do, but that familiar warning at the back of your mind stops you. This is one thing he can never make manageable for you. It's better to keep it contained, secret. You clutch your bag against your belly.

By the time the train pulls in to your stop, everything is normal again. You tell him about your new friends, and he asks you to come to an event with him the following week. You've been avoiding the society rooms in case you run into him, despite Fiona and Matt's invitations. You'd been holding back, blocked off. Now, as your lives slot back together, you breathe a sigh of relief. Lorcan walks you to your door, just like he did so many times after school, and you're smiling again.

Fifteen

The bird isn't dead, but it will be soon. Its marble eyes are unemotional about this fact. There's something unnerving in how it moves its head from side to side. It lets out a mournful chattering as it struggles to get to its feet, a gash cut across its breast. You stare at the place the flesh should be. You meet its gaze, and your hand goes to your own gut.

Luna is sitting on the kitchen table. Her yowling is what alerted you to the situation, but she's quiet now, and the silence is oppressive. This bird is so alien to the scene that it makes your kitchen feel like an unknown place, where anything could happen.

Luna licks her paw while looking right at you. There is a small bloodstain on the white fur around her whiskers. She mews, then gracefully slinks out into the garden, the cat-flap closing behind her.

You return your attention to the bird. The room, now cat-less, seems much smaller, the space between the bird and yourself tiny. You take out your phone and begin googling helpful questions. *Bird dangerous Ireland? Irish magpie disease? How to scare away bird Ireland?* The last one leads you to several websites selling plastic hawk replicas.

'Evan?' you call, but there's no answer. You walk out into the hall and try again. 'Evan. Hello?'

You go upstairs and bang on his door as the bird resumes its chatter down below. You hear his phone go off inside the room, but he doesn't open your message. You try the door handle, but it's locked. You imagine what he might be doing inside. In your head, the lights are never on in his room.

You try one more time. 'Evan?' You press your ear to the door, listening hard for the squeal of a chair that might give away some movement, but you hear nothing.

You scroll frantically through your phone on the way back down to the kitchen, trying to figure out what to do and whether this is some kind of omen. You send messages into every group chat you're in. People laugh-react to your message, but don't offer any helpful advice. You trip on the second-last stair and your phone flies out of your hand. Definitely an omen.

You call Lorcan. The magpie hops up onto the table and shits on your laptop, and you listen to the dial tone, contemplating your next move. The humane thing to do would be to kill it, but you couldn't stomach the sick crunch of its skull beneath your shoes, or the clean-up after.

Lorcan answers after a few rings, as you knew he would.

'What's up? I'm just having dinner.'

'You have to come over right now.' You'd meant to be more tactful, more mature, but your brain has decided that urgency must be communicated first and foremost.

'Now?'

'Right now.'

'Why?'

206

'There's a bird and I don't know what to do.'

'A bird?' He sounds confused, as though this isn't a matter of great importance. His question almost makes you doubt whether the last fifteen minutes has really happened, but you're still staring at the bird. And it's still staring at you. 'Is that what those messages were about?'

'Yes, a bird, are you listening to me?'

'Okay, okay, I'm at home so just give me a minute.' You hear some noise in the background, the sound of a chair scraping across the floor. 'I'm leaving now, I can be there in ten minutes.'

'I'm not sure the bird will last that long.'

'Fine, it'll be easier to catch then.'

'You're not funny, you know.'

After you hang up, you close all the doors and trap the bird in the kitchen. You can't hear it any more, which stills the beating of your heart, but you've trapped your-self with nowhere else to go. The hall is dark, so you turn on the light. It blinks faintly and begins to light up, but you're still standing in darkness for a minute or two, waiting. It's an energy-saving bulb your dad bought because 'those things last for ever', and he was right.

Lorcan shows up five minutes before he said he would, and he's winded.

'Did you run here?'

'Did you not say it was an emergency?'

'Fair enough.' You're thankful you've called him now, that he's taking this seriously even if he also finds it funny. Lately you've been trying to not need Lorcan; you're all too aware of the things he might misunderstand. This thing between the two of you is feeling more and more precious, as though one wrong move could shatter it.

There's been a lightness to your relationship, almost a childishness, that reminds you of the pretend games you used to play. Last summer you'd stayed on the beach late into the evening just talking, your feet in the water. You think it might have been the safest you've ever felt. You hadn't wanted to return to the house, not with your parents in separate rooms and your grandmother too ill to make the drive. Meteors had streaked across the sky, and you'd wished on every single one. The beach is the only thread of continuity in your life.

'Plus, I can't resist a damsel in distress,' he says, bringing you back to this moment.

'You're a prick.'

'But I'm a prick that's here.'

'Did I mention I love you?' The words are out of your mouth without conscious thought, buoyed along by the banter, but Lorcan doesn't react as though you've said anything out of the ordinary; patterns are difficult to break. You look him in the eyes, doing your best to radiate an aura of platonic normalcy. You ignore the undercurrent that passes between you, as you always have. Out of sight, out of mind.

'Not often enough.' He hangs his coat on the hook by the door and asks, 'Where's the bird?'

You point him in the direction of the door, but make no move towards it. He shakes his head at you, but you stand your ground.

'And it's alive?'

'It was.'

'It was?'

'Before I locked it in.'

'Right, and why isn't Evan dealing with this?'

'You know how Evan is . . .'

'Yeah, fine. But just so you know, after this you can't call yourself a feminist.'

'I don't need feminism any more, I need a big strong man to get rid of birds for me.'

'And I'm a big strong man?'

'Well, you're at least one of those things.'

He opens the door and the bird is nowhere to be found. You try not to picture rotting bird corpses under the sofa and behind the fridge. The thought of meat makes you think of your stomach, of what's festering away there. There's a small pile of feathers on the table, the only evidence that you haven't hallucinated the whole thing.

'Do you have a bag or something I can put it in?'

'We don't know it's dead yet,' you say, as you hand him a reusable bag. It has good sturdy handles; you're sad to see it go.

'And something to scoop it with?'

'Scoop it? Yeah, cool, I'll just get out my comically huge ice-cream scoop.'

'Like a dustpan?'

'Oh, yeah, maybe,' you say, and retrieve the dustpan from under the sink.

Lorcan peers into the cupboard with you, his shoulder brushing yours. You stand up quickly and take out your phone to show him some of the results you'd found earlier, and he pretends he isn't paying attention to you. You pretend you don't notice him pretending. It's a delicate balance, one you're not sure when and how you got stuck in. You read aloud to him for something to say. One of your targeted ads is for birdseed.

'I think I can handle it,' he says, though it's obvious neither of you are confident in that.

The bird chirps from behind the sofa.

'Was that . . .?' he asks.

'Yes, indeed it was.'

Lorcan approaches the sofa, bag and dustpan in hand. He'd been calm before, but you can see fear slowly creeping into his posture. He's beginning to question why he'd agreed to come here, and you're starting to wonder the same. He slowly pulls the sofa away from the wall.

'Shit!'

The bird jumps up, injured wing flapping wildly, beak razor sharp and searching for boy flesh to tear into.

'I thought you said you could handle it!'

'It's not nearly dead!'

'It is, or it was earlier!'

'Well, what am I supposed to do?'

'Why did you come here?'

'I don't know, masculine responsibility?'

'Well, deal with it then.'

'Now that my masculinity has shifted gears from performative to active I think I've lost my taste for it.'

'Too bad.' You push him forward slightly. You see Lorcan's eyes flash down towards your hand before you release him.

He approaches the bird, and it hops at him again, more pathetically. Lorcan recoils in horror and looks at you balefully, but you just urge him on. Now that it's not your responsibility, the whole thing is kind of funny.

'Fine, but open the back door.'

'You're not going to kill it?'

'Kill it?'

'Yes, kill it.'

'Are you serious? No.'

'But that's what you're supposed to do. It's going to die anyway. It's cruel.'

'Call it natural selection.'

'Cruel.'

'Fine, you kill it.'

The contents of your stomach fight against you. 'Fine, let's go with natural selection.'

You open the back door for him, and together you usher the bird out. It hops slowly, and as soon as it's out you shut the door again.

The two of you stand there, looking after the bird. The air is still, and neither of you says anything. You're thinking of something to say to Lorcan, some way to break the silence. You make eye contact with him, he smiles slightly, and Evan walks into the room, startling you both.

You look at Evan expectantly, but he ignores you. He's wearing the same t-shirt as the last time you saw him, but you're not sure how long ago that was. It could have been yesterday, or last week. You're rarely home for dinner any more, not that your family eat together when you are.

Evan is quiet while Lorcan speaks, and then interrupts the first syllable you say to speak over you. Lorcan meets your eyes as Evan does it. He's the only thing stopping you from feeling utterly invisible. Listening to the two of them talk gives you an insight into Evan's life you haven't had for years. He speaks in complete sentences and tells Lorcan he wants to study science. You had no idea what he put down on his CAO form.

You explain the bird situation to Evan when you finally get the chance, and then he goes back to his room, shrugging the entire time. It's like he exists in some sort of dimension that runs parallel to your own, where you can perceive him but he can't see or hear you.

'Weird,' says Lorcan.

You're relieved that he noticed and that you don't have to explain these things to him. He's also witnessed the change in Evan. With your parents, it's like they can only see the child he used to be, and they're always surprised by his reactions to things. It's like his personality, which you barely got the chance to know, retreated somewhere deep inside.

'Yeah, I know. He's really withdrawn. He's been shut up in his room all year. I can't even get him to look me in the eye any more. Maybe starting college in September will help him, bring him out of his shell? That is, if he gets in anywhere.'

'You said he spent the entire year studying?'

'That's what I thought at the time, but maybe he was just watching porn.'

Lorcan laughs, as though you're not serious. 'Yikes. You worry too much. You know how it is: teenagers are barely people. I'm sure he'll fly through first year no problem, make loads of friends, whatever.'

'I just wish he'd tell me what's going on.'

'He'll grow out of it. Give him a chance.'

Lorcan reaches across to you, and you diplomatically side-step him. The ease with which he tries to touch you speaks to how simply he views the world. You're not sure if he's aware of his body, or the effect it has on the people around him. To him, nothing is complicated.

'Evan!' you yell in the direction of his room, 'Lorcan's leaving.' There's no response. Lorcan is sheepish in the hall; you know he doesn't know what to say, so it doesn't matter that he doesn't say anything. There is relief in sharing this moment with him, as though him experiencing it too makes it more solid, more real, and therefore easier to let go. You don't have time to consider any of the implications; the way love and friendship can get tangled in the brambles. You can't look at him when you think these thoughts, however, because if you told him how much you loved him he'd read all the wrong things into it.

Sixteen

You and Lorcan are walking to Fiona's birthday party. It's the end of summer, not yet cold, but autumn hangs in the air reminding you that time passes. He's just back from two months of travelling and he's telling you about it: Paris, Amsterdam, Berlin, Prague. You've missed him, although you kept in constant contact while he was away. You had a running joke where he'd collect a pressed penny for you in every city he went to. It felt like you were there with him, and you've heard all these stories before. He's finished his masters and starting a real job soon. You're not prepared to return to college without him. The two of you walk side by side, laughing, and people step into the bike lane to avoid you.

At this point in your life, you feel stable, and maybe even happy. You've made yourself at home in the limited life you've allowed yourself, but you can't recognise that's what you've done yet. It feels almost comfortable. You're not aware that things could feel better: college is fine, you've stopped wanting to cry all the time, and you've become an expert at repressing all the things you don't have the capacity to think about.

Fiona lives in one of those big houses that still has a servants' entrance. The door is open when you arrive, and you follow the signs of life down to the kitchen and out the back door. There are bowls of tortilla chips and dip on every surface. Matt and Fiona are lounging on deck-chairs in the last of the evening's light, a bottle of wine open on the ground between them.

'You're early!' Fiona says when she sees you.

'You told us to be.'

'Here, take a photo of us.'

Fiona hands you her phone immediately. You're used to this behaviour. On the screen, Fiona and Matt transform. You see a light enter her eyes, and his arm snake around her back to take hold of her soft side. The screen is another reality, one where they're happy. You smile at them weakly, and take a few photos from different angles. Fiona grabs Matt by the arm and leads him further down into the garden. You follow them, snapping candid shots.

'See if they're okay,' you say, at the exact moment Fiona says, 'Thanks, that's great.'

Watching them is oddly disturbing. You wonder if she sees what you see in the photos, or if they somehow obscure reality from her, instead of making it painfully evident. Maybe you're just primed to see the cracks in relationships; that's the reason you tell yourself you've avoided them. You've yet to encounter a happy one. Lately, Fiona's been posting a lot of selfies of the two of them. Sometimes, when she's drunk, she'll send one into the group chat. You watch them now, the coldness more evident without the eye of the camera.

You like that Lorcan isn't active on social media: he

doesn't even have Instagram. You've never had to see him as anything other than he is.

'Hello? Are you listening?'

Lorcan is waving his hand in front of your face. He's been saying something, but you're not sure what.

'Sorry, I was a million miles away.'

'Am I really that boring?'

'No, I'm just thinking about them.' You say it quietly, under your breath, but Lorcan understands your meaning immediately. Fiona and Matt are further down the garden, taking selfies with their wine glasses.

'Yeah,' he says, 'it's a pity. They don't know what they have.'

'What do you mean?'

'Just like, someone who really knows them.'

He's looking at you; you can feel the heat of it on your face. He's been looking at you like that more and more often, as though he's on the cusp of speech. You know what he'd say, and you've been avoiding it. You know what Matt and Fiona have, and the idea of it terrifies you. You never want to give away control to another person, to allow them to impact your life. Not again.

You've heard your dad talking on the phone, when he thinks no one else is home. You're good at becoming invisible, existing in utter silence. You know he's looking at buying an apartment, and you know your mum doesn't know. You've chosen to believe it's for you, maybe once you graduate college, and have filed the information away in your brain under that label. You've been avoiding having any direct conversations with him about it. But thoughts, even carefully stored ones, are heavy.

More people arrive, and the garden fills up. You drink

wine and move between groups, your thoughts ricocheting like pinballs. At some point, Fiona appears and asks you to join her for a smoke. She links her arm in yours and the two of you head to the bottom of the garden. You go with her silently, still thinking. She hops up onto the wall at the end, and you stand there watching her, trying to find your way back to the present. You've been getting more and more trapped in recollection lately, or projections of the future. Your phone shows you memories and they all feel like they happened to a different girl.

'So tell me everything,' she says, lighting her cigarette as she does.

'Everything?'

'Yeah, about Lorcan.'

You don't stop yourself from laughing. 'You've asked me this before, and I don't know how to say nothing is going on any other way.'

'He texted you every day for two months. He doesn't text anyone! Matt says he didn't hear from him at all.'

'We're friends,' you say, tired.

'Are you that stupid?'

'Excuse me?'

'No, sorry, I didn't mean it like that. It's just, I've known you for over three years, right?'

'Since first year, yeah.'

'Since first year,' she confirms, 'and that's basically for ever in college years. I know everyone you know.' She uses her cigarette for emphasis, her hands held wide, palms open.

'Where is this going?'

'What I'm trying to say is I know you, and I know people who know you, and none of them have ever been as in love with you as Lorcan is.'

'Ah, come on.'

'I'm serious, and I know you know it too. You can't even argue with me. In all that time, I've never even seen you go on a date.'

'There was Kevin—'

'You never cared about Kevin! Honestly, you were using him to make Lorcan jealous, and we all knew it!'

She's half right, at least. You'd thought it was fun messaging Kevin, having someone to talk to and about with your friends. But it had only ever been a game to you. It's always only a game.

'We're just friends, really.'

'Sure, okay, fine. I mean, what's stopping you?'

You look at Fiona in the darkness. The words are on the tip of your tongue, they're half formed, and in the silence you think you're actually going to say them. You picture the hole inside you, the way you imagine it swirling and festering, and no words come out. The moment stretches, and she stamps her cigarette out on the ground.

'I wish you'd tell me what the problem is,' she says, her voice on the verge of sadness. 'I just want to understand.'

You have nothing to say, so you say nothing. She leaves you with a hug, and you let her go; there is never any malice in Fiona. You wait a while, scrolling through your phone, checking random notifications, trying to convince yourself that you inhabit your body. Your phone hasn't been working the way it used to: it doesn't offer you enough any more. The updates from your friends are boring and the constant stream of news is exhausting. At one point, you're sure it used to be entertaining to scroll, but those feelings are lost to you now.

You use the light of your phone to pick out the stones

in the grass, and make your way back to the group. You felt adrift in the darkness of the garden, and there is warmth in returning to the party. People look at you as you walk by them, and it feels good.

'Where were you?' Lorcan asks you.

'Just off performing some dark ritual.' Then seriously, 'Actually, it's kind of funny . . .'

'Oh?'

You take a seat beside the tastefully arranged fire pit, and the light dances off Lorcan's features as you lean in to talk to him, worried that someone will overhear.

'Yeah, I was just with Fiona there. And anyway, she started off on this big rant—'

'And Fiona loves her rants.'

Your hackles rise at the interruption. For one brief second, you remember Pat interrupting Mary at some family dinner, when you were too young to really understand what was happening. You see the scene as a shadow that passes over Lorcan's face. You blink, the light changes, and you banish the past to where it belongs.

'Yeah, anyway—' The words tangle themselves up on their way to your mouth, but you think if you acknowledge them they'll fizzle away; that's how you've learnt these things work. 'She seemed to think – well, she had this whole idea, anyway – that you were in love with me.' You mean for the sentence to be longer, to convey more meaning, but the end of it gets lost and you stop abruptly.

He laughs. 'Trust me, if I were in love with you, you'd know it.'

You laugh then, because he expects you to, and he clutches your hand. Your stomach begins to ache in a hollow sort of way, and you can't quite meet his gaze. Of course you know it.

'Are you okay?' he asks you, and you smile, willing the pain away, willing it to vanish into nothing. You want to believe that what he said was true, you want it with every fibre of your being.

But you're not an idiot. You've become perceptive as a means of self-preservation. You've known him for nearly your entire life, for all the parts of your life that ended up mattering. And you know the way he looks at you, you know the eagerness with which he responds to your requests and your jokes. You've done your best to shut down sentences before he can even think of confessing them to you. You're balancing a hundred different meanings, trying to pinpoint what each one might signify to him, and everyone else.

You're saved from having to respond to him by a notification. Fiona has tagged you in a post, giving you photo credit. You like the post and comment a random selection of meaningless emojis and words: *Obsessed*, fire emoji, star emoji, dancer emoji.

No one else at the party reacts, but you can feel the moment it happens. There's a stillness to the two of them, Fiona waiting for Matt to see, Matt silently holding his phone. You can't quite catch the whispered conversation, but you can taste the emotion of it. It reminds you of your parents. You unlock your phone again and look at the picture, taking it in fully this time. Fiona has captioned it *Thankful this boy is finally paying attention to me*.

You show it to Lorcan and he shakes his head.

'It's just a caption,' you say, 'it doesn't mean anything.'

'You know I think that, but you also know what Fiona

was doing. It means something to her, to the two of them.'

'Yeah,' you say. You're all too aware of the complicated ways the internet shapes meaning and context into something new. You've been thinking about it more lately, but you don't know what to do with the thoughts. You'd once hoped it would open an avenue for you to shape yourself into something good, but now you're thinking that you've been wrong. You're not sure what it's shaped you into, but you know that it left you with holes.

You glance back over at Fiona and Matt. Matt is fed up, his gestures sharp. He stands up and walks away. You don't know if the message itself had any meaning, or if some new meaning was entirely generated inside Matt; you don't know whose fault it is.

'Right, I better go follow him,' Lorcan says.

Right now you feel more connected to Lorcan than anyone else at this party. Your smile fades when your hand goes to your gut, and you shake away whatever thoughts you're having.

Fiona waves at you. You think you see something in her eyes, some kind of heavy meaning as she looks back towards the front door and the two boys beyond. But you're not sure if she means anything, or you just want her to mean something. Fiona motions with her head, and you go inside with her to the bathroom. Your inability to pinpoint the essence of the moment panics you.

As soon as the door closes, she bursts into tears. You lean against the wall and wait for it to subside. You pass her scraps of toilet paper, which she uses and then tosses on the floor. You move the bin beneath her, but she doesn't notice. Another piece of soggy toilet paper hits the floor.

The only thing that calms her is her phone. She takes it out and scrolls through her social media apps. After a while, her breathing slows.

'Matt's not happy with me,' she says.

Her face is puffy, and she keeps swiping at her eyes. The simple sentence is off-putting and out of character. You give her the opportunity to explain, but when she doesn't elaborate you ask, 'Why?'

'That stupid caption.'

'You knew it would annoy him.'

'Yeah, obviously, but he never fucking reacts to anything I do otherwise. He's like a brick wall. And then he reacts too much. I just can't read him any more.'

In her hands, she's flicking through pictures. She's moving through them so quickly they blur, as though she's searching for something in particular and not finding it.

'See this one?' She holds up a filtered image of them sitting on a park bench. They're both smiling, and in the next one Matt is kissing her cheek. 'I had to beg him to touch me. Fucking beg him.'

'That's not . . . good.'

'I fucking know that.' The breath goes out of her, and she says, 'It's over anyway.' She wipes at her eye with the sleeve of her top. This isn't the first time they've broken up at a party, and you're pretty sure it won't be the last. Three weeks ago, they'd got into a screaming match outside Brian's apartment. Everyone could hear every word, even over the music.

Fiona slides down the wall, and you sit with her. She shows you photo after photo and tells you the backstory behind them. It's worse than you knew, but you don't let on that you knew anything at all. Instead you say things like 'I had no idea' and 'That idiot'. You'd long suspected something was going on; the vibes of their relationship started shifting around the same time that she started posting more, but to call that out goes against all etiquette.

You let Fiona talk. You share your wine with her and take turns swigging from the glass. You know from experience that she's good at calming herself, talking herself into resolution. You just nudge her in the right direction.

'We have to do something about the group chat. I post all my best content there, and I don't want Matt in it any more.'

'Sure,' you say, 'let's do that now.'

You start a new group chat, adding everyone in the old one except for Matt. You set the name as a string of emojis, and wait for it to take on a life of its own. You watch Fiona visibly relax as you do it, as though the chat was the last thing holding her and Matt's relationship together. You remember how the group chat you had with Jack went dead, and how it came to life again. A lesson in how things only stay buried for so long online.

'Much better,' she says.

As she's talking, her eyes now dry, your phone lights up with a message from Lorcan.

Where are you?

Fiona looks over at you, deliberately sly. 'Who's that, your boyfriend?'

You shrug. 'It's just Lorcan.'

'That's what I said.'

'Stop it,' you say. But you see now a twinkle in her eye, and you know this topic will distract her. 'Now you're single, maybe you could ask him out.'

'And be third wheel between the two of you?'

'It would be a nice change, for sure.'

'Please, just tell me why you won't even try? Then I'll stop bringing it up.'

She's drunk, but there's a clarity to her expression. Your eyes meet. You think *maybe now*. You can feel the ripeness of the moment, nudging a confession. The words are there: the thing you've never been able to say. Your hand is clutching your stomach, kneading the space around the absent flesh. You are going to tell her.

Before you can form the syllables, Fiona says, 'You know, I'm so jealous of you.' This startles you, killing the words before they've had a chance to live. She senses it, so she says, 'You've just always seemed so together, so strong, like you know what you're doing. And you've never needed any guy to tell you that. You're just watching the rest of us bumble around, making mistakes, when you're like this totally complete person.'

You don't tell her. You love Fiona, but she misunderstands who you are entirely. And it's your fault. Later, when you remember this part of your life and recognise the loneliness you felt, you'll know why. But you don't know why now. So you raise your shields again, smile blandly at her, and say, 'I've never had a friend like you.'

'Me neither.'

When you re-enter the party, Lorcan and Matt are nowhere to be seen. You reply to Lorcan's message, but he's not online any more. Fiona decides to go take a disco nap. She's drunk enough to not be crying, but you know as soon as she's alone the floodgates will open. You see her to the staircase, unsure if she will make it back down them. The cake hasn't been cut yet.

225

In the kitchen, you slip into a group of people you know. Ross is here, and you haven't seen him since he graduated. He's still in some of the group chats you use, but you're surprised he's shown up tonight. He greets you with a hug, casually. He's talking to a girl called Emily, someone you only know because she follows Lorcan around at society events. She doesn't hug you. You think you recognise some of yourself in her hand movements, the ways she moves her hips.

Ross tells you about his masters, how he's liking the UK. It's nice talking to him; you laugh about the stupid things you did when you started university, you're even brave enough to say 'You', and watch him blush. Your bottle of wine slowly drains, and you begin to enjoy yourself. You touch his shoulder, the intent clear, and watch it register on Emily's face.

Someone asks where Lorcan is, and you say you don't know. You look at your phone, but he hasn't messaged you. Emily seizes the moment, recognising potential weakness. When the attention of the group focuses on her, she does what you recognise as an impression of you. She shifts her weight slightly and opens her eyes wide. She says Lorcan's name in a singsong voice, placing the back of her hand against her forehead in a fainting gesture.

It doesn't bother you: it's a flimsy parody, meant to make you seem like something you're not. You know the smart move here is to not react, to say nothing, as you always do.

But you see some people laugh, and Emily knows she's hit on something, because she smiles and gets louder. Then her impression of you heightens, and she holds her arms against her stomach, as though she's clutching it. Your hands move to your side; you hadn't been aware of their placement until now. It feels like betrayal from Emily, even though she never owed you anything in the first place.

'I'm going to get some air,' you say.

'I'll join you,' Ross says.

Success. A small moment of success. Emily's expression falters. Her hands drop. Your face is unsteady, but it just about holds. You grab a blanket off the sofa on your way out, and stand outside in the cool air.

'Do you smoke?' Ross asks.

'No. It's killing my grandmother. You?'

He laughs a little. 'No, sorry, I don't know why I said that.'

'Lost for words?'

'You're very intimidating.'

'I'll take that as a compliment.'

'You should.'

He's close to you now, you can feel his body heat. You want to lean in. You want Emily to see you lean in. It would be a mistake, but it's hard to think of that now. Your sense of control is slipping, and you need something to direct all of this emotion towards. You know what happens when you let it boil over.

Ross moves his hand near yours, and you watch it with a kind of excited detachment. You want to see what he's going to do next; you might just let him do it. The front door slams, and you jolt back into yourself. Lorcan and Matt come in. They cheer when they enter the party, and the party cheers back. Matt stumbles against the kitchen counter.

'I should go see what that's about,' you say.

'Of course.'

You leave Ross outside and step back into the party. Lorcan didn't text you to tell you they were on the way back. Matt is carrying a slab of cans, the plastic already ripped into.

You pull Lorcan aside. 'Is this helping?'

'I was keeping an eye on him.'

'You're so irresponsible I don't even know what to do with you.'

'He had to blow off some steam.'

There are very few moments when it feels like you don't know Lorcan, and it's mainly when this side of him comes out. He can't say no to people, he can never be the bad guy. Another way he reminds you of his father. Matt comes up to the two of you then, putting an arm around both your shoulders. You can smell the alcohol off him.

'Where's Fiona?'

'She's asleep, and I suggest you leave her at it,' you say.

'Fuck,' he says. 'Just fuck it.'

'I think you should go home, Matt.'

Matt pulls you in close, drawing you and Lorcan together. He's inches from your face now, they both are. At some point, maybe, in your most chaotic of thoughts you'd imagined being this close to either or both of them. You remember the time you tried to video yourself naked, how you'd fantasised about it, and how disgusted you were when confronted with the reality of it.

Matt is slurring his words, but he's suggestible. You disentangle yourself from the two of them and lead him towards the hall. He grabs his bag from the floor and heads out the door. You follow him and watch it slam in your face.

'Well, that's that,' Lorcan says, having followed you out.

'Someone should go after him,' you say, but Lorcan's not listening.

He pulls you close and puts his arm around your shoulder. He smells like booze and sweat. Everything he does reminds you of his physical form, how he flaunts it, and how you're fading away. It makes you angry at him, at all the ways he does not understand you. You're rarely angry with him, but when you are it's when he reminds you that no one has ever truly known you. Especially not him. You see his father in him now. You shrug him off and he shrugs back at you. Behind him, people are mingling at the party.

'What?'

You're annoyed at him for being drunk now, and for invading your personal space so obviously. You're annoyed that you waited so long to see him, and this is how he acts. You walk past him and into the kitchen. Now everyone is looking at you, and you feel like they're beginning to see you differently, like your carefully painted mask is cracking. The party is ruined; it clings to your skin like a sheen of sweat. It all feels too tight.

You start clearing up, grabbing empty cups and plates, just for something to do, hoping it ends the party. Time, you think, must be circular, because you feel so small again. Lorcan sits down with Emily on the couch and laughs loudly. You feel solitary, alone in the moment, but also observed.

'Hey!' It's Lorcan calling you. Emily's legs are over his lap, but he seems oblivious to it. 'Come here for a second.'

His eyes are unfocused, and his words slur. You hate Lorcan's unpredictability, his inability to understand situations. Control to him comes naturally, because he gives in to his impulses, and no one expects better. You know the same isn't true of you; you don't have that protective layer. Loss of control erodes you.

'I'm going home,' you say. Emily is laughing at Lorcan's jokes again, and he's no longer paying attention to you. You are nearly invisible.

Ross catches you on your way out of the kitchen. 'Everything okay?'

'It's just been a long day, long party, long year, I don't know.' You rub your eyes with the heels of your palms, and then stop when you realise you've probably smudged your eyeliner. 'Do you ever feel like everything you do is always the exact wrong thing?'

'Oh, all the time,' he says with a smile, because he thinks you're joking.

'The thing is I know I'm not doing the wrong thing, I never allow myself to do it. But I still feel this way.'

The two of you are standing in the dark hall, his body tantalisingly close to yours. You're not thinking of Lorcan, or Fiona, or the hole that burns inside you. You're not thinking at all.

You grab his hand, feel skin on skin. Everything happens very quickly. He calls a taxi, and you step out into the night. In his room, you keep the lights off, and when he moves his hands along your body you direct him away from the parts he shouldn't touch, and he doesn't say anything.

He asks you a few times if you're okay, or if he's hurting you. You don't say anything, just shake your head. You wonder if he expects you to feel anything at all, if he'd be disappointed to know that you don't. Jack had taken all feeling away from you; he'd made your body his, because you didn't want it any more.

Now you want it, but it's not there. You are formless.

Seventeen

The funeral is expected. You weren't surprised when your mum came in to wake you up one morning to tell you your grandmother had died. The previous day you'd been in to visit her and death had been all over the hospital room. You smelled it in the air and heard it in the way she breathed. You remember thinking how sad it was that this would be the last time you saw her, that this will be how you'll always remember her. You'd wanted to leave the room, but you'd stayed and held your mum's hand. The light was watery through the window, as though it too did not have the energy any more. Your dad had sat in the reception waiting for you; you don't even know why he bothered to come.

You put on the dress you bought a month ago. You've been preparing for this for a long time, and you go onto autopilot now.

You walk to the nursing home with your mother in total silence, the weight of the things you do not say to each other hanging over the two of you, as it always does. You wonder if she just doesn't have the words to protect you from the life she has found herself living. The two of you stand side by side with your grandmother's body, witnesses to you're not sure what. Your mother rests her hand on the side of the coffin, but she does not touch the corpse.

You see the waxy skin, the stitches under the jaw, the rosary in her blue hands. It doesn't seem like real life; everything has the quality of an image, a reflection. You cannot process it. And everywhere, the smell.

Later, your dad drives the four of you to the church. The car ride is silent; your parents don't speak to each other. Everything is shrouded in a fog, a grey film, like a silent movie. If Evan notices, he doesn't say anything.

Outside, you stand amongst your cousins and mingle. It's weird seeing them here, like they're out of context. Your cousin Jenny has had another baby, who clings to her hair as she talks to your mum. She's talking about smartphones and the internet, and the problems she's having with her oldest. 'You just don't know what they could be looking at,' she says. Then she nudges you. 'You must be glad to have grown up without all this to worry about.'

She's talking about her own childhood, not yours, but you nod. You observe it all from the detached perspective of a visitor to the zoo. You're afraid to get involved, afraid to lose control and what it might do to your sense of self. Time moves all at once and then not at all, and you can nearly feel the fabric of it getting snagged.

You don't cry during the mass. Your mum's voice cracks when she delivers the eulogy, and you want to reach out to her, but you don't cry. If anything, it makes you feel better, which surprises you. You'd fought with your parents when you were a teenager and said you didn't believe in God any more. You haven't been to mass in a decade, but you still remember the ritual of it. There is a comfort in communal grief, in knowing the words to say and saying them at the same time as everyone else. You actually like losing yourself in the collective; instead of taking something away from you, it makes you feel more present than you have in a long time.

You don't cry as people come up to you to express their condolences. So many sorrys are uttered that they lose all meaning. Your grandmother had been the matriarch of the family, and it shows in the turnout. Lorcan and his parents make their way to the top of the church, and he holds you tightly. You haven't seen the three of them together in years. You wonder if grief changes things, if it's somehow the equal and opposite to love. You don't cry now either.

You do cry, however, as you are leaving the church. You and Evan are walking side by side, looking up at the rose window, and the organ starts to play her song. The song she would sing to herself as she made apple crumble in the kitchen. The song she would be called upon to sing at any family gathering. She hadn't been able to remember the words properly for the last few years, but all of you had joined in to help her. And now she would never sing it again. You would never hear her sing it again. You transcend recollection, and live each memory again in a moment, with more detail and emotion than you ever have before. Somehow it brings you back to here: to now.

You cry, and weave your arm through Evan's. He's surprised, but when you look at him there are tears in his eyes as well. He's been lost to you for so long, you've been lost to each other, it's startling how easily you can find each other now, even for just this moment.

Out in the fresh air, you rub at your eyes. For the first time in your life you don't feel ashamed or stupid for crying, as you always have before when too much emotion threatened to overwhelm you. Instead, you feel lighter. The mood is different out here in the open, and people are joking and laughing, catching up with each other. You see Fiona standing to one side talking to Lorcan.

A woman approaches you, now that your eyes are dry, and it takes you a second to recognise her.

'Kate?'

A few years ago you'd gone on to one of her profiles and seen that she was living in London. You're not sure what she was studying, and you were too ashamed to reach out to her. She had always been a good friend to you, but at the time it was just easier to let her go. You had been too overwhelmed to know that then, though. Those feelings have faded with time, and what remains sizzles away in the heat of the afternoon. She's standing before you wearing black jeans and a blazer, and you don't know what to make of her.

'How are things?' you ask. You genuinely want to know. You've spent so long repressing parts of your past, it's fascinating to watch one walk right up to you. You'd thought you'd feel differently, hold some amount of shame or regret, but you don't. You've never felt like more of an observer to your own life; you're curious what might unfold next.

'I think I should be the one asking you that. My mum saw the death notice on RIP.ie and I thought I'd come along. I hope that's okay?' Kate is uncomfortable, and the words seem rehearsed. You remember how anxious she was in school. Suddenly you remember a lot of things about her. You look at her hands, and the skin is pristine.

'Of course. What are you up to now?'

She adjusts the strap of her bag. 'I'm a nurse.'

'That's what you always wanted, isn't it?' It's funny how the memories come flooding back, as though you're inhabiting the body of your old self; or your old self is rising up from somewhere deep inside. You remember all the conversations you had with her, the stresses over exams and boys. You remember how you felt back then as well, how intense everything seemed. The way she talks reminds you of yourself, and you think that it's funny the people we carry with us through life, even when we no longer talk to them.

'And you seem to be getting on well.'

'Oh, I'm doing okay.'

'You were always the smart one in school. I bet you're doing better than okay.' She laughs at your reaction, then says, 'No, really. I was just talking to Mark about you the other day.'

'Mark "afraid of the tampons in the girls' bathroom" Mark? You're still in touch?'

'Still dating, yeah.'

'Oh shit. What's that been, three years?'

'Five.' She laughs. 'Who would have thought it, I know. God, I was so stupid when we were in school.'

'We all were.'

There was a point where you would have given anything to be able to relive your teenage years, but do it right. You think now, though, that there isn't a right way. You were always going to end up like this, you're just living with the consequences. That intensity that burned through you had left you maimed, less than whole, and your body still hasn't recovered. It hasn't got worse in years, but you're terrified every day that it might.

'Not you.' She shakes her head. 'Are you joking? I was always so jealous of how confident you were. So together.'

You laugh at that, at her word choice. And you suppose some part of you had known she'd felt this way, had enjoyed it even. You'd always loved when people saw you for the way you wanted them to, which was so at odds with how you were feeling inside.

This Kate is a different woman to the girl you knew. She carries herself with a quiet confidence, and you don't know her any more.

'I wasn't that confident.'

'Please, you had us all wrapped around your finger. Do you see anyone from those days?'

'No, not since—' You're at a loss for words, so you gesture vaguely '—everything.'

'Yeah, everything.' She pauses sadly, and the two of you look at each other. 'I should have handled that differently. If it makes you feel any better, everyone thinks Jack is a prick now.'

It does bring you some amount of comfort, but the scar tissue is too thick to fade away. It's something you'll always carry with you. At the same time, you both say, 'I'm sorry,' because there is nothing else to say.

A wall has risen between the two of you, one built solid over years and years. You don't know how to reach over it, to go back to the place you used to live in together; you're too separate now. So you don't. You smile at her, and laugh, and then someone else comes over to talk to you, and you excuse yourself. You see her slip out of the church car park and vanish behind a line of trees.

In the car on the way to the burial, your family is silent, letting the grief settle. Your father turns the radio up. You take out your phone. You load Kate's social media profiles and flick through them. On her Instagram, she has photos with a lot of people you were in school with. In the third one, there she is in some pub with Ella, who has blonde hair now.

You want to know if they all remember the past, if they still think of you as the person you were when you knew them. Maybe you had been wrong: maybe the only way to remove yourself from your past is to grow alongside it. By leaving it behind, you've left so many people who still think of you in that way, preserving it.

Your thumb hovers over the follow button, and in your head you draft a message to her. But you don't send it, and you don't follow her back. You scroll through all of your followers, and think about them. You wonder if they see your posts, if they care, and what they think about you. They've always seemed like an unknowable audience to you, but now you're imagining each and every one as an individual, and finding you don't know what to post any more.

You're struck by the transience of things, by the way that people walk in and out of your life and who you are while they're in it. You think of your grandmother and how you'll never be the exact same person again now that she's gone. Memories come rushing back, warping time and space so they feel as though they happened concurrently: her making you a hot chocolate on the beach, her driving you to the pharmacy and letting you pick out whatever colour of nail polish you wanted, you sitting at the computer ignoring her, her sitting at the dinner table watching you use your phone. You don't have a name for the feeling that washes through you; grief and shame and love approximate it, but could never be strong enough. It's a loss you'll never be able to quantify.

Your family gather around the graveside, and as she is lowered into the ground you feel just how empty you are. For one moment, you picture yourself jumping onto the coffin, either to pry it open and check she's really dead, or else to be buried alongside her.

'Oh, my brother's here,' your dad says, pointing at a grave further down the row. 'I didn't know that.'

Your father never talks about his grief, about the things that he carries with him. In truth, you don't know how your uncle Simon died, only that it was before you were born and your mother says your father was never the same after. Your mum links her arm with your dad's then, and he lets her, which surprises you. You're not sure of the last time you saw them be tender towards one another, if they ever were.

Nearly everyone shows up to the pub for a cup of tea and at least one quarter of a sandwich. You all sit, telling stories about your grandmother, about what a great woman she was. The fragments of stories enrich your memories, fleshing them out, allowing you to see her as a woman instead of an obligation. You see her differently in your memory now, younger, and picture your relationship as it was when you were a child. You remember hugging her, which you haven't done in twenty years, and never will again. Everyone is laughing, and you realise she must have been a different person to each of these people as well. And maybe it isn't a bad thing.

Lorcan sits next to you, silently filling your cup with tea when it empties and handing you tissues under the table. He makes a joke for Evan, and for the first time in a long time you see Evan laugh. He intervenes when people ask you too many probing questions about what you're going to do with your life and breaks any silences that engulf the table. You think about who you are to him and who he is to you.

As the afternoon draws to a close, you all sing your grandmother's song together, and it's like she's there with you, made up of everyone's recollections of her. You understand, maybe for the first time, the value in being made whole by other people.

Eighteen

You already know what you're going to wear tonight, but it takes you a long time to put it on. Your body feels slow, as though it's not your own. You stare at yourself in the mirror, running your hands over the fabric stretching across your navel. You've been feeling better lately, you think. But the hole hasn't gone away.

You've spent years agonising over it, ignoring it, trying to fix it. Now you're apathetic to it. It's regrettable, but it simply is. It's something you have to live with for the rest of your life; it's something you can never show anyone else. It's part of your identity now, one formed long ago. You've been thinking more and more about what an identity is, and how you came to have this one. Your choices feel constrained by ones you made when you were too young to fully understand them, and all you want to do is break free from them.

You sit on the edge of your bed, phone in hand. You take some photos and look at them, wondering if the fabric of your t-shirt is thin or it's just your imagination filling in the gaps with what you know is underneath. You think you've lost weight, but it's hard to tell. There's nothing there to push the fabric of the t-shirt out any more.

You pose yourself in front of the mirror. You lean on one elbow and hold your phone up. The screen captures your movements, freezing them in time. When you look at the photos, you're happy, and you post them. You think about whether this is an act of identity formation or an embodiment of what you already are. You've become wary of your phone over the last few months, since graduation, and the way it makes you feel about yourself. These thoughts aren't enough to stop you posting, from scrolling through endless videos, but you take no joy in it. It's an addiction.

You leave your room and stand outside Evan's. You knock, and he says nothing. You're tired; you're tired of the silences, the way he ignores you. You remember him as a child, and how you were always the one he turned to when he was upset. You'd hated it then; it had made you feel like you were responsible for him. You miss it now. You decide, fuck it, and open the door. The room is dark and smells musty. Evan is sitting at his laptop, the screen visible from the doorway. Some of the words on the screen burn themselves into your mind. *Females. Whores.*

'Jesus, what are you reading?'

Evan moves quickly, closing the window and standing up. His form fills the doorway, and you take a half step backwards.

'Nothing.'

'Um, okay.' A moment passes between you. 'I'm leaving now, if you want to come with me.'

'No.'

'Okay. Lorcan said he might like to see you.'

The words fall out of your mouth and all but clatter to

the floor. Evan closes the door in your face. You're not sure exactly what just happened. You think maybe you'd imagined it, but then you see Evan's movements again, the expression on his face. He looked like a person who'd been caught doing something they shouldn't. And you know from experience what he was looking at, and it makes you sick. It reminds you of Jack, and you feel small. Too small.

These thoughts occupy you as you walk to Lorcan's new apartment. You remember the way the boys in school used to talk about you, how they'd stared at your body. The act of remembering is peculiar. Although these memories have always lived inside you, it's only when you're looking back with hindsight that you see the effect they've had on you. A few months ago you'd stumbled onto the dark part of the internet. You'd gagged, bile burning the back of your throat; you used to not react at all. You wonder, for the first time, what effect the internet has had on Evan. Perhaps you'd seen it all along, but you were as powerless to stop it as you were to see it in yourself.

Lorcan's apartment is in the basement of an old house. There are roses in the front garden, so you stop. You take some pictures of the buds, trying to capture the pink to orange gradient. Lately you've been trying to notice beautiful things. You think you'd be happier if you lived a beautiful life. You post the photos to your Instagram story and immediately forget their exact colour. It's as if the act of taking a photo removes you from the present, and you're always experiencing moments through the lens of the future or the past; how you think you might feel someday, how you realise you actually felt at the time.

The door is under the staircase to the main entrance.

Through the window, you can see the sitting room and Lorcan beyond. He's painted yellow by the light and moving along to some song you can't hear. You like that Lorcan is always Lorcan, no matter who's watching. As long as you've known him, he's been a steady presence, standing strong against whatever digital tide had buoyed you along.

You ring the doorbell and wait, anticipation bubbling inside you. Lorcan opens the door to you, and you're so overcome by the emotions rising inside you that you hug him, pulling him close against you. You wonder if he could get through to Evan, save him somehow. Lorcan startles and freezes, and then his arms close around you. You're still, among the coats and shoes.

He leans back and takes a look at your face.

'What's up?'

You find it hard to come up with the exact words, so you say, 'Evan.'

'Well, what's new? Is he coming?'

'I don't know.'

Lorcan looks at you, concerned. You're aware that you still have your arms around each other, so you step back stiffly.

'I'll talk to him later, if you want.'

You wanted him to say these words, to understand without needing you to explain, and yet it's not enough to fight back the panic. You're afraid that Evan is lost; in fact, you know that he is.

You want to talk more, to explain properly, but you don't have the words and you can hear other people inside the apartment. Moments fade quickly, especially when you're not ready for them, and this one passes. You feel as though things are slipping away from you, as though things you previously had control over have revealed themselves to be entirely wild. You want to talk to him about Jack, to finally confide everything in him. It's a reckless feeling, one that is threatening to overcome you. You imagine lifting up your top, showing him the hole. It's an impulse that goes through you like a shudder, one that you fight against with everything you have.

'Matt's coming tonight, by the way,' Lorcan says, the change in subject sharp. 'I know you've been worried about him.'

'He's been really off lately.' You say the words slowly, catching up with the conversation. There's been a strange undercurrent to your interactions with Matt. You're not sure how to act around him now that he and Fiona have broken up and it's actually stuck. It's nothing tangible that you can adequately explain, but you sense it all the same. He messages you a lot; you think he probably just needs someone to talk to. You've told Fiona, and she's pretended she doesn't care.

'Well, he hasn't been talking to me about anything.' Lorcan is looking at you, his head to the side. He leans back against the wall. 'I know that you're just looking out for him, but that doesn't mean that's how he sees it. If he wants to read into things, he will.'

'I can control my actions, but I can't control how people perceive them? That sucks.'

'That's life.'

'Your philosophy degree has ruined you.'

'Thank you for acknowledging that I wasn't ruined before.'

'I didn't say that.'

Brian arrives, and Lorcan turns away from you. You

go through to the sitting room, conscious of every movement you make. Lorcan's only just moved in, and the room doesn't have much personality yet. A blue sofa from Ikea, two lamps, and a white coffee table probably also from Ikea. The apartment belongs to his mother's friend, who agreed to rent it to him for the cost of the mortgage, cash in hand. You're jealous of him; you'd give anything to escape your parents. You feel something else as well, something hard to pinpoint, that comes out of your desire for stability.

You message Fiona, and she says she's running late. She sends you photos of her outfit options, and you give her advice. She'd told you she was leaving half an hour ago, but that's Fiona.

It's easy talking to people at the party; you know most of them. You flit in and out of social circles, and you relax a little bit. You have three jokes for each person, and you can tell they feel like they know you. You know you're good at this, and your body takes over even if your mind is elsewhere. You're good at performing for an audience.

Matt arrives, and he approaches you. He has the feeling of a man carrying around an unacknowledged sadness. You sympathise with him, and the Fiona-shaped hole in his life. He keeps talking about moving; to Barcelona, or maybe Lisbon. He doesn't know what he wants to do, but it's obvious he doesn't want to be here any more. He sits down next to you and leans in so he can speak quietly.

'Don't worry, nothing is going to happen tonight. It's going to be a normal, drama-free evening.'

'Famous last words,' Lorcan says from the door.

Matt jumps. He moves back from you, and now he's unnaturally far away. You're moving without thinking, so you close the space again. You want this party to be normal; you crave it. But the more you seem to act like things are normal, the stranger they get.

'Did I interrupt?' Lorcan says.

'What?'

You can't shake the impression that there is something going on that you can't see. There are darker thoughts here that you don't indulge, don't think about, as you sip from your plastic cup. There's something nice in being an object of desire, something that someone wants. And Fiona had once wanted Matt, which makes his attraction a particularly potent drug. But you're not thinking about that, not acknowledging that feeling. You are a creature of pure logic, interpreting and responding to stimuli. Emotions have nothing to do with it.

Matt is saying something to you, but you're not paying attention to him. You've just seen Evan walk through the door.

'Sorry, I have to go,' you say, and leave Matt standing by the sofa.

'I thought you weren't coming?' There's an edge to your voice, one that you forget to soften.

He shrugs. He always shrugs. Jack used to shrug too. You'd thought you'd left the past behind you, forgotten it somehow. But ever since you met Kate at your grandmother's funeral you've been having nightmares where he's still touching you. Evan moves through to the kitchen, and you've never felt further away from him.

You're starting to feel overwhelmed now. Your flight response kicks in, and you want to banish the present to your past and forget about it. Maybe moving on is the only way to get yourself out of this rut. Maybe you could move to Barcelona or Lisbon. It's as though Matt's words and dreams are becoming your own, and you're manifesting them into reality. It will be a normal evening.

Your body knows what it should be doing. It's carrying you along, and you're impressed by it. These are movements you learnt long ago, and you know the steps. Inside, however, you're putting two and two together and hoping what you're coming up with is five. Maybe what you'd seen Evan looking at was nothing; maybe it was something, but merely the usual misogyny of the internet, and it had slid right off his brain without leaving a trace. But you're thinking now, your mind calling up memories of Evan's behaviour, his language use, the way he disappeared into his room at some point and none of you could reach him. You wonder now what Evan would do if he met Jack again, if he'd like him this time around.

You take yourself into the bathroom to calm down. You don't like feeling like you don't know someone, like they've surprised you and you don't have them figured out. It makes you think about yourself in a way you don't like. You begin to feel that familiar ache, that fizzle that eats away at your flesh, and take a deep breath. You press the heels of your palms into your eyes so forcefully you see red. Not today.

You return to the party. You do your best to get lost in it, to play the part you know how to play. You listen to someone tell you about their new job in consulting and hear yourself asking questions as though you're interested. Your phone is heavy in your hand, and every time you look at it you panic, so you put it in your pocket.

You have a message from Fiona but you can't bear to open it. You remember what you used to use it for: the photos you'd take of yourself, the men you'd message. It's tainted, somehow more responsible for your actions than you are. You need to breathe. You need to calm down.

You need to find Lorcan.

But he's nowhere to be seen. He's always been good at helping you figure things out, and making sure you don't overthink.

You walk through the party as though in a dream. From the outside you're impressed with yourself, at how easily you're navigating this situation. You feel caught between everyone, stretched thin. You're glad when you see Matt still in the sitting room, because you're looking for familiarity. It's quieter in here, most people having moved out into the garden, so you close the door.

You open your mouth to talk to him, but no words come out. You think about telling him about Evan, about Jack, about the hole, about everything. There is too much to say, so none of it comes out. He sits beside you, saying nothing, and then suddenly leans in close to you again and kisses you right on the mouth. His tongue is cold and tastes like beer; you wonder if he was drinking before the party started. For one sickening moment you feel his thumb run over your nipple before you're able to move and jump up. His hand falls away, brushing against your torso as it drops. A shudder goes through your entire body. You feel with a deep certainty that, at one point in your life, you wouldn't have moved away. You would have let it happen.

'What the fuck?'

'What, you'll kiss Ross but not me?'

Pure shock makes its way through your body. You get up and leave the room, shaken. You feel like you've badly, even terribly, misunderstood everything. You're nothing like the person Matt thinks you are, if he thinks you'd get with him in Lorcan's sitting room. The idea that who you are and who you are to him could be so vastly different makes you hyperventilate. You wonder if it's your fault, if you've become so unaware of your body and your actions that you could actually have done something to make him think you'd want this.

Lorcan. You need Lorcan.

He's not in the kitchen or standing outside. It's his party, and he doesn't seem to be at it. The edge of your vision is blurry, like you might faint, and you have a stabbing pain in your stomach. The smell of smoke is making you miss your grandmother and reminding you of her sickness. Someone asks you if you're okay, and you say yes. You ask them if they have any plans for the weekend and leave when they are mid-sentence.

You find Evan in the garden. He looks at ease until you approach. He knows what you saw on his screen: he must. He's talking to a girl you recognise, and after a moment remember that her name is Emily.

'Have you seen Lorcan?'

'Not for ages,' she says, adding, 'not that I was paying attention.'

You reel yourself in and take in the scene in front of you. You see the way Emily is looking at Evan and recall his expression before you announced yourself. As if to echo your thoughts, Emily grabs Evan's hand and pulls it around her shoulder. All you see are the words on the webpage Evan was looking at. You want to shake her, warn her, take her hand and save her from the same fate as you. But you are paralysed, unable to move, unable to affect the events that are unfolding in front of you, as you always have been.

Evan raises his eyebrow. 'I think I saw him go into his bedroom.'

'Thanks.'

You think you might actually faint now. You've never had a panic attack before, you didn't think that kind of thing happened to people like you. You're not sure how it all even started. You think you might be crying, but you're not sure; you're not sure of anything.

You walk through the kitchen and out into the hall, the whole time imagining how you're going to say all of this to Lorcan, and what he might say to you. Your hand reaches under your t-shirt, feeling the familiar emptiness of the hole. You rest your hand inside yourself, and breathe until you have the energy to open the door.

'Oh god, I'm so sorry,' you say, frozen in the doorway, reacting before your brain has time to process the image. You cover your eyes and say 'Pretend I saw nothing, eh, carry on!' and close the door behind you.

You've retrieved your coat and bag and walked out the door by the time you hear Lorcan's door open again and him calling your name. You're out in the cool night, the air fresh on your skin. You think it was Fiona with him; you're sure it was, but that doesn't make sense. You struggle to put your coat on, but one of the sleeves is caught inside out and won't budge.

'Hey!'

You stop, your back to the house. You feel Lorcan reach out, and so you turn to him. He's hastily dressed, with a coat thrown over his bare chest.

'I don't want things to be weird between us,' Lorcan says.

You laugh. 'Well then, maybe don't fuck my best friend?'

He runs his hands through his hair. 'Fuck.'

You're silent.

'I've been trying so hard not to fuck this up but I keep making it worse.'

'Yeah, what's wrong with you?'

His face is pained, his hand gestures wild. 'Well, you haven't been making this easy. With Ross, and Matt tonight.'

'Matt tonight?'

'I saw how he was looking at you!'

'Oh yeah, how was that?'

'The way everyone does.'

You get your coat on properly now, shoving your arm into the sleeve.

'I literally have no idea what you mean.'

You think you're yelling, or else your voice is echoing in your ears. Lorcan takes one step back towards the house, as though he's going to go inside, but then changes his mind and steps closer instead. His face is inches from yours, and he looks pained.

'You're my best friend, do you know how hard that is?'

'Sorry, I didn't realise I was such a burden.'

'No,' he pauses again. '*Fuck.*'

You stare at him, wondering where he is going with

this. Lorcan is rarely at a loss for words. You can smell the sweat off him now and something that you're worried is Fiona.

'It's hard, because I don't know what I'd do without you, and I can't lose you, but I'm in love with you and can't keep going on like this. I can't keep pretending like I amn't.'

His words go through you like a cold wind.

'Oh,' you say.

'Yeah, and maybe if you thought about it for a minute, you might realise you probably love me too. Look, I—' He falters, searching for the right words '—I just wish you could see yourself the way I do.'

'Right,' you say, lamely. 'I have to go.'

And you take off running down the street. You're not aware of what Lorcan does, or if anyone else heard, or anything at all. You're not aware of how you must look sprinting down the street, your green coat billowing out behind you. You're just aware of the feeling inside you that's growing.

The moment you get home, you run upstairs to your room. You close the door behind you and lean against it. You feel feverish and sick. It's an all-too-familiar feeling. You close your eyes tight and bend over double. Silently, you scream. Your body aches; you're ripping apart.

Lorcan always makes you feel this way; he always has. Maybe he's the root of your problems, the way he seems to poke you when you're most vulnerable. Your thoughts aren't coming clearly; they're covered by the wave of emotion that overcomes you.

You strip off slowly, deliberately. You're prepared now for what you know you'll see. It's almost funny, you think, that you're fading away. You walk over to the mirror, your hands covering your stomach. You breathe in once and then reveal the hole.

It's there, definitely, but it's not bigger.

You think, somehow, that it might be smaller, even. But that doesn't make sense. You sit down in front of the mirror, cross-legged, and examine it. You've always had a sick fascination with it, but this feeling is different.

You thought you had a handle on what was happening to you, as much as you could, but maybe you don't. Nothing is what it seemed to you.

Evan isn't just some quiet recluse. And Lorcan isn't just your best friend. Your dad never offered you an apartment. You shut your eyes tightly, focusing on the black, trying to drown everything out. You can't remember the last time you felt sure of anything. Maybe it was on the beach, or some sunlit day in your kitchen at home, your mum cooking. It all slips away from you now, the harder you try to grasp at it.

These feelings don't make sense.

You crawl into bed and bury yourself beneath the covers. Your phone is in your hand, and in the heat you google everything you've googled before, and none of it brings any answers. You try *Girl reappearing*; *Girl closing up*; *Girl unvanishing*.

When you reach the dead end, you start with things like: *Could I be in love with my best friend*; *Does my best friend love me*. You know there are things the internet cannot answer, but that doesn't stop you from trying. The sum total of the human experience is distilled into the questions you ask Google in the middle of the night.

You fall asleep with your phone in your hands, and

when you wake up, it's pressed to your face and out of battery.

You'd dreamt of Lorcan, you know that, but the content of your dream fades quickly from your mind. It was like you lived all the events of your life simultaneously, and they had folded in on themselves, creating little rhyming moments. In each one of them, each significant one, there is Lorcan. In the post-sleep fog, you wonder if maybe you are in love with him. You've never even fully considered it as an option, not since you became old enough to know better. All those times you refused to call something love didn't make it not love though. It just made it painful. All those times you thought you were settling for love, intimacy, friendship, didn't make it those things either.

The one person you want to talk to about this is Lorcan, but you're afraid. You shouldn't have run away, but it seemed like the only thing you could do. You're always running, avoiding, disappearing. And it has never once made anything better. Sometimes you can be such an idiot. Your emotions fade away, slowly, and then all that's left is the voice in your head telling you to do something about it. It sounds like your mother.

You get out of bed heavily, your body aching.

When you look in the mirror, you think maybe the hole is a little smaller. There's a mole visible that you haven't seen in years. It's unsettling; you'd longed for the hole to recede, to fill up, to go away, for as long as you can remember. But now that it's happening, it doesn't feel right either.

You plug your phone in to charge and wait for it to come to life in your hands.

You see a stream of notifications, but they can wait.

You want to get your own head straight before talking to anyone.

Lorcan said he wished you could see yourself as he does. But as far as you'd been aware, you controlled how he saw you. You'd carefully curated the part of yourself you'd presented to all your friends. But maybe none of that had worked.

You spend your time looking at photos, trying to understand the timeline that led to you being here, now. You find a photo of you and Kate from school, and remember the girl you were, and wonder if you're still that same girl, if somehow you'd never not been her. You flick through your profile pictures, watching yourself get younger, then older, then younger again.

Some of these photos have a lot of likes. You click into the list of them now and see the names of people you haven't thought of in years. You have over two thousand friends, but in real life you think you probably only have two. The general feeling of disgust that lives inside you transfers from your body to this internet persona you've created, who seems to have always cared about the opinions of these people. You're tired of it. You start unfriending people, tentatively at first, but with each one you begin to feel lighter, and you speed up. A lot of time passes, and when you're done your list has shrunk to under a hundred people.

You read through some of your old posts. At the time, they had felt like entries in a private diary. Now they are a living time capsule of the ways you've tried to forge your identity. You've always been desperate to have someone to share yourself with, and you'd tried to satiate that need by sharing yourself with everyone, until there was nothing left for you. You gave everyone what they wanted of you, exactly what they wanted, and it was never enough. You think of your grandmother, and how she'd shared things with other people that somehow made her greater.

Some of the posts are unintelligible to you. Clearly, at the time, they were loaded with coded meaning, meant for particular people to understand in a particular way. Now, though, they mean nothing. You think about the ways you've painted meaning onto everything you've read online, and how it's subjective. You wonder if people feel the same way about your posts, if they aren't picking up on any of your carefully constructed meanings. Every time you've posted something just for one person, it's been seen by hundreds.

You sit with your top pulled up, examining the hole inside you. The edges of you blur into nothingness, the boundaries unclear. Perhaps they're becoming more unclear. Perhaps your skin is reaching across the space, knitting itself together.

You're looking at an old video. It's so old it's a recording of a grainy TV. The original has probably been lost to time. You and Lorcan are on the beach, and so small. You remember that day, and how tall you'd felt he was. But he doesn't look tall at all.

There's more. As the video goes on, your nostalgia turns bitter as you remember how this video had made you feel. You'd felt pinned down, subjected to another form of reality. Maybe this was the first time you realised you had a body and what that could mean. It was the first time you'd experienced yourself as someone else's object. You didn't realise it then, but you do now.

You're scrolling through your photos again, selecting

random ones as they fly past. The first time someone had left a mean comment on your Facebook profile. The first time you'd sent a nude to someone. Your body doesn't look like that any more. But in this photo it still does, frozen behind glass. For ever.

You pause and wonder whose eyes you've really been seeing yourself through.

You think you have a name for that feeling now, the one that spills through you: self-hatred. You'd never been able to pinpoint it before, never known its source. Now you know it's because it doesn't just come from you, it comes from everywhere else as well.

These experiences shaped you, and you're not sorry for how you acted. You had limited information, and emotion clouded your judgement. You were just being a person. Not logical, but rational; actions spurred on by past experiences.

You are still just a person.

Sometimes, you think, you lose sight of that. It's easy to convince yourself that you have to be who everyone thinks you are. It's easy to live your life for who you are on the outside and forget who you are inside.

You think that maybe, somehow, you've managed to separate yourself into two halves, trapping some part of you locked deep inside. And maybe that part of you has been eating away at your flesh all these years.

You're tired of feeding it.

The first messages you see are from Fiona.

Im sorry
Im sorry
In srry

And then, sent later, ones that are more legible:

Can we talk?
Last night meant nothing, obviously
I was just stupid and trying to get back at Matt

This, at least, is something simple.

It's okay
I'm not mad at you at all

You watch the typing bubble appear and disappear. Minutes go by, and you get fed up. You call Fiona.

'You're really not mad?' She's breathless. 'Because it really was nothing. And he was only inside me for, like, five seconds.'

You laugh at the absurdity; it's classic Fiona. Your laugh draws a nervous response out of her. You're looking at yourself in the mirror, at the hole inside you. Your fingers move around the edges.

'I'm not mad.'

'Really? Can I ask . . . why? Not that I don't believe you, but I find it hard to believe.'

You think, for a moment, on what you should say to her. You suppose it is weird that you're not mad, that you're in no way threatened by her. Instead of trying to spin the story, you breathe out and say, 'Because I know no one can come between me and Lorcan. Except maybe Lorcan himself. Or maybe me.'

She laughs. 'I always did wonder if you were ever jealous of all the attention he got.'

'Not for a long time.'

You love Fiona, you love how straightforward she is. You don't know why it took you so long to realise that you could be honest with her too. Your friendship was never a power game. It is comforting that there is no ill-feeling between the two of you, that this isn't something you need to carry with you for years. You can simply be united. You tell her about your conversation with Lorcan, and she squeals.

'What are you going to do?'

You hold the bridge of your nose in one hand. 'I don't know.'

'You have to do something. Please, I'm begging you.'

'Part of me thinks that Lorcan can't love me, that he's not really capable of loving anyone. I've never seen him be in love with any of the other girls.'

'The other girls aren't you. I've been waiting for this to happen for years, you realise? *Years.* We all saw it. Matt and I used to joke about it, we'd always call it a double date when we hung out with the two of you.'

Her voice stumbles over his name, and you flash back to the party.

'I'm just not sure it's possible for men to feel love without confusing it with sexual desire, and I'm not sure they can feel sexual desire without treating women as objects.'

You're not sure you can feel it either, without treating yourself as an object. You think over the events of your life, the way you've been treated, the way you've allowed yourself to be treated. You want so badly to recognise them as wrong, as perverse, as abusive, but it's so hard to recognise it when you didn't feel it at the time. It will be a long time before you're able to process these feelings.

Fiona is quiet, and then says, 'Maybe, I don't know, but they can definitely feel sexual desire without love, and it's different.'

You decide to tell her about Matt, because right now communication is flowing freely and without judgement between the two of you, for perhaps the first time ever. She takes a moment to say anything, and the silence stretches out, so you say, 'He's a total dick.'

'He really is. I suppose it's the kick I need to finally get over him.'

'That's the spirit.'

'Anyway, thanks for not minding that I kinda half fucked the love of your life.'

'I don't even know how you want me to respond to that.'

'Stunned into silence, just how I like it.'

After you hang up the phone, you smile. You feel lighter than you did before. And you feel more like yourself. Fiona had expected you to be mad at her, and it would have been so easy to hold on to that feeling and weaponise it. But you don't want to do that any more. It's easier to let it go.

You get dressed and head downstairs for some water. Evan is sitting in the kitchen, waiting for his toast to pop. You don't say anything to him; you're so tired of his attitude. He looks over at you once, then twice, and you ignore him.

'Not going to say anything?' He's goading you, and you know it.

You stop and look at him. You really look at him, searching for the boy you once knew. He's so tall, so different to how you see him in your mind's eye. He's standing by the kitchen counter, and behind him you can see the two holes in the wall that used to hold up the phone. Time folds in on itself once more, creating another flashpoint.

'So, do you like Emily?'

He snorts out his nose.

'Evan, I don't want to do this.' You think about calling him out, shaking him, trying to get him to see your point of view. But then you stop. Tears are at the edge of your vision now, and you say, 'When did we stop hanging out? I don't want to fight with you, I really don't.'

Your body is still tired, your mind carrying you down too many tracks. There's nothing you can say to him to change him, to get him to see the world the way you see it. At least not yet. Not when your relationship is like this.

'What are you doing later?'

The change in tack surprises him. 'I don't know, playing a game.'

'Which game?'

'Does it matter?'

'Yes. I'd like you to teach me how to play. Or at least let me watch you.'

He pauses, considering. 'Okay?'

'Okay.'

You nod, fill a glass of water from the sink and leave. He seems confused, bemused even, but you feel a little bit better. You may not like him now, may not like the person he's becoming, but you still love him. And maybe it's you who has to bend to meet him first. You, more than anyone else, know how the internet can worm its way inside you, shaping you. Maybe you're the one who can reach him, not Lorcan. It's worth a try. The fact that he's considering letting you play gives you hope, and you like the feeling of hope.

Back in your room, the real problem raises its head. You're surprised that Lorcan hasn't messaged you, but at the same time you aren't.

Can we talk?

Give me 15 minutes.

You sit for a while, thinking about what you're going to say. Then, less than fifteen minutes later, there's a knock on your door. And there is Lorcan, shadows under his eyes, shirt incorrectly buttoned.

'You ran here?'

'I walked quickly.'

'Eager much?'

'I suppose so.'

'Why are you smiling?'

He leans against the doorframe. 'Oh, I've just realised I have nothing to lose. I bared my soul to you last night, finally came clean, and so I don't have to worry about what to say next. It's all on you.'

'Presumably, though, you're worried about what I'm going to say?'

'Oh, terrified. But I also like having the upper hand, for once.'

'Never.' You laugh, and then the two of you go silent. Lorcan's right: it's your turn. You look back through the hallway into the kitchen beyond and see Evan.

'Maybe we should go for a walk?'

You keep glancing at Lorcan, as though something has

changed. You can make the contours of his face with your eyes closed, you've always been able to. Maybe the change isn't in him; it's in you.

'Please stop looking at me like that.'

'Like what?'

'Like you're trying to figure out what to say.'

'Aren't you here to talk to me?'

'You know what I mean.'

You keep walking, the conversation relatively light, until you get to the green space in the centre of the village. It's not that you're avoiding the conversation, but both of you are waiting for the right time to say something. You sit on a bench, the sun alternating between shining and hiding behind a cloud. Two children on scooters are whizzing along the path, their dad chasing after them.

Lorcan leans back, his hands behind his head, relaxed.

You turn to him, your hands in your lap. 'Are you sure you're in love with me?'

'I'm not sure I've ever been more sure of anything. Or I guess I'm not sure I've ever been sure of anything else before.'

'Okay.'

'You've said that one before.'

'I'm just buying myself some time.'

The children catch your attention again. The girl is laughing, easily outpacing the boy. You're conscious of how much time has passed and how much more of your life you have to live. You want to step into that life, to live it to its fullest. You have control over what happens next, and it doesn't matter what anyone else thinks.

You're also aware of Lorcan beside you: both now and

the role he's had in your life so far. He's the one constant that's always been there, the one person you've always wanted to talk to. And the one person you know you want by your side in the future.

It's terrifying, really. And then, at the same time, it's not.

You look over at Lorcan, at his easy charm, the way he always knows what to tell you, the way he infuriates you only because you know he can do better. And you think about why you've held yourself back from him for so long. It's as if you've always been able to see how he slots into your life, and so you've kept him at arm's length. Not any more.

'I think I probably am in love with you too,' you say, and he smiles. 'For some time, actually.'

'I fucking knew it.'

You slap him on the shoulder and laugh.

'You could have said something earlier.'

'I knew I had to let you come to your own conclusions.'

'You fucking didn't.'

'I was getting pretty tired of you trying to resist me.'

You're laughing now, and then you kiss Lorcan. You just do it, as though it's the most natural thing in the world. You feel him catch his breath and then pull you close. It feels, you think, like how things were supposed to feel all along.

You pull back. 'Just wait until I tell Fiona this. She's going to lose her mind.'

Your hand is on your phone, about to unlock it.

'Maybe we can hold off on the status update for, like, five minutes,' Lorcan says.

It's hard, breaking your social media habit, trying to

live your life for what's in front of you instead of what people might be saying about it online.

But really, here with Lorcan, it's not actually that hard. You put your phone away.

Nineteen

You love this place. You have always loved this place, and you always will. Love, you are learning, does not have to be difficult. You carry your shoes in your hand, a tote bag slung over one shoulder. You're wearing a dress and a raincoat, just in case. The sun has just peeked out from behind the clouds, and you can feel the warmth of it on your skin. The air smells like the ocean and sun cream and wet grass. The laneway welcomes you home. You are always surprised when you see it, the memory of the place diluted in the months since you last walked it. Photos don't do it justice. The montbretia is in flower, the black-berries are about to ripen, and everything is alive. You see it all with fresh eyes and childlike wonder.

Lorcan is beside you, carrying a cooler in one hand and your towels in the other. Your parents are somewhere behind you, but they're out of sight for now. Last month you'd caught them laughing about something together, quietly, just the two of them. At times life seems unbelievably complicated and then impossibly simple.

This little space, for this one second, is for you and you alone. And him.

For your entire life you've had a sense of being observed,

of knowing how to perform for an audience and how to fall to pieces when you're alone. When you're with Lorcan, it doesn't feel like either of those things. Private and public meld, and you become whole.

His head is lit from behind by the sun, the sunburn on his neck apparent. You don't think about whether or not you should reach out to him, you just do. At times it doesn't feel like you're separate people. You spend every possible moment together. He's held your hair back as you've vomited and you've held him as he's cried. You do the crossword together every day and argue about what shows to watch. He's stopped cooking fish because he knows you don't like it, and you've driven him to the airport at four in the morning.

His hand is in yours, and you run your thumb along his knuckles.

'You know, I used to be a bit embarrassed we came on holiday here?' you say.

'Yeah?'

'Yeah, I don't know. Some of my friends were going off to Florida or Portugal. And we always come down here to sit in the rain.'

'It doesn't always rain.'

'It mostly rains. But it's funny, I wouldn't trade this place for anything in the world now.'

'Neither.' Lorcan nudges you with his shoulder. 'It's our place.'

'It's my place,' you say, 'but you can be here too.'

Down at the beach, the tide is all the way out. A world of seaweed has revealed itself. Seeing the rocks is like greeting old friends. You meet Lorcan's mother in her usual spot, and she hugs you when she sees you. She always hugs you when she sees you and asks you if Lorcan is treating you right. She's stopped dyeing her hair, and she looks old, but not in the way that society thinks women should diminish as they age. She looks happier.

'Just about,' you always say, and then you exchange a look with her that carries more than you'd ever dare to put into words. But there's much more of his mother in Lorcan than his father. You can see her in his eyes and the way he insists you take an umbrella with you any time it rains.

You throw a towel down on the sand and stretch out. You wave at your cousins. Every year, your family multiplies in this place, each generation of children creating their own memories. When you think about it now, the things you love about this place are the things you could never quantify. You remember trying to preserve this beach with the video camera, but film could never capture the feeling of digging your fingers through the sand, or the sound of the sea foam as it dissolves on the shoreline. The image is too flat, lacking in context and sensuality.

Your family arrive and set up in the sand next to you. Evan sits on a rock, his face shaded by his blue baseball cap. He's not dressed for the beach, in jeans and shoes that need socks. He's pale, but not as pale as he used to be. Across his face is a constellation of freckles.

'Hey,' you say, 'you're reading that book I told you about.'

'Yeah—' He holds it an arm's length away, as though it might jump out at him '—I'm actually really liking it.'

'Good.'

Lorcan nudges you, amazed. You spend a lot of your evenings talking about Evan, but Lorcan doesn't mind. You have him over for lunch most Saturdays, and although he doesn't say much, he hasn't stopped coming. The three of you sit around the little glass table in the apartment, and it feels like reaching back through time, healing the rift of the last decade.

You smile at Lorcan, not needing to verbalise how much this tiny victory means to you. Lorcan didn't say anything when you told him about your relationship with Jack, not at first. It hadn't come out in the right order anyway. He'd sat opposite you, and listened, and quietly taken your hand when you didn't have the words any more. You hope that Evan gets as much out of that book as he can. Last week he told you he broke up with Emily, something about her being too clingy, and you'd taken it as a positive sign.

You spend the day taking your little cousins and second cousins and third cousins by the hand, leading them in a long line and showing them all the parts of the beach that you love. You show them how to walk across the rocks, the way that you tried to show the video camera when you were their age. This, you think, is real. This memory will live on with them, and you, and these places will shift and reform countless times with the retellings. These children will make their own worlds, not caring about the one you tried to save for them.

You get a message from Fiona as you're eating a roll. She's booked time off work and is going to come down next week. She's started seeing someone, but she hasn't told you she's in love with them yet. So, you're taking it seriously. You think she might need a place like this, and you've told her that. Lately you've been trying to assume less about what people need and instead make open suggestions to them.

You and Lorcan are sitting on the edge of the rock, your feet in the ocean now. Your head is resting on his shoulder. You put your phone away in your pocket. It's not your life line any more; you don't need it to interpret the sea, or the rocks, or the boy beside you. You lean back against the brown stone. It's still comfortable, even though you've grown significantly.

'I always think this place will have changed by the time we come back, but it never does.' Lorcan says this without looking at you, running his hands over a patch of barnacles. He's gazing out over the horizon, the ever-churning waves.

'It changes,' you say, 'but so do we.'

'You've gone very deep all of a sudden, very poetic.'

'I've just been thinking about it a lot lately. I used to want to control everything, to make sure everyone thought I was this perfect person who was always calm and indifferent, that I could do that by posting the right picture or whatever. But I think I was spiralling. I was so afraid of change, I froze myself as well.'

'I never thought you were calm or in control.'

You splash water in his direction. 'Ha ha.'

You're feeling self-conscious now, not because Lorcan will judge you, but because you're judging yourself. You're so sad for who you'd spent so long trying to be and for who you actually were. When you look at photos from that time, you don't recognise yourself.

'Can I ask you something?'

'I've never been able to stop you before,' you say, and he splashes water back at you.

'That time, right here, when you kissed me. Why did you stop?'

'Ah.'

'I spent like five years being confused by it.'

You laugh, and he shakes his head at you. You tried so hard to convince yourself that it meant nothing to you, but for years it played on a loop in your mind. You had been obsessed with it, but your desire was too difficult to touch and acknowledge. He's always been good at just admitting the things you deny to yourself.

'Me too.' You watch the seaweed sway with the waves and the small fish darting around the edge of the rock. 'I suppose I was afraid you'd see me for how I was, and you wouldn't like it. Because I didn't like it.' You say it with a shrug. In the abstract it is sad, but you feel only the truth of the words and the relief that you've let the feeling go.

'I meant what I said. I never saw you the way you wanted me to. Sometimes I could tell you were trying your best to hold it all together, so I never said anything.'

'Oh, thanks, that must have been pathetic.'

'No, I mean I thought you were so strong, and I never wanted to pry. But your little tricks never worked on me.'

'Are you sure?' You know the answer, but you ask anyway. You know he saw through you the entire time, even though you spent years trying to convince him of things about you. You'd learnt to shape your identity online, and Lorcan had never really cared for that space. He never believed that was the authentic you. At one point this would have terrified you. Now it's comforting. You want to live offline; you crave unobserved authenticity more than anything else.

'I knew you loved me before you knew you loved me,' Lorcan says.

'Love is a strong word.'

'And isn't it so nice that's what we have?'

It's easy to admit you love him, something you would have felt deep shame about in the past. You've never told anyone else you love them, not Jack and not your parents. You've never truly known what it meant until now. You think, maybe, it's impossible to know how to love anyone else when you hate yourself so deeply. You want that to change; you want to live loving life.

'We wouldn't have worked then, anyway,' you say, and you know it's true. You don't have to look at him to know the expression he's making, but you do anyway. His hand is on his chest in mock-shock, playful, but he's told you his insecurities, his fears for the future, and so you say, 'Because of me.' Then, because the smirk is predictable, you say, 'Okay, don't get too smug, because of you too. I think it had to happen this way.'

'I'm glad it finally did.'

He helps you to your feet, and the two of you walk back over the rocks. The tide is in now, and the beach has been transformed. There's only a narrow strip of sand where people are sitting, the rest all underwater. Change is constant in this place; you don't know how it took you so long to realise and embrace it. You wade through the water, your feet sinking into the sand, your footprints there for a moment and then filled in.

'Looks like it's time to jump off the rock. Are you in?' Lorcan asks.

'Yeah, I think so, if you jump with me.'

You change into your swimming togs, and when you run your hands across your stomach all you feel is smooth flesh. You're not afraid to jump any more.

ACKNOWLEDGEMENTS

This book was a funny one to write. The story came to me all at once, but also in little fragments I had to piece together. It was like I always knew the story I had to tell; it's not my own, but it could have been. I could tell it in my sleep: maybe I'm always telling it, and always will be. The problem was figuring out how it needed to be told. Several things had to fall into place before I found my way there, and I couldn't have done it myself. I owe the book you hold in your hands to a number of things, some impossible to define. But I will do my best.

I am so delighted this book has a home at Canongate. The entire team have shown unwavering support for my vision for the story. In particular, I want to thank Leah Woodburn for helping me hone my ideas into what they are today, and Jamie Byng for his continued faith in me. I couldn't have got this far without my agent, Marianne Gunn O'Connor, and her championing of my work.

In some ways, the writing of this book was an act of recollection. Of thinking back over my own life and wondering how I got to where I am. For a long time now I have been thinking about the effect of social media on my life, and doing my best to explore it in my work.

Very few people's lives are interesting enough to fill a novel, and very rarely do they follow a satisfying narrative. This book came out of endless conversations with my friends, over wine and coffee, in person and online. This book is not my story, or theirs, or anyone's; but it could be yours. I'm so thankful to every single one of them for sharing their thoughts, fears and unpleasant memories with me so that I could sketch out this story and shine a light on them. Collectively, this is how we remember it, and it feels important to share that. You all know who you are, and I hope the pieces of you that I borrowed and wove into this story are well represented.

Throughout the course of writing this book, I became obsessed with little rhyming moments in my own life. The events that seemed to chime with one another, building in significance with each reoccurrence. I felt this most strongly when I returned to places I hadn't realised were significant at the time. There's something about landscape that has the ability to shape thought and emotion. The beach that I return to every August that grows with me and stretches back through time through my mother to my grandmother, and farther still. Over the last two years, since the world began opening up again after the pandemic, I have felt myself retracing my steps, finding myself in places where I used to be a different person. Returning to my old school had the effect of transporting me back through time, and reminded me of feelings that had long lay dormant. I had the idea for the structure of this book in 2019 while talking with a friend in the Parc de Bruxelles. At the time, the story felt too expansive to tell, too difficult to capture. I've since had the chance to return to that park, to taste the moment again, and to map my life now against what it once was. I am grateful for each and every place I get the chance to return to. The same beaches, the same cafes, the same skies, the same people. Yet, different somehow. Changed. It seems weird to thank a series of locations, but without them I wouldn't have the words to write this story. What is less weird is thanking the people who let me stay with them as I re-explored these places and made memories in new places that I hope to return to again one day: Nora, Catriona, Robyn and Katie, Dee, Lex, Kilian and Ina, Doireann, Paul, Sunny and Brian, Clare and the Hanlons. Thank you for your homes, for meals and coffees and conversations.

If there is one thing that is clear to me now, it is that there are many different ways to experience recollection. As much as change is important to map, so are constants: the places I never had to leave for so long that I started to change without them, the people who've never left my life since they entered it, who see me with clearer eyes than I have for myself, the people that I've found my way back to again after the pandemic and all things becoming unstuck, the new people in my life, that I meet as they are now, and they me, unaware of how far I've come. I am made up of all of these people, and so they are in the very fabric of this novel. There are too many of you to name, but I am grateful for every one of you.

And you, as always, the reader and central character to this story. Thank you.